ACT

OF

VENGEANCE

Books by Chris Carver −

We're not Afraid of Lions, (Autobiography).
Pursuit of Evil Series −
   (Book 1) Act of Vengeance.
   (Book 2) For Better, For Worse.
The Talented Miss Turner.

ACT OF VENGEANCE

Book 1 of the
PURSUIT OF EVIL Series

A novel by
Christopher Carver

Cover image: The Old Bailey
Central Criminal Court, London

For my dear wife Moira

MAIN CHARACTERS

James Johnson. MI5 Officer. Code reference "Zero Eight".
Anita Hussein. Young British born Pakistani recruited as an agent by James Johnson. Code name "Delia".
Colonel Rutherford. Ex Commanding officer of the SAS. Now liaison officer between Intelligence and Security services.
Mrs B. Full name Mrs Beatrice Gordon. Controller MI5.
Sarah More. Mrs B's personal assistant.
Counter Terrorism Command. (CTC). Investigation branch of Metropolitan Police Service which specialises in cases with political or terrorist ramifications.
Commander Birch. Head of CTC.
Detective Chief Superintendent Arthur Fitzgerald. Senior Investigating Officer and team leader.
Detective Inspector Robin Catchpole. Fitzgerald's deputy.
Detective Sergeant Luke Macdonald. Member of team.
Detective Constable Sidney Fox. Member of team.
Usman Khalid. Member of a terrorist organisation. Known as "Suleiman".
Aisha Khalid. Usman's wife.
Rhana Khalid. Son of Usman Khalid. Known as "Lewis"

Foreword

Anita was in her flat, pregnant and feeling lonely. She had heard nothing from her husband, Raji, visiting relatives in Pakistan and was annoyed that he had not contacted her. Suddenly there was a loud knock on the front door which made her jump. She opened it and was met by an elderly Asian man, wearing traditional clothes, whom she did not recognise. There was no greeting, introduction or explanation as to who he was, he just announced in heavy accented English. 'Your husband has been martyred. You must revenge his death. You will be told what to do.' He turned and limped away.

1

The mobile phone rang with two muffled blurs. Johnson immediately grabbed it and clicked Receive. He heard a female's voice which he recognised. 'Plaza Hotel. Wolverhampton. Tonight.' The line went dead

'At last!' he said to himself wondering if he had finally struck it lucky. This was the call he had been waiting for. He swung his legs out of the bed and sat up. He hoped she was now cutting up the SIM card and replacing it with a used one, as he had instructed.

He looked behind him at his partner for the night whom he could just see in the darkness. She was fast asleep. Josephine, she said her name was. She was rather nice, he thought, I wouldn't mind seeing her again, but knew he couldn't and wouldn't.

He stood up, slipped on a dressing gown, picked up his phone and barefooted, quietly left the room, shutting the door behind him.

He went downstairs to his glory hole, a storeroom that doubled as his office. He opened the door of a wall cupboard, removed a box and exposed a telephone, his direct line to headquarters, and dialled a number. It was answered by a sleepy sounding female voice.

'Scramble,' he said. There were a few clicks and then the same voice answered again, more alert this time. 'Put me through to the colonel.' After a short while a man's voice came on, 'Rutherford,' he barked in an assertive manner.

1

'Zero Eight sir. Message from Delia. Plaza Hotel tonight.'

'Right' was the abrupt reply and the call ended.

Johnson went back to the kitchen and loaded his percolator to make a mug of coffee. The wall clock said it was two-thirty in the morning. Whilst it was heating he thought of his new agent, Anita Hussein. He had given her the code name "Delia". He was anxious as this was her first assignment and he hoped she wouldn't mess up. Anyway, she was all he had so he would have to make the best of it. The percolator started hissing and giving off a rich aroma.

He went over in his mind the operation he was working on.

MI5 had uncovered a new organisation. al-Abdullah, which was started by the head teacher of an Islamic religious school in Birmingham. The teacher insisted that their sole purpose was to attract new members to Islam. However, a special branch agent had advised that this teacher was having secret meetings with someone from London and was hatching a plan to radicalise the new recruits and use them to "make jihad against *kuffars*". An MP, David Robinson, was touring the country holding public meetings warning of the dangers of Islamic fundamentalism and had been named as a target. He, Johnson, had been tasked to find the London contact. So far, he had drawn a blank, but now with Anita, he had high hopes that the meeting tonight would bear fruit. He realised he could be in for a busy day.

The percolator boiled; he poured out a mug and added a slug of whisky, but it was too hot to drink so he sipped it whilst gazing at the other end of the room which was in semi-darkness. Eventually his eyes rested on an empty wine bottle lying on the floor. There was something else on the floor next to it he could not recognise. He got up and switched on the overhead light and smiled. It was a bra. He picked it up and hung it over the back of a chair. He was still smiling as he recalled the high jinks he and Josephine had been up to. It was all her idea but, yes, it had been fun. He drank his coffee, turned off the lights and went quietly back to the bed so as not to wake her.

He awoke at ten past seven. Josephine was still asleep, so he got out of bed quietly, picked up some clothes from a chair, padded into the bathroom to get dressed and then went downstairs.

He would normally go for a run now, but he didn't want Josephine to wake up and find she was alone in the house. Instead, he did his exercises on the floor; then, feeling exhausted, he lay flat on his back for five minutes to let his body recuperate. Finally, he got up, loaded his coffee percolator again and soon smelt the rich aroma. He poured out a plate of cereal for breakfast. He preferred a cooked breakfast but only if someone else would cook it and it was obvious Josephine wasn't going to do any cooking.

Suddenly Josephine appeared barefooted and wearing nothing but one of his shirts which was far too big for her – blond hair tousled and all over the place and her face with a distinct "morning after" look.

'You look as if you could do with a good mug of coffee,' he said pushing his mug across the table towards her.

'Do you know where my clothes are?' she asked.

'Your clothes? No. Why should I know?'

'Because you took them off.'

'Ah ...There's a bra over there ...' pointing to the chair.

She picked it up but continued looking.

'What are you looking for now?' he asked.

'My shoes.' She pulled the sofa sideways. 'Ah. Here they are,' bent down and picked up her knickers, waving them at him.

Johnson shook his head. 'You're dangerous. You should carry a warning ... '

'What's the time?' She interrupted him.

'Ten to eight,' he said looking at the wall clock.

'Christ, I've got to be at work by half past,' she cried and dashed to the stairs.

'I'll make some coffee for you,' he shouted after her.

Fifteen minutes later she came down, fully dressed, hair tidy but still with a remorseful look on her face.

'Here drink that,' he said and pushed a mug of coffee towards her.

3

'Milk and sugar are there if you want them.' She picked it up and drank it, black.

'I'll drop you off on my way to work but we had better get a move on if you have to be there by half past eight because of the traffic.'

She had told him she worked as a check out at a supermarket the other side of town. He had told her he was a welder in the industrial area. He always used this as a cover story. It was not a job that encouraged further probing and it was not too far from the truth because he had done an apprenticeship before joining MI5.

He went through to the glory hole and picked up a dirty pair of overalls and a duffle bag. He always took them when he left the flat in the morning to make his cover look authentic. Josephine put down the mug, half drunk, and together they left the flat.

Johnson's flat was one of three in a converted Edwardian house. He lived in flat 3 at the rear, in the old kitchen and servants' quarters. The kitchen had been converted into an open plan family room; the pantry was his glory hole and office and upstairs were two small bedrooms with a bathroom in between. Ideal for his situation and the best part was that entry was at the back so he could come and go virtually unnoticed.

They walked around to the street where his car was parked, a scruffy looking Ford Escort. He threw his gear into the boot and got behind the wheel. Josephine slipped into the front passenger seat and he pulled away from the curb. His car's appearance belied its true worth for beneath that scruffy exterior was a highly tuned very powerful motor making it capable of a top speed of 120 mph.

They drove to the end of the treed avenue where he lived, turned right, up a short incline and filtered onto the main road which was solid with traffic. Progress was very slow – stop, start all the time. Josephine became very agitated.

'I've already had two warnings for being late,' she cried. 'One more may be one too many.'

Johnson, who knew the road layout well, made a sharp left turn at the next junction and, darting down side roads and back alleys, came up behind the supermarket only to find his way blocked by a large delivery van.

'I'll get out here and run,' she said. With that she leant across, gave him a peck on the cheek. 'Thanks, it was fun,' opened the door and was gone.

He smiled to himself. She was a nice girl. He wondered if her name really was Josephine.

He did a "U" turn and retraced his route. His headquarters were in an innocuous unmarked block of offices with an underground car park on the Thames Embankment. Weaving through various commercial and residential areas he made his way avoiding main roads and the traffic as much as possible. He eventually arrived at the office building and drove down the ramp into the car park, getting past the barrier with his swipe card. He parked, locked his car and walked to the lift.

The lift was always manned by an attendant whom he knew was a security guard armed with a weapon under his jacket. The guard recognised him, so he did not need to use his identity card. He rode to the second floor and got out. He walked down the corridor to office number 26, knocked once and entered.

'Hello my darling. You're looking as ravishing as ever. We really must have a date and paint the town red.'

He was addressing Sarah, the receptionist. Sarah was about his age, thirty-two, very good looking and always immaculately turned out, but did not have an ounce of humour in her make up.

'You're expected,' she said without looking up from her computer.

Johnson knocked on the intermediate door and went in. Mrs B, his controller, was sitting behind her desk, her grey hair in a bun as always and wearing her favourite navy-blue suit with a gold necklace.

5

2

Mrs B. Real name Mrs Beatrice Gordon, fluent in French, German and Spanish, had many years of experience in the service and was highly regarded. She controlled several officers. Johnson treated her with profound respect. 'Good morning Mrs B.' he said.

'Good morning number eight.'

'I got a message from Delia early this morning.'

'I know. Colonel Rutherford has been on to me already.'

'I assume this is another Robinson job.'

'Yes. He's holding a public meeting at the Old Plaza Hotel in Wolverhampton this evening. He's then spending the night at the hotel and going on to Manchester tomorrow. He has been warned that there's a threat against him. This is not the first time, as you know.'

'Yes, but I still have no leads.'

'Has Delia given you any names yet?'

'No. Only "Suleiman" which is not his real name.

'What about addresses?'

'No. He always contacts her after prayers at the mosque.'

'I thought you said she wasn't a Muslim?'

'She's not but when her friends deserted her after it was known her husband had been a Taliban, the only person who showed her any kindness was the imam. So, she continued going to Friday prayers.'

'Well I hope she doesn't develop any hostile Islamic ideas. Keep a careful watch.'

'Don't worry, I am. What do you want me to do about this meeting?'

'I want you to attend. Contact a Sergeant Nelson, who is one of Colonel Rutherford's men, and in charge of operations at the hotel. He will be acting as an usher. You will recognise him by his moustache, a small Hitler-like one. He knows you will be there.'

'OK. I'll need some money,' he said.

Mrs B. opened a drawer in her desk and took out a wad of notes. 'Here is £400. I want the receipts and any change.' He grinned. He knew the procedure. She would be lucky to see any change, and she knew it.

'When you speak to Sergeant Nelson use an alias, not your real name,' she said, 'and your password is Fishguard.'

"Fishguard", he thought; that's a strange word. 'I'll use my grandfather's name, Abdul Nazir.'

He saw that Mrs B had an apprehensive look on her face. 'He's passed away,' he said.

'I'm sorry.' She relaxed.

'That's all right. It was six years ago. I'd better be off. I'll be going by rail.'

He got up and left. As he passed through the receptionist's office Sarah was sitting at her computer, as usual, and did not even look up. 'I'll give you a ring when I get back; if I get back; and we'll make a date.' There was no response.

Johnson always kept a suitcase in the boot of his car which contained what he called his smart casuals and a haversack with emergency night things. It meant that in circumstances like this he could change into suitable clothing without having to go back to his flat. He retrieved his suitcase, took it to the guards' changing room in the basement and changed into slacks and a black blazer. He put his old clothes into the suitcase, locked it in the boot of his car and left the building by the car park ramp carrying his haversack over his shoulder.

On the road, he hailed a taxi to take him to Euston railway station. He checked the timetable and found a Virgin train that would take him to Wolverhampton off peak, leaving at twelve-thirty pm and bought a first-class ticket at an automatic ticket machine. The journey would be about three hours.

He looked at his watch. It was 11.20 am. There was over an hour to kill so he went to a news stand and bought a newspaper and a motoring magazine and then looked for a cafe to get a proper meal. He ordered a "Full English" breakfast. This was what he wanted this morning had Josephine been able to cook it. Josephine! Josephine. He recalled the night of passion with her. Yes. She was very nice and very experienced. He wondered where she had learnt all her tricks.

'. . ow do yer want yer coffee then?' said the waitress, plonking a full plate of food in front of him. He was so engrossed he hadn't seen her coming.

'Large black please,' he replied. He realised how hungry he was and got stuck in. 'Dya then,' she said a short time later as she banged down a large mug of black coffee. Her manner was not conducive to good customer relations, he thought, and wondered if anyone understood a word she said.

At twelve-twenty he left the cafe and walked to Platform 6 where the train was standing and boarded a first-class carriage which was almost empty. He selected a window seat and made himself comfortable. At exactly twelve-thirty the train pulled out of the station.

The journey was uneventful. Johnson took the time to think and plan about the operation tonight. The organisation they were investigating, al-Abdullah, had first come to notice about a year ago and was recruiting people to convert to Islam. Nothing illegal in that and quite harmless; but then it was discovered that some of their converts turned up in Afghanistan fighting for the Taliban, Anita's husband being one. Later they received a tip-off. Due to the amount of hostility against Muslims in the media they decided to act. Their plan was to radicalise their converts and use them to assassinate any suitable target in the UK. The MP, Robinson, was touring the country holding public meetings warning against the dangers of Islamic fundamentalism and was thought to be high on their target list. So far, no attempt had been made, but they could not take chances and had to cover every meeting. Thanks to Anita, this was the first time they had had a positive tip off.

Anita had been unaware of what had happened to her husband and was horrified when told. She was also frightened when warned she must 'avenge her husband's death and will be told what to do'. Johnson assured her he would not let her come to any harm. He hoped he would be able to speak to her, alone, at the hotel.

The train made numerous stops. At no time was his carriage more than one third full and no-one took any notice of him. At three forty-five the train arrived at Wolverhampton, fifteen minutes late. He disembarked and went to a bookstore on the platform to ask for directions to Old Plaza Hotel. He asked the cashier, a young Asian girl, if she could direct him.

'It's half hour off Birmingham Road,' she said, and pointed it out on a map. He was always amused when people gave distances in time.

Half hour walk was about two miles. The sky was clear with no sign of rain so he decided to walk to stretch his legs after the long train journey, and set off at a brisk pace. He headed into the town centre and then turned left down Birmingham Road. There were a lot of car sale yards on the road which seemed busy.

He walked at least a mile down Birmingham Road and then turned left into a side road. He passed rows of terraced houses and flats. This was obviously a residential area. After two hundred yards, the road curved and there was the hotel.

The Old Plaza Hotel was old, probably built before the war, he thought. It was four stories high with wooden sliding windows. It had once been a very smart place with a wooden portico and an old-fashioned glass revolving door at the entrance. Looking through the glass on the door he saw a large foyer with a receptionists' desk to one side manned by Asian male and female staff wearing smart wine-coloured uniforms. He noticed the hotel had three stars.

He entered through the revolving door into the foyer. It was very large with a grand wooden staircase leading up to the first floor. In the corner, next to the entrance was a table with a large display of flowers. Opposite the receptionists' desk were the lifts. He saw the "toilets" sign near the lift shaft. He went to the receptionists' desk.

'Is a meeting being held here tonight?' he asked, admiring the receptionist's smart appearance.

'Yes, in the ballroom,' she said, smiling as she pointed to a double door.

'Do you have any spare rooms?'

'Double or Single?'

'Single.'

'Yes. Plenty. Do you want me to book one for you?'

'Not yet. I'm waiting to meet someone and if he comes, I will come and see you again,' he said with a smile.

He walked across to the ballroom and looked through the door. Members of staff were laying out the chairs, he guessed it would hold more than two hundred people. At the far end was a small stage with two chairs, a table and a lectern on it. The bar was next to the ballroom. He asked a waiter where the dining room was and he pointed to the stairs. 'The Blue Room cocktail bar is also up there,' he said.

His watch showed the time as five-forty. The meeting was at seven pm so he had time to kill. Next to the bar entrance were some easy chairs and tables. He found a chair which had an unobstructed view of the foyer, unfolded his newspaper and made himself comfortable, hoping to see Anita. A waiter came and asked if he wanted anything. He ordered coffee and a plate of sandwiches.

He settled in for a long wait, his newspaper open, but watching what was happening in the foyer. He noticed that all the staff were Asians. From six-thirty onwards more people started coming into the foyer. They were mostly white men and women, but with a scattering of Asians; only three blacks. Most of them made straight for the bar.

He looked at his watch, wondering if Anita was going to appear. At six fifty-five people started streaming out of the bar and making for the ballroom. Johnson got up and joined them. He found himself a seat in the middle on the right-hand side so that he was nearest to the door to go out to the foyer if he needed to. As he sat there, he watched people being shown to their seats by several ushers. He looked carefully. Only one had a small Hitler-like moustache so he presumed he must be Sergeant Nelson. He got up and quietly walked to the front and stood near him. Nelson dealt with a couple ahead of him and then turned to him.

'Take a seat here sir, if you will.'

'Fishguard,' said Johnson.

Nelson looked perplexed and then obviously remembered. 'The gents are through that door sir,' he said and turned to the next couple.

Johnson returned to his seat and waited. After five minutes the speaker, Mr David Robinson, appeared on the stage and was greeted with loud applause. He was accompanied by the local party chairman. The lights dimmed and the chairman rose and introduced the speaker. More loud applause erupted.

Johnson noted that Sergeant Nelson was seated at a table to the right and just in front of the stage with a door immediately behind him. After the speaker had got into his stride and the meeting was properly under way, Nelson went out through the door. Johnson quietly moved to the back of the room to go out to the foyer. As he left, he had a good look around but still could not see Anita and wondered whether she was present as she had said.

He went to the gents and there met Sergeant Nelson who was alone and introduced himself, 'Nelson,' he said putting out his hand. 'Abdul Nazir,' said Johnson taking the proffered hand and shaking it.

Nelson asked if Johnson knew anyone present or whether he was expecting anyone to which Johnson replied. 'No'. He then asked if he knew what was going on. Johnson replied he only had a brief idea.

'Mr Robinson, the MP, has been holding public meetings around the country about Islamic Fundamentalism.' Nelson explained,

11

'Apparently, he has upset an organisation called Abdullah something-or-other, who want to scribble him. We have received a tipoff that tonight is the night.'

'So, what are we doing?' asked Johnson.

'I've got five details filtered in amongst the audience, some are my men, some special branch. One is a bomb expert. Robinson has two police protection guards. They are sitting at the side of the stage behind the curtains. Robinson is due to stay the night here. We have booked him a suite of rooms on the first floor and he has been asked not to use any of the public rooms but to ring for room service. We have provided the waiter who will serve him. Robinson likes to mingle with members of the audience at the end of his meetings, but we have asked him not to do so tonight but to go straight to his rooms. Unfortunately, he has got form and tends to ignore Police warnings and do his own thing.' He shrugged his shoulders and continued. 'We can only do so much.'

'What do you want from me?' asked Johnson.

'I hope you may be able to identify anyone of interest and tip us off.'

'I'll do what I can but can't promise anything.'

'I'll give you this wire so you can contact me if you see anything.' Nelson pulled out of his pocket a small black cloth bag and took out a small earpiece and throat microphone which he helped fit to Johnson.

'They are switched on all the time so I can hear everything you say,' he said. 'You don't have to talk loud, just whisper and I'll hear you.'

They tried it out and it worked fine. 'If we want to meet, I suggest we meet here,' said Nelson.

They left the gents separately, Johnson first and Nelson five minutes later. Johnson returned to his seat but before he sat down had a good look around the room to see if he could spot Anita, but couldn't see her anywhere. He was now getting worried.

Johnson was sitting next to a white man who had curly hair and a very ruddy complexion – obviously liked his booze. All the way through the speech he kept muttering, 'bastards, bastards,' to himself but loud enough for his neighbours to hear. He suddenly turned to Johnson and asked, 'Are you a Muslim?'

Johnson replied, 'No. I'm a Christian.'

'I didn't know there were Christian Muslims,' he said. Johnson said nothing. It was getting complicated.

The meeting was due to last an hour and then there would be questions. Ten minutes before the end he got up to go to the gents, this time because he needed to go. He did not tell Nelson.

As he was walking back to the door he saw Anita. She was wearing a green dress and cardigan, looking quite relaxed and sitting in the middle of the back row. Next to her was an Asian man whom he did not recognise. She gave no indication that she had seen him. He had no means of getting hold of her apart from phoning her on her mobile which he did not want to do in these circumstances. The arrangement was that she would contact him using the mobile phone he had given her when it was safe to do so, and then destroy the SIM card so that no-one could trace the call. He made a mental note that he must organise a better way of getting hold of her for the future.

He relieved himself in the gents and took the wires out of his clothing. As it was obvious he would be spending the night, he went to the reception desk and booked a single room. The pretty receptionist had gone off duty and he was attended to by a young man. He was given room 411 on the fourth floor and handed the keys.

The meeting ended and people started to stream out of the ballroom and leave the hotel. Johnson stayed by the door hoping to see Anita but she did not appear. He had no idea where she was but assumed she must have left whilst he was in the gents. He wondered whether this was the time they were going to act. He contemplated telling Nelson but decided against it. They were already alert and he had no additional information.

When everyone had left, he went to the bar. There was a small crowd already there. He found a space and a stool and ordered a beer and a cheese and onion sandwich. He was just about to eat his sandwich when Nelson came and stood next to him and ordered a whisky and soda. Johnson took his keys out of his pocket and put them on the counter so that the number 411 was clearly visible. He also took out the little black bag and put it next to the keys. Nelson said nothing but took the little black bag and went to find himself a seat at the rear of the bar.

At ten past ten Johnson decided to go to bed. His room was on the top floor. It was small with a single bed and very basic furniture but quite adequate for his needs. He turned on his mobile, undressed, climbed into bed and turned out the light.

3

David Robinson, Conservative MP for a North Hampshire constituency, came down from the stage when the meeting ended and mingled with members of the audience who gathered around him despite having been warned not to do so by the Police. His two Police protection officers, Detective Constable Grimstone and Detective Constable Burns, each armed with a revolver in a shoulder holster, stayed close to him keeping their eyes skinned for any unusual or suspicious movement.

Robinson was making small talk with the crowd around him and seemed to be joking about the fact that threats had been made against him and he needed police protection. At least he had the grace not to point out the two policemen standing with him. After a short while he said he had to go to his room as he had been warned not to use the public rooms. He invited the chairman and two other committee members to his room for a drink giving them his room number on the first floor, Room 113. The two police officers grimaced when they heard this. Anyone nearby would have heard. He asked his guests to give him half an hour to have a shower and change and to meet him in his suite at nine o'clock. He left with the two officers and took the lift to the first floor.

Robinson had been booked into one of the hotel's Premier Suites consisting of a double bedroom, en-suite bathroom and small sitting room. He undressed, had a quick shower and changed into casual clothes. He prepared to receive his guests, rang room service and ordered a bottle of red wine and four wine glasses to be sent up. He also ordered his dinner to be sent up at ten o'clock.

His two police officers had been booked into a room directly opposite Robinson's suite and would spend the night there, taking it in turns to keep awake and keep watch. At the end of the corridor, opposite the service lift, was a butler's pantry where room service received its orders. In there was Detective Constable Ted Baxter dressed in the hotel's waiters' uniform. He had been placed there by Sergeant Nelson. It was DC Baxter who had taken Robinson's order.

At nine pm the guests arrived and were admitted into the suite by Robinson. DCs Grimstone and Burns were watching through a crack by leaving their door slightly ajar. At five past nine DC Baxter, pushing a trolley with a wine bottle and glasses, knocked on the door which was opened by Robinson.

'Your wine sir,' he said.

'Oh. Thank you. Please push it over there,' indicating a corner of the sitting room. He put his hand in his pocket to pull out a fiver to give to Baxter but saw it was a tenner by mistake.

Too late, he handed it to Baxter who thanked him and left. No-one had ever given him a ten-pound tip before.

At nine-fifty the guests left, seen off by Robinson. As soon as they had gone he rang room service and asked if he could have his dinner early. Baxter answered the call and promised to see what he could do. He phoned down to the kitchen but they said it was not ready – they would do it as soon as possible. At 10 pm the dinner arrived in the service lift on a trolley and Baxter pushed it to Robinson's suite, removing the first trolley.

In the meantime, DC Grimstone, who was the senior of the two, told Burns to lie down and he would take the first shift. Burns got onto the bed, took off his shoes but otherwise fully clothed, lay on his back. Grimstone pushed a chair so that he could look through the crack in the door to the suite opposite and made himself comfortable with a book. There was a murmur of voices and movement downstairs, otherwise it was quiet.

At eleven-ten the door burst open and Robinson stood there, looking annoyed. 'I have been trying to get hold of room service,' he said, 'but there is no reply. I want another pot of coffee because the one I've got is cold. Would you go and see what's happening?'

'I'll chase it up sir,' said Grimstone. He turned to Burns who had woken up with the noise. 'Nip down to see Baxter and find out what he's up to.' Robinson returned to his suite.

Burns put on his shoes and walked down the corridor to the pantry and saw the door shut. He opened it, DC Baxter sitting on a chair but slumped over an open newspaper on a table in front of him. Burn's blood went cold as he felt something was wrong. It was too still and too quiet. Cautiously he went over to Baxter and just stood looking at him. There was no sign of breathing or movement. He pushed his hand into his collar and felt for his carotid artery; there was no pulse and the body was cool, and there was a small puddle of blood under the head. He gently tilted the head off the paper. The eyes were shut, the face deathly pale and there was a very small hole in the middle of the forehead with a little blood seeping out. Baxter was dead.

'Bloody hell,' he said to himself, in shock. 'Bloody hell.' He gently replaced Baxter's head as he had found it and left the room, shutting the door behind him. He hurried back up the corridor to their room.

'Baxter's dead. He's been shot in the head,' he said to Grimstone who was still sitting in the chair. There was a long silence as Grimstone tried to digest what he had just heard.

'Are you sure? Dead?'

'Yes. He's not breathing and there is no pulse and there is a hole in his head,' pointing to his own forehead.

'Shot, did you say? He's been shot? I didn't hear any gun shots. Did you?'

'No. I didn't hear a thing. Maybe they used a silencer.'

'Christ. I'd better tell the boss.' Grimstone got up and opened the door. 'Watch my back,' he said to Burns. He knocked on the suite's door.

'Come in.' Robinson was sitting at a coffee table with a whole lot of papers strewn around in front of him.

'I'm sorry to bother you,' he said. 'One of our Constables has been shot.'

'I'm sorry to hear that. Is he hurt?'

'He's dead sir.'

Robinson was silent, looking shocked as he stared at Grimstone. 'Who is he?' he asked hesitantly.

'DC Baxter, sir. He's the one who brought you your drinks and food.'

'Crikey. That old man. He looks like someone's grandfather.'

'Yes sir. He was due to retire quite soon.'

'He was here – what – less than an hour ago.... I'm sorry.... Poor bugger. What happened?'

'We're not sure yet. I think we must assume there are some very dangerous people around and your name has been mentioned as a target. I would like you to remain in your room. Shut and lock the doors and don't let anyone in, anyone, except for Burns and myself. We will announce ourselves by our names.'

Visibly shaken Robinson did not argue. As Grimstone left he heard the doors being locked; he went back to their room. 'I'd better tell Sergeant Nelson,' he said. He picked up the internal phone and dialled Nelson's room number.

'Yes.'

'Grimstone here, Sarge. We've got a problem. Baxter's been shot and killed.'

There was a long pause. 'Don't touch a thing. I'll be right down.'

Five minutes later Sergeant Nelson appeared. Grimstone and Burns told him what they knew. Leaving Burns to guard Robinson, they went to the pantry. Nelson inspected Baxter's body without moving it. He then felt his hand which was lying on the table. It was now cold and rigor mortis was starting to set in. 'I will have to tell the local CID. They will be swarming all over the place. Have all your details ready.' With that he left and went to an internal phone and

18

rang room 411. Johnson, who was just drifting off to sleep, answered. He heard a voice say, 'Nelson here. I'm coming up now,' and the line went dead.

Johnson put on some clothes and waited. He could tell by the tone there was something wrong. A few minutes later there was a knock on the door and Nelson entered. He briefed Johnson on what he had seen and what he had done. 'Are you sure there was no-one you recognised this evening?' he asked.

'No,' Johnson lied. He did not want to expose his agent unless it was essential, and anyway she had told him nothing they did not already know. Nelson left, clearly not believing what Johnson said.

Johnson waited ten minutes and then called Mrs B. on his mobile. They scrambled and he told her what had happened. 'The local police are bound to want to speak to me. What should I say?' he asked.

'Don't give them your real name, give them your cover name and any believable London address and play it by ear. Don't obstruct them but don't give anything away. You have done this before I'm sure. In the meantime, I will get onto Colonel Rutherford and suggest he asks the Met's CTC to take over the investigation. They specialize in this type of situation. Keep me informed,' and rang off.

He went back to bed but could not sleep. At 1.50 am his mobile rang – two muffled blurs. He answered immediately and recognised Anita's voice, speaking in a whisper.

'What happened?' he asked.

'They cancelled it.'

'Why?'

'Because there were too many police around,' she answered.

'Where were you?

'I was in the front, collecting money.'

'Do you know a constable was shot and killed?'

'One of the men went ....' the line went dead.

'Damn,' he said to himself looking at his phone in disbelief that it should cut out at this critical time. He thought of dialling her but decided against it. He hoped she would ring him again but there was no call. He put through a second call to Mrs B. and told her what he had heard.

'How did they know there were a lot of policemen present?' she asked, 'I thought they were supposed to be anonymous with false identities.'

'Exactly,' he agreed, 'I would like to know as well.

4

By two-thirty in the morning the whole road was swarming with Police. Police cars and vans with flashing blue lights were everywhere. The front of the hotel had been closed off with blue and white tape and turned into a crime scene. Uniformed members had surrounded the entire block, checking anyone moving around at that time of the night. Undertakers were present with a stretcher and body bag ready to take the body away. The whole street was awake and a small crowd of spectators was gathered on the opposite side of the road being supervised by two uniformed policemen. Rumours were flying around and somehow the message had got out that there had been a murder in the hotel.

Nelson had previously called the hotel manager, Mr Ranjid Japour, and advised him of the murder. Mr Japour was an Anglicised Indian, educated at Harrow, married to an English woman and lived away from the hotel. He had previously been put in the picture about Baxter's role and Nelson told him what had happened and asked him not to tell the police who Baxter was but to say he was a temporary waiter brought in from an agency and not to even mention his name. He would sort it out with the police. He felt Mr Japour could be trusted.

The person in charge was Detective Superintendent Davies of the local C.I.D. Sergeant Nelson was liaising with him. He told him that he and the two constables looking after Robinson were from the

Police V.I.P Protection Unit in London. No mention was made of anyone else.

Davies had a team of detectives with him. The hotel was about half full which meant there were 15 bedrooms unoccupied. From reception, he got the names of the guests staying in the hotel and putting one of his women detectives on the telephone, told her to ring every guest and tactfully explain that there had been an incident in the hotel, asking them to stay in their rooms and a police team would come and see them to explain. He then organised two teams to visit each room and briefly question the guests as to whether anyone had seen anything suspicious and a third team to question the staff.

He also organised another team to visit all the unoccupied rooms and check if anyone was in them, or any sign that anyone had been in them. This team was handed skeleton keys by the reception.

In the meantime, a scenes of crime team in protective clothing, together with a pathologist, were in the pantry carrying out a detailed check and search for evidence. Numerous photographs were taken. They checked for fingerprints everywhere and took DNA samples wherever they could. The trolley with the empty glasses and wine bottle was still there. The glasses and bottle were placed in plastic bags for checking later. They looked for but did not find any expended cartridge cases. At five-thirty am they finished and the undertakers were called. They put Baxter's body in a body bag, placed it on a stretcher; put it into their van and drove off to the mortuary.

Meanwhile the team checking the empty rooms, Sergeant Joe Swift and Constable Barry Jones had some surprises. Four of the alleged unoccupied rooms were in fact occupied by hotel staff. Some of them pretended that this was allowed as they were on duty in the morning. Others admitted that it was not authorised and begged them not to tell management. Swift took all their names. It was not his job to sort out the hotel's problems.

One room on the second floor, a double room, was occupied by a man and woman in bed. As they entered the woman sat up and was protected only by a sheet pulled up in front of her. She was mortified at being caught. 'Please don't tell my husband. Please don't tell my husband.' She begged.

'Who's your husband?' Swift enquired.

'He's the chef.'

Swift smiled. The man just lay in bed under the bedclothes and seemed to be amused by the whole incident. Swift took their names and left them to it.

'That's what we call "in flagrante delicto". Are you familiar with the law Jones?' he asked.

'No Sarge. What's it mean?'

'Caught in the act to you and me. If we told the chef, he might Bobbitt that bloke.'

'What's that mean?' asked Jones.

'It is an American case. Mrs Bobbitt found Mr Bobbitt in flagrante delicto with another woman so she got a kitchen knife and chopped off his delicto; so now it is called being Bobbitted.'

'Is that a legal term?'

'No but it sounds good.' He inserted the key into the door of the next room which was empty.

Johnson had been in his room all the while. He looked out of his window and saw all the flashing lights and activity. He had received the telephone call from reception and waited for someone to arrive. At five-thirty am he shaved and got dressed. There was still no sign of the police.

At six-thirty am there was a knock on the door. He opened it and was met by a woman Sergeant with a male colleague.

'We're sorry to bother you sir,' said the Sergeant, 'there has been an incident in the hotel.'

'Oh dear, not serious I hope.'

'There has been a death sir.'

'Oh dear. Anyone important?' He asked, looking shocked.

'One of the staff members, sir. We are asking all residents to please stay in their rooms until we have finished checking the area which shouldn't be too long now. Would you give me your name and address and tell me what you are doing in Wolverhampton?'

'Abdul Nazir. 121 Coventry Road. Hackney. London. 0208 634 4344. He gave his uncle's address – his father's brother – who had a garage and used car business where Johnson had done his apprenticeship. His uncle knew he worked for MI5 and had agreed to provide an emergency address if needed. He would confirm his bona fides if anyone rang.

'Did you see anything suspicious last night sir, for example after the meeting?'

'No. I went to the bar and had a couple of beers and then came up here and went to bed. I saw and heard nothing.'

'Thank you, sir. We may need to get in touch with you later.'

'What about breakfast?'

'The Super will let us know when it is all clear.'

He went back and lay on his bed. Breakfast wasn't until eight and it was only seven forty-five now. He was wondering about Anita. Why had she not contacted him again after her phone cut off?

At eight forty-five he received a call from reception to say breakfast was being served. He went down. Afterwards, there was nothing for him to do so he paid his bill and left for the railway station. There were still policemen all around but no-one took any notice of him. He had no idea where Sergeant Nelson was. He caught the first train for London.

At ten am the telephone at Wolverhampton Police Station rang and was answered by the receptionist. 'This is Commander Birch of the Met. Counter Terrorism Command. Would you put me through to the Regional Commander?'

The call was put through to Deputy Chief Constable Michael Carter. Commander Birch introduced himself again. 'We have been instructed by the Prime Minister's Office to take over the investigation of the murder at The Plaza Hotel. I understand that your men have already got the ball rolling. I am sending you Detective Chief Superintendent Arthur Fitzgerald and a team. Would you ask your man to hand him all the documentation and give him whatever assistance he requires?'

'Certainly. Tell him to come and see me first and I will point him in the right direction.'

Good, he thought as he put the phone down, that should save us a lot of extra work and save on manpower. They had had to cut back on manpower due to austerity and were in the process of re-organising themselves so any saving was very welcome. He put a call through to D/Superintendent Davies who had just returned from the hotel and gave him the news. Davies was not pleased.

5

Johnson arrived back at his flat at seven pm. It had been a long slow journey back, stopping at every station and he had then to go to his headquarters to collect his car. He thought of going up to see Mrs B, but decided against it. He would go in the morning when he felt refreshed. He called in at a supermarket on the way home to get some provisions.

He had had very little sleep the previous night and was feeling very tired. He decided to have a long hot shower and then a light supper and go to bed. He made beans on toast followed by the usual mug of coffee with a slug of whisky. He finally went to bed, turned on his mobile in case Anita rang but quickly fell asleep. There were no calls in the night.

At six am he awoke, feeling refreshed. He donned a track suit and trainers and went for a 5-km run. He had another shower, shaved and then dressed and went downstairs. As he had fresh ingredients, he decided to break his rules and cook himself breakfast. He was eating when the phone rang. It was Mrs B.

'Good morning number eight. Did you have a good trip?'

'Good morning, Mrs B. Yes, I did. I got home at six thirty last night.'

'I would like you to be at my office at nine o'clock to tell me all about it.'

'Fine, I'll be there,' he promised. He had been expecting this call.

Johnson drove to his headquarters by the back roads to avoid the early morning traffic, arriving at eight-fifty. He parked his car in the underground car park and took the lift to the second floor. He walked down the corridor to room 26, knocked and entered. 'Go through,' said Sarah, without looking up from her computer.

'Sour puss,' he thought, 'someone needs to break her shell.'

He knocked on the intermediate door and entered. Mrs B was sitting behind her desk and sitting in a chair facing her was Colonel Rutherford.

'Ah. Number eight. Do you know Colonel Rutherford?'

'Yes ma'am, I do. Good morning Colonel.' Rutherford did not seem to hear. Johnson sat in the only other chair in front of her desk.

'I would like you to tell us in your own words what happened in Wolverhampton,' she said.

'Have you heard from Sergeant Nelson, sir?' This addressed to the Colonel.

'I want to hear what you have to say,' he replied.

Johnson paused for a moment to collect his thoughts. Then he started. He told them in detail everything that he had done from the time he arrived at the hotel on foot until the time he left. Mrs B and the colonel listened attentively without interruption. Eventually the colonel spoke.

'Did you tell Sergeant Nelson that you had seen Delia in the auditorium?' asked Rutherford.

'No sir'

'Why not?'

'Because I did not want to compromise my contact. I didn't have any additional information to pass on. He already knew as much as I did and I didn't see him again after he left my room.'

'Huh.' Obviously, Rutherford was not impressed.

The Colonel and Mrs B started talking to each other. The big question was how did the terrorists know that there were any policemen present, let alone how many, and how did they know that Baxter was a policeman and not a waiter? Also, was the person sitting next to Delia a terrorist or a member of the crowd?

'You will have to get hold of Delia and question her on what she knows. She must know more than she is telling you,' said the Colonel addressing Johnson.

'Yes. I can only contact her by ringing her mobile phone which might be dangerous. I told her I would not call unless it was absolutely vital as she is our only contact.'

'Well you'll have to find a way,' said the Colonel.

'What about her money?' Johnson asked Mrs B. 'We said we would pay her.'

'But she hasn't told us anything.' The Colonel exploded.

'She told us the meeting would take place and she was right there, and I know she is desperate'.

'Give her a hundred pounds to keep her quiet. She can get the rest when she tells us the whole story,' said Rutherford.

Johnson looked appealingly at Mrs B. 'We'll give her two hundred and fifty. It would look highly suspicious if she is suddenly flush with cash.' As she said this she pulled out some notes from a drawer and counted out two hundred and fifty pounds which she handed to Johnson who was then told he could leave. He left without saying a word to Sarah as he passed through her office.

Colonel John Rutherford was ex S.A.S with an exemplary record. He had been due to retire but cancelled it after "nine eleven" as he thought his services and experiences might be useful. He became the liaison officer between Special Services and the Intelligence Services. He was a crusty old timer and known to be sceptical about Intelligence Services protecting their sources by not passing on information.

Anita lived in a council flat in Tower Hamlets. She was the daughter of a solicitor who was employed by a partnership in the area. Her mother was not working. Her father had not been pleased with her marriage but after the death of her husband he agreed to help financially by paying her rent. She supplemented her income by working three days a week at a local fruit and vegetable shop. Johnson first heard about her from Janet Butler, an old girlfriend, to whom she had told the story about a stranger telling her that she must "avenge her husband's death." Johnson arranged a meeting with her at Janet's flat.

Johnson had worked out the contact arrangements between them using a mobile phone and gave her an old Nokia pay-as-you-go phone. He emphasised the importance of security and the danger of the phone being checked for calls. To prevent this, he said she must change the SIM card after each conversation with him. He gave her some old used SIM cards to put in the phone. They prepared them first by putting bogus conversations in her voice on them. He decided that her own mobile would not be safe and would be much more likely to be stolen.

He would now have to find another way of contacting her. He set off for home thinking of ways he could do it. He could telephone her at her place of work but her employer was an elderly Pakistani of the old school and probably would not approve. He could go and see her and pretend to be a customer but dismissed this as too risky.

As he was driving home his car's engine suddenly started to splutter and misfire. Bugger, he thought. He would have to take it to his uncle again and put it on the tuning machine. His uncle would complain, he always did, but he could be sweet-talked into letting him use it. His uncle! His uncle! Of course! Why had he not thought of it before? He would get him to telephone Anita.

Johnny Johnson, his father's elder brother, owned a garage and used car business in Hackney, not far from Tower Hamlets. He was very popular with his customers and known as "JJ" or "Mister JJ". He had agreed that Johnson could use his address and telephone number in an emergency and he would vouch for him. But he said he did not want to become involved with "all this MI5 stuff" as he put it. In fact, the two got on very well and he always helped Johnson out when his car had problems. Johnson trusted him absolutely.

On arrival home, he parked in the street outside his flat. He lifted the bonnet to see if there was anything obvious that was causing the trouble but saw nothing untoward. There was no alternative, he had to talk to his uncle. He let himself into his flat, sat down and tried to think out a plan. He would have to be very diplomatic and not let on that he was on a case for MI5.

"Unc" was always teasing Johnson about finding a decent woman, settling down and getting married. 'You're thirty-two now,' he would say, 'you can't go on working your way through all the women in London. You'll wear yourself out and be no good for anyone.'

Perfect. He would tell him that he had met a woman whom he would like to take out but she worked for her father in a vegetable shop and he was very strict and would not let her meet any man without a chaperon being present. He was sure Unc would co-operate. He would work out the details later. First, he had to find out what days she worked at the shop and the only way was to telephone the shop himself.

He looked up Towers Fruit and Vegetables in the directory and telephoned. A man's voice answered. 'Could you tell me what days Anita is working please?' he asked.

'She'll be here tomorrow,' came the terse reply. He cut off the call immediately so as not to get involved in a conversation.

He then telephoned his uncle. 'Hi Unc. I've got problems....'

'That bloody car of yours again,' Unc cut him off. 'Why don't you flog it and get a newer one. I've got plenty in the yard.'

'It just needs a bit of tuning. Can I bring it round? I'll do it myself.'

'Come this afternoon. We are using it now.' He was referring to the Sun Tuner which was used to tune up all makes of cars.

'Thanks, Unc. You're a star.'

Johnson had worked out his plan. He would go around before lunch and take prawn sandwiches, which he knew were Unc's favourite, and some cans of beer and over lunch put his plan to him.

He put on his overalls and left the flat. He drove to the nearest shop and bought two packs of prawn sandwiches and four cans of beer, after which he drove out to the garage, arriving at twelve forty-five, just before the lunch break.

'You're early,' said Unc, sitting at his desk. 'I said come this afternoon,'

'I know but I want to talk to you. I've brought lunch.'

JJ raised his eyebrows. It all seemed very mysterious. Johnson closed the office door shutting off the workshop area. He produced the sandwiches and beer and sat down opposite his uncle.

'I've met a girl whom I like very much and I want to take her out but I can't because she works for her father who is of the old school and won't let her out without a chaperone.'

'Is she British?'

'No – Pakistani but born in Britain. Her father, though, is an immigrant and old- fashioned in his manner. He owns and runs a fruit and vegetable shop in Tower Hamlets and his daughter works for him there. She can't go anywhere without his permission.'

'So, what do you want me to do?'

'I know they do deliveries locally using an old delivery bicycle with a large basket on the front. If you could place an order with them and ask for it to be delivered here then I am sure Anita will do the delivery and I would make sure I am here to meet her.'

'But I don't want any fruit or vegetables. Is that her name, Anita? It doesn't sound very Pakistani.'

'I'll take them off you and I will pay.'

'So, when do you want me to place this order?'

'Half past four this afternoon and she will deliver tomorrow because she is not at work today but she will be tomorrow.'

'How do you know that she'll do the delivery?'

'Because I can't see her old man riding around the streets of London on a delivery bicycle. He's too old and doesn't have the right build.'

JJ was silent for a while as he pondered the plan. 'O.K, write me out a list and I will do as you ask. You had better make sure this is the right one because I don't like telling lies to people.'

Johnson wrote out a list including apples, pears, bananas, a cauliflower and some plums. It had to be big enough to justify a delivery but not so big that Anita wouldn't be able to manage it on her own. He wrote down the name of the shop and telephone number and gave it to his uncle.

Johnson spent the rest of the afternoon tuning up his car on the Sun Tuner. It was a tricky job but he had done it so often that he was used to it.

At 4.30 pm JJ called him into the office. 'You had better listen whilst I put this order through,' he said. He dialled the number and read out the order. He asked if it could be delivered before two o'clock tomorrow and received an assurance. 'That was very easy,' he said to Johnson, 'let's hope it works.'

'I had better be here early tomorrow in case the delivery is early,' Johnson said. 'Could I use the time to give my car a service?'

'So long as you pay.'

'Thanks. I'll see you tomorrow.' He drove back to his flat very pleased with progress so far.

The following morning at nine am Johnson arrived at the garage dressed in his overalls. He had to wait until there was a gap before he could put his car on the ramp to do the service. When he had finished the service, he decided to give his car a thorough clean and vacuum the inside. He finished everything by midday. Just after midday he saw a bicycle with a large basket on the front approaching. It arrived at the office entrance, being ridden by a teenage youth. Johnson went to meet him.

'Your fruits and veg,' the lad said to Johnson.

'Thank you. Who are you?'

'I'm Usman. My father owns the business. He told me to bring your order.'

'I didn't know you worked in the shop. What's happened to the

32

young lady?'

'She's sick today. She said she will be in tomorrow.'

Johnson picked the cardboard box out of the basket. 'How much is that?'

'Eight pounds sixty please.' He gave him ten pounds. 'Keep the change.'

'Thank you, sir,' said the young man and rode away.

Johnson took the box through to the office where JJ was sitting behind his desk. He was spluttering with laughter. 'What now?' he choked. Johnson put the box down, thoroughly despondent. He couldn't think what to do. Eventually he put the box in his car and drove to his flat. When he unpacked the box, he noticed one of the apples was slightly bruised, otherwise everything was fine. But it gave him an idea.

The following morning, he was back at the garage again with the box. JJ was sitting behind his desk as usual.

'What, back again? What's the matter now?'

'I've got an idea. I'm not very happy with the quality of some of the fruit and would like it replaced. Would you ring the shop again and tell them? I would like to replace all the apples and the plums.'

'Why don't you do it? It's your fruit?'

'Well you gave the order and he might be suspicious if I telephone him and not you.'

JJ shook his head. 'I'm not happy about this. I'll do it this once and will leave it to you to do the arguing if there's any trouble. What's the number again?'

He rang the number. A young woman answered. 'Towers Fruit and Veg, Anita speaking. How can I help?'

'Oh, hello. My name is Johnny Johnson of Johnson Motors. I gave you an order yesterday for some fruit and veg. which was delivered, but I am afraid I'm not happy with some of the quality. Could you replace it for me?'

'I'm sorry to hear that,' she said, 'what would you like us to replace?'

Johnson could hear the conversation and held up an apple and the box of plums. 'The apples and plums,' JJ answered.

'I don't think that will be a problem. I'll just speak to the owner.' The line went quiet as she obviously covered the microphone with her hand. After a short while she came back. 'Not a problem, sir, I will bring them out myself after lunch.'

'That's very kind of you.' JJ nodded at Johnson. 'You've got the luck of the devil. I wouldn't ride nearly a mile to replace a few apples and plums. I would have told you to drop them in yourself. Anyway, she sounds a very nice young lady. You had better make the best of it.' Johnson smiled. It was now just a matter of waiting.

Just before two pm he saw her approaching on the bicycle. He remained in the office. She stopped by the door and propped up the bicycle on its stand, took the packet of apples and plums out of the basket and opened the office door. Johnson was standing just behind it. She came in and stopped right in front of him, said nothing, just opened her mouth in amazement.

'Hello Anita. Come in here,' indicating the cashier's office next door. She went in with the packets and he shut the door behind her.

'I'm sorry to do it like this but I have to speak to you and this seemed the safest way to contact you. He's my uncle who owns this garage. You can trust him. I told him you were my girlfriend and your father would not let me see you so we had to meet secretly.'

So far Anita had said nothing, just looked stunned. 'What shall I do with the fruit?' she asked.

'Nothing. It is fine. Oh. Leave that here and tell your boss that you managed to talk me into keeping the damaged fruit and sold me the other as well. That should impress him.' He gave her another ten pounds to pay for it. 'I don't want any change. You can keep it. We've got to talk about what happened at Wolverhampton. I think the best way is for me to take you out to lunch at some remote pub and we can have a private chat. Is that alright with you? After all you are supposed to be my girlfriend,' he said with a twinkle in his eye.

'Yes. O.K. When?' she asked.

'What about this weekend, say Saturday.'

'Alright. I'm doing nothing. Where shall we meet?'

'Can you get to the Millennium Dome? I'll pick you up from there.'

'Yes. That's easy. What time? Eleven?'

'Eleven will be fine. I'll pick you up from the car park in my car,' pointing through the glass panel to his blue Ford Escort in the workshop.

'See you then,' she said and opened the door to leave the office. Johnson accompanied her out and saw her off on her bicycle. He went back into the office. JJ was still behind his desk.

'Thanks, Unc. We are meeting on Saturday.'

'Well you certainly know how to pick 'em. She looks very nice indeed.'

Johnson gave him a cheeky grin, got into his car and drove back to his flat.

6

Johnson couldn't wait for Saturday to come fast enough. He wanted to see Anita again. There was something about her that he found attractive. He looked at a map of London for a location here he could take her and be private. Dartford looked interesting. It was on the outskirts of the town and easy to get to, essentially just down the A2.

He opened his computer and Googled "Pubs in Dartford". Eventually he decided on the Rose and Crown, a family run pub and not too expensive. It had a garden to sit out in and a car park. He telephoned and booked lunch for two on Saturday.

Today was Thursday. He had two days to wait. He went over in his mind all the things he wanted to ask her. He would take his tape recorder to record what she said. He remembered that at Wolverhampton he had wondered whether he could trust her and recalled Mrs B's warning. He had done some background checks and her name did not come up at all, but her husband did. He had been radicalized by al-Abdullah, had travelled to Pakistan and was killed by the Taliban in Afghanistan. Otherwise, he was of no interest.

He cast his mind back to when he first met her. He was called by an old girlfriend, Janet Butler, who had known Anita at school. Anita had contacted her after the meeting with the strange old man and was frightened when told she must "avenge her husband's death". Janet suggested she tell the Police, but Anita was very hesitant about getting the police involved. When Janet was alone she telephoned Johnson. He suggested she should invite Anita around to her flat and he would suddenly arrive as if by chance. He trusted Janet who was aware of his true role.

Janet arranged the meeting and Johnson laid on the charm, telling her he was in the Crime Prevention Unit. Eventually Anita told him her story. She did not know the old man, had never seen him before and had not seen him since. Johnson told her he would pass the word around his colleagues. In the meantime, if she heard anything more she should get in touch with him. Johnson reported his meeting to Mrs B and she suggested he should try and recruit Anita as an agent.

A week later he arranged another meeting with Anita. He told her that it was suspected the old man was a member of an organisation trying to convert non-Muslims to embrace Islam and that they were holding secret meetings to do this. The police were very interested in this organisation and asked if she would be prepared to pass on any information to him.

Anita hesitated before replying. 'Will I be safe? I'm not sure I trust that old man.'

'It will be quite safe for you. I can assure you I will not let you come to any harm,' he replied. He also told her she would be paid for anything she passed on, which pleased her because she was very short of money. He gave her a Nokia mobile telephone and taught her how to remove and destroy the SIM card after speaking to him. He emphasised the importance of secrecy and not being caught with the telephone. He said her code name would be "Delia".

Johnson finally made up his mind as to what he wanted from her when they met on Saturday; names and phone numbers were the most important. The only name she had given him so far was Suleiman," which was a code name for the person who contacted her. He also wanted to know what the plan had been for Wolverhampton. He telephoned Mrs B and advised her of his intended lunch with Anita. Mrs B told him that the police at Wolverhampton were not getting very far with their investigations so anything he could pick up would be welcome.

Saturday dawned. Johnson woke at six, put on his track suit and went for his normal 5 km run. On getting back to his flat he showered, shaved and dressed in clean clothes. It was now nine o'clock. He was meeting her at eleven. It would take half an hour to get to the Millennium Dome so he had an hour and a half to kill. He checked that he had enough money and almost forgot the two hundred and fifty he had to give her. He checked he had his tape recorder and that the batteries were charged. He was ready and had high hopes of getting some useful information at last.

Finally, at ten-thirty he went out to his car and drove off. As there was very little traffic he got to the Millennium Dome quicker than he expected. He looked around for Anita but there was no sign of her. They had agreed to meet by the entrance to the car park so he found a parking space where he could see the entrance and waited in his car. Eleven o'clock came and went; no sign of her. Five past eleven; ten past eleven; he was he getting anxious and wondered whether she would come. Finally, at almost a quarter past he saw her walking towards the entrance.

She stopped by the entrance and started to look around for him. He thought she looked stunning. Shoulder length hair pulled back behind her ears, plain green dress with a dark green cardigan and small brown boots. He started up and drove towards her. She smiled when she saw him. He stopped, leant across and opened the door for her. She was still smiling when she got in.

'I'm so sorry,' she said, 'I didn't think it would take so long to walk to the Dome.'

'Not at all. It's my fault. I should have realized that it was a long walk.'

'Anyway, I'm here now so let's get going,' she said. Johnson engaged gear and pulled away.

'Where are we going to?' She asked.

'A nice little country pub. It's a surprise.'

They drove in silence for a brief time whilst Johnson negotiated his way through the traffic. He then got onto the A2 and knew it was a straight run to Dartford.

'I'm sorry I had to do this cloak and dagger stunt to contact you,' he said, 'but I couldn't think of any way I could get you without someone knowing.'

'Was it you who rang my boss to ask when I would be at work the other day?' She asked.

'Yes. I'm afraid so,' he replied.

'Well he was very unamused and gave me a scolding to tell my boy-friends not to telephone me at work.' He looked at her. She had a smile on her face so was obviously amused by the whole thing. 'I didn't realise it was you. I thought it was Suleiman,' she said.

'Does he speak to you by phone?'

'No never. He only ever speaks to me after prayers at the mosque, but he was the only person I could think of who may want to speak to me.'

They drove on. To make conversation he asked her what schools she had gone to.

'I was born in Reading,' she said, 'and went to a private school for juniors in Berkshire. In those days, my father was a partner in a firm of solicitors and we could afford it. Then something happened to his firm and we had to move to London. I finished my schooling at a grammar school in London.'

'And after that?'

'I wanted to be a lawyer but didn't have enough 'A' levels so had to settle on being a teacher. I went to the L.S.E. where I met Raji. He was also training to be a teacher. He was very handsome and I soon lost my head and my heart to him. We just seemed to click. However, my father was not pleased. Said he was too low class. His father was very anti too, saying he had to marry some girl in Pakistan – obviously, an arranged marriage which Raji knew nothing about. We decided the only way to stop this was for us to get married as quickly as possible and so we did. We were far too impulsive.'

'And now?'

'Raji's father will have nothing to do with me and as I'd been left with no money I had to go and beg forgiveness from my father. He was not very forgiving but agreed to pay my rent.'

'That's a terribly sad story,' said Johnson. 'I hope things work out for you in the future.'

They arrived on the outskirts of Dartford and thankfully the satnav guided them to the pub which was tucked away off the main street. He pulled into the car park. It was now midday.

'What a delightful looking place, it looks like an ordinary house.' Anita said.

They went into reception and booked in. 'What time would you like lunch, sir?' asked the receptionist.

'One o'clock,' said Johnson looking at Anita who nodded. 'In the meantime, can we have some drinks and I think we would like to sit out in your garden if that's alright.'

'Of course, sir. If you would like to find yourself somewhere to sit I will bring your drinks out to you. What would you like?'

Anita ordered an appletizer, Johnson a beer. They found themselves two seats with a table and an umbrella under a large overhanging tree. It was a fine sunny day and they were the only ones sitting in the garden. Johnson took out his tape recorder and placed it on the table. 'Do you mind if I record our conversation?' he asked, 'It is the best way to ensure I get everything right.'

He had decided to tell Anita what he was doing, to be in the open. He did not think she would appreciate being kept in the dark. So far as she was concerned he was just a policeman and he intended to keep it that way. 'Who will be listening to it?' she asked.

'It's for my boss.'

'I thought you said you were a policeman. I have never seen you in uniform.'

'No, I don't wear uniform. We wear plain clothes and our job is to prevent crime happening as far as we can... Let's get started,' he said, 'let's start with Wolverhampton. No, first tell me as much as you can about Suleiman?'

Anita's face dropped and she became very solemn. 'I don't know much about him. He seems to be the main organiser. He is the one who told me to go to Birmingham with him but did not tell me what they were going to do. He said we would be at The Plaza Hotel.

'Is "Suleiman" his real name?' asked Johnson.

'No. I don't think so. We have all got code names. He said we must not talk amongst ourselves unless we use our code names.'

'What's your name?'

"Rubai." As Johnson looked blank she continued, 'it means poetry in Urdu.'

'Do you speak Urdu?'

'No. Only English. He told me what it means.'

'Are you sure he said Birmingham and not Wolverhampton?'

'Yes, I am sure he said Birmingham when he first mentioned the trip.'

'OK, what happened next?'

'Suleiman said he would pick me up outside my flat at eight o'clock. He said we would be staying the night and that I should take some night things. He arrived at eight o'clock in his car.'

'What type?'

'It was silver.'

He lifted an eyebrow, 'no, what make was it?'

'I don't know. I'm not very good at cars. I think it was a BMW but that is the only car I know.'

'OK. what happened then?'

'He first drove to somewhere in North London. I don't know where, but I saw a sign that said Barnet. He stopped outside a large house and told me to wait in the car. I waited for about an hour and eventually he came out carrying a small suitcase which he put in the boot. We set off and after about three hours we arrived in Birmingham. He parked in the street. He said he might be a long time and I must wait in the car for him.'

'Do you know where he went?'

'No. He walked off down the street.'

'Did you see the name of the street or anything that would indicate where you were?'

'No nothing. I don't know Birmingham. I have never been there before.'

'OK. What happened after that?'

'I sat in the car for about half an hour but as we had had nothing to eat I got out and went into a newsagent which I noticed about twenty yards down the road. There I bought myself a sandwich and bottle of water.'

'Did he give you the money for that?'

'No. I paid for it myself.'

'Did he give you the car keys so you could lock up?'

'No. He had the keys with him. I left it unlocked.'

'Go on.'

'I also bought myself a magazine and then went back to the car. He eventually came back at about half past three. He did not say where he had been or what he had done. He just got in and drove off.'

'Did you see any schools in the area?'

'No. But as I came out of the shop two schoolboys came in. I say "boys", they looked like young men as they had beards; but they were wearing black blazers with a badge on the pocket looking like a school uniform.'

'What happened after that?'

'We eventually arrived in Wolverhampton.'

'Do you remember the time?'

'I think it was about five o'clock.'

'Go on.'

'We booked into the Holiday Inn. Suleiman said he wanted me to be his wife. I was alarmed. I didn't know if he meant pretend to be his wife for this venture or whether he had other things in mind. He booked a double room and we were taken up by a waiter who took our suitcases for us.'

Anita paused while she collected her thoughts and then continued.

'The room had twin beds, not a double bed which I was relieved to see. When the waiter had gone, I told Suleiman that we were to stay in our own beds for the night. He did not answer, just smiled.'

'At six o'clock he looked at his watch and said we must go. I had no idea where we were going to. We drove down some back road and drove past the Old Plaza Hotel. I saw the sign over the entrance. He turned the corner at the end and stopped in the street opposite some shops. There were parking bays there and he pulled into one of them. Again, he told me to wait in the car and he walked back around the corner towards the front of the hotel. I sat for about half an hour. It was getting dark and the street lights suddenly came on. He returned, opened the boot of the car and took out a collection tin. He gave me the tin and said he wanted me to collect money in the front of the hotel. The tin had "Afghan Orphans" written on it in large letters.

'Where did you do this collecting?'

'I stood inside by the front door, the revolving door, and pushed my tin at people who were coming in. There were quite a lot of people coming through the door. Some put money in my tin, but most ignored me.'

'How long were you there?'

'I don't know but it seemed a long time. I had heard that there was a political meeting going on in the hall and that was where everybody was going. Eventually Suleiman came to me and said I should put my tin on the table by the door – the table with a large bowl of flowers on it – and follow him. We went and sat at the back of the hall and listened till the end of the meeting.'

'Do you know where Suleiman was whilst you were standing in the foyer collecting money?'

'No. Somewhere in the hotel.'

'What happened then?'

'When we saw that the meeting was about to end, we got up and left. He told me to go and wait in the car for him. I waited for him for ages. I don't know how long but I was getting very cold. Eventually he arrived carrying the tin which he handed to me. It was very heavy. He was smiling and looking very happy. I asked him why he was smiling and he said, "We've got one of them". I asked him what he meant. He said, "killed one. Shot a policeman." I was stunned. I didn't know what to say or what to do.'

'So, what happened next?'

'We drove back to the Holiday Inn and went up to our room. There Suleiman forced open the tin and counted the money. There was a lot of money in it. I saw a lot of notes. He was very happy at that. I then asked him to tell me what happened to the policeman. He said one of his men went to see where the politician was sleeping but there were a lot of policemen around so he shot a policeman. He didn't explain any more than that.'

'How did you feel about that?'

'I was shocked. This is not what I thought his organisation did. Anyway, I now realised that he was a dangerous man so decided to be very careful. I didn't ask any more questions. I went into the bathroom and took off my dress and put on my night dress over my underclothes. I kept them on just in case. I then climbed into my bed, turned my back on Suleiman who was still fiddling with the money and I pretended to be asleep. At about one am I heard him snoring so I quietly got out of bed and went to the bathroom with my mobile and phoned you. I hadn't seen you anywhere and didn't know where you were. I didn't even know if you were in the hotel.'

'I was actually in a room on the top floor of the Plaza. When I answered, you suddenly cut off our conversation. Why did you do that?'

'I was sitting on the toilet and I heard Suleiman moving. I thought he had woken up and I didn't want him to hear me talking and then come into the bathroom and catch me on the phone.'

'What happened then?'

'I went back to bed. He hadn't woken up, just turned over, but I wasn't going to take any chances, so I didn't try ringing you again.'

'OK, so it is now about half past one in the morning. What happened after that?'

'I didn't go to sleep. I couldn't sleep. I just lay in bed wondering what mess I had got myself into and wondering how I could get out of it but must have dozed off because at six o'clock Suleiman woke me up. He gave me a shake and said we must leave for London straight away. I got up, dressed and we left without having any breakfast. I think he paid for our stay with the money from the tin.'

'Is that the end?

'He dropped me off outside my block of flats. He said I must not tell anyone what had happened and drove off. I haven't seen or heard from him since.'

'Well that is very helpful, Anita. I am sure my boss will be very pleased with the information you have given us. Are you happy to go on helping us?'

'So long as I am safe. Yes.'

'Don't worry about being caught up in the mess, as you put it. I will help you and keep you out of trouble.'

Johnson and Anita were so engrossed in their conversation that they were surprised to see the waiter walking across the lawn towards them. 'Lunch is ready sir,' he said.

They walked to the dining room and were shown to a table in the corner. There were only five other tables with customers. The menu for them to choose from was on the table. Johnson said, 'don't be shy. Order what you want. Let's celebrate. Have a starter and a main course. We can choose desserts later if we want them.'

Anita was a bit shy about appearing too greedy, so he chose for her. 'What about a prawn cocktail for starter?' He suggested.

'Yes. I love prawns,' she replied.

'And what would you like for main? What about steak and kidney pie?'

'Yes please. I love steak and kidney pie also,' she said.

'I'll have the same.' He ordered two prawn cocktails and two steak and kidney pies.

'Would you like another drink?' He asked. 'What about another appletizer?'

'Thanks.'

He ordered one appletizer and a half pint of bitter for himself.

Whilst they were eating their lunch their conversation drifted to her late husband. It was obvious that she had been very fond of him and was devastated by his death. She now knew he had been radicalised but had not realized it at the time. She said he spent a lot of time on his laptop before he went to Pakistan. Since then, all her friends had dropped her because the story had got out that her husband was a member of the Taliban. Coupled with being disapproved of by her parents and ostracized by her parents-in-law, she gave the impression of being a very lonely lady.

'What's happened to his computer?' he asked.

'Nothing. It's lying at the bottom of my wardrobe.'

'Do you ever use it?'

'No, I haven't even opened it since he left.'

'Would you mind if I had a look at it?'

She thought for a while. 'No. But I would like it back when you've finished with it.'

'Of course. I will be personally responsible. When can I get it?'

'If you drop me off near my flat I will run up and get it and you can have it straight away,' she said.

'Thanks. We'll do that.'

They finished their meal and then left for home. They chatted all the way about their school days. She loved sport, hockey and tennis. He told her that he liked football and cars. They arrived at Tower Hamlets and he stopped some distance away from her block where he found a parking space. She ran off and appeared fifteen minutes later with a laptop in a carrying case. He got out and thanked her for being so frank and then he remembered her money. He leant into the glove pocket and took out an envelope and gave it to her.

'There is only two hundred and fifty in here,' he said. 'My boss said it would be too risky if you suddenly came into a lot of money at one time. The rest will be held in credit for you and we will pay it to you in dribs and drabs. If you want any at any time, just call me.'

She didn't look very happy but accepted it. He felt a bit of a heel after her being so frank with him. He would speak to Mrs B. He was sure she would be pleased to get the laptop. He would see if he could squeeze a bit more out of her. Anita thanked him for the lunch and the lovely outing and walked back to her flat.

He arrived back at his flat at four-thirty and immediately telephoned Mrs B. He thought what he had was too important to leave until Monday. She answered immediately, even though it was Saturday afternoon.

'Can we scramble Mrs B? Number eight here.' There were some clicking sounds as she encrypted her phone and he did the same.

'You had a good meeting I assume,' said Mrs B.

'Yes, very good. I've got some tapes and a laptop. She gave me her husband's laptop which she hasn't used since he went away. I've got it on condition that I return it when we've finished with it.'

'Bring them round first thing tomorrow morning. I will meet you at my office at nine.'

The following morning Johnson arrived at Mrs B's office with his tapes and the laptop.

'I was going to bring Colonel Rutherford in,' she said, 'but on reflection I think it would be better if I listen to the tapes first and bring you in for a discussion later. We'll have him here then. I think the laptop could be quite interesting.'

'I want to talk to you about Delia at the same time.'

7

Fitzgerald put the phone down. 'ROBIN,' he shouted. He was calling his number two, Detective Inspector Robin Catchpole. Catchpole put his head round the door.

'That was London. I think we've got a breakthrough.' He looked pleased and relieved at the same time.

Detective Chief Superintendent Arthur Fitzgerald was the senior officer despatched from the Met's Counter Terrorism Command with a team of one Inspector, Catchpole, and two Sergeants. The rest of his team was made up of personnel seconded from the local C.I.D. An incident room had been set up at Wolverhampton Police Headquarters. Sergeant Nelson, from Special Forces, had stayed for two days and then left for London.

'Apparently, they had a spook at the meeting, an Asian woman with an Asian male companion. After the meeting, the male boasted that they had shot a policeman,' said Fitzgerald. 'We don't know if they were part of or connected with al-Abdullah or not. They had apparently been staying at the Holiday Inn. Have we checked out the Holiday Inn?' Fitzgerald looked at him with an enquiring expression.

'No sir. It was right off my radar.'

'Right then we will have to do that ... What's the time?' looking at his watch, 'half past four. At the morning briefing tomorrow, we'll have a full discussion with the whole team and work out a plan. Make sure everybody is there. Don't say anything to them beforehand.'

Catchpole left the office. Fitzgerald spent his time collecting his thoughts for the briefing in the morning. He was fully aware that they had spent a whole week on the investigation and got nowhere. He was determined not to let this opportunity slip by.

He also knew how important it was to keep all members of his team fully briefed as to what was going on. He insisted that there was a briefing every morning at nine am which had to be attended by every member unless they were on active investigations elsewhere, but on Mondays, at the start of the week, everybody had to be there for a full briefing so that they were all 'singing from the same hymn sheet' as he called it.

The following morning everybody assembled, sitting around at their respective desks or tables. Fitzgerald came in five minutes later and took up a position by the incident board. Catchpole was sitting beside him, facing into the room.

'Good morning Ladies and Gentlemen. We've had a break.' There was an audible sigh of relief from everyone. 'Before I come to that let's have a round-up of what we have got so far.'

'Steve?' pointing to Detective Sergeant Steve Francis. Francis had been tasked with contacting as many people as possible who had been at the meeting. They knew there had been 204 chairs laid out in the hall, most, if not all, had been occupied. They had put out an appeal over the media for people to call a special phone number.

'Only seventy-nine persons have responded so far. Most left immediately after the meeting, some went to the dining room for dinner. No-one saw or heard anything untoward.'

'Smethers?' Woman Detective Sergeant Jane Smethers had been assigned the task of contacting all the hotel guests. She was local to Wolverhampton. Eighteen rooms had been occupied. 'I've managed to contact all bar three couples who have apparently gone abroad. Most did not attend the meeting and most did not have dinner at the hotel. They had other things to do in town. Again, no-one saw or heard anything suspicious.'

'Luke?' pointing at Detective Sergeant Luke Macdonald. His

assignment had been to check the hotel staff. 'I've spoken to all the regular staff, but I have to say they did not strike me as being very co-operative. I had to draw any information from them. They did not volunteer anything. I had to put assorted options to them and they either replied "Yes" or "No". Apparently, there were some casual staff present on that night, but the regulars were remarkably ignorant as to who they were. The casuals were interviewed by the local CID immediately after the incident and had now left. I got the impression they were trying to hide something.'

'It could be because one of their number was killed, or someone whom they thought was one of them, and they think the finger of suspicion will be pointed at them,' said Fitzgerald. 'You know how people are. We'll come back to them later.'

'Right, we've had a break,' he said again. Fitzgerald then gave them all the information he had. He had everybody's full attention. 'It's not much but it's all we've got so let's not waste it. It looks very likely that Baxter's murderer was someone from an extreme organisation, possibly, but by no means certain, Islamic. Now that we've got something to work on I would like to start again from scratch. I think we'll concentrate on the staff. Robin, I would like you to work with Luke on this. In the meantime, I will have another chat with the manager. One other thing. Sooner or later, I will have to face the press and I want something to tell them. At present, we have nothing. OK, let's go to it.'

Catchpole asked. 'Did Sergeant Nelson know about this spook when he was here?'

'I don't know. He certainly said nothing to me,' Fitzgerald replied.

'I wonder sometimes if we're all fighting the same war,' Catchpole remarked. With that everyone left the room.

They all knew that in his younger days Fitzgerald had a fearsome reputation. It was said he never gave up and never lost a case. That was why at the age of thirty-four he was a Chief Superintendent.

Catchpole, on the other hand, at thirty-six and with two more years' service, was an Inspector, three ranks below him. Everybody knew that Fitzgerald would not tolerate mistakes or cock-ups. They would have to be very thorough.

Fitzgerald telephoned the hotel manager, Mr Japour, and asked if he could come and see him in his office. An appointment was made for two o'clock. At two o'clock on the dot he arrived and was shown in by Japour's Personal Assistant. They had met before and had got on very well together. Fitzgerald knew that if you want to get co-operation from people it is far better to interview them in their own environment rather than ask them to attend the police station. Attending a police station seems to carry stigma with it.

'How's it going?' asked Japour.

'We've got a slight crack to work on which is why I'm here.'

'Good. How can I help?'

'I'm sorry but I have to interview all your staff again,' said Fitzgerald.

Japour looked shocked. 'Not good news. You know it causes an awful lot of disruption.'

'Yes, I know but we did not have this new bit of information when we first spoke to them and I feel sure that one of them may be able to help. Just one point, when my man, Sergeant Macdonald, interviewed them originally, he said they did not seem very co-operative, almost as if they had something to hide.'

'Well, I hope none of them are involved. It could be a language issue. Half of them do not have English as their first language.

'Just as a matter of interest, how many staff do you have?'

'Let's see. Two chefs and two assistants in the kitchens; two full time barmen; three receptionists – two male one female; six waiters who work in the restaurants and bars. Those are my full-time staff and then we have four ladies who come in in the mornings to make beds and contract cleaners who come as required. The cleaners and bed makers are always gone by five pm at the latest. If we need any more staff I get agency staff from the employment agency; and finally, we have Lewis.'

'Who is Lewis?'

'He's the under manager. He was a student doing a course in Hotel Management and did his practical here. We took him on permanently when he graduated. He's been here now about thirteen months. He's settled in very well. That's not his proper name, by the way. He is Bangladeshi. I think his proper name is Khalid.'

'Did you get any agency staff for the meeting last Friday?'

'Yes, six. Lewis's job is dealing with all staff matters and he holds all their records. I'll tell him to liaise with you when you want to interview the staff. No. I'll tell you what, you can use his office which will, I hope, speed things up.'

'Thank you very much. I make that sixteen permanent staff, including Lewis, plus six agency workers here on the night. Twenty-two in all?'

'Yes. Sounds right.'

'Which employment agency do you use?'

'Able Employment in Birmingham. We've been using them for years. They know what we want.'

'What about CCTV?'

'We have cameras in all the public rooms. Lewis's job is to look after them.'

'Thank you very much Mr Japour. It's very kind of you. I would like to start tomorrow and we will cause as little disruption as possible.'

'Good bye Mr Fitzgerald.'

Fitzgerald returned to the incident room and called Catchpole into his office.

'I've just had a very interesting chat with Japour and organised for you to start interviewing the staff tomorrow. He's giving you the under-manager's office. There were twenty-two staff there on Friday, sixteen hotel staff and six agency workers.'

'Did you say twenty-two staff?' asked Catchpole looking at a file in his hand. 'I've only got twenty names here.'

'Yes; definitely twenty-two.' Fitzgerald paused. 'That's two missing ... I wonder why? Oh. He said the lack of co-operation could be language problems. You'd better check the names carefully tomorrow. Now what about the Holiday Inn? We'd better check that out. Send Joe Swift.'

'I've already sent Jane Smethers. She's not getting very far with the guests, so I've taken her off that for a while.'

Fitzgerald continued. 'I believe the post-mortem is being done tomorrow so with a bit of luck we'll have some information on the type of firearm used. That'll give us something else to follow up.'

Catchpole left and Fitzgerald turned to his Investigation Diary. He kept a detailed log of everything that was being done during the investigation especially tasks he allocated to his team, so that he could check that he got a follow up report from them. He was concentrating on his diary when suddenly Catchpole put his head round the door. 'Boss. You had better listen to this.'

The way it was said gave Fitzgerald a surge of excitement. Catchpole stood aside and ushered Jane Smethers into the office.

'I was checking the reception at the Holiday Inn, sir,' she said, 'in particular those who left early on Saturday morning. The hotel was about two thirds full. The occupants from six rooms left early, before breakfast. Three paid up the night before and it's not known when they left. The other three came down just after six when the reception opened.'

She continued, 'I made a note of all their names, addresses and car registration numbers and then checked them out. Five tallied but the sixth did not. Their names were Mr and Mrs S. Khan. The address given was in Edinburgh, but it doesn't exist. The car registration given was Y434HBS. This is a Ford Escort Van that was scrapped in Bristol four years ago. Also, the receptionist said the man was very agitated, asking why it was taking so long to complete the paperwork. He had a very young wife who stood in the background and said nothing. She did not think that the girl was his wife.'

'What nationality were they?' asked Fitzgerald.

'The man was Asian, middle-aged with a small moustache. The girl was also Asian and looked in her early twenties. She was very pretty and looked a bit shy.'

Fitzgerald looked at Catchpole. 'I said we would crack it sooner or later.' To Jane Smethers, 'well done Jane. Wonderful work. You might as well continue and follow up on the van. Interesting that it was scrapped in Bristol!'

'Thank you, sir.' They both left the office.

8

Baxter's body had been transferred from Wolverhampton to Westminster Hospital in London, and placed in the latest high technology mortuary, the Ian West Forensic Suite, for an autopsy. This was to be carried out by Professor Robert Fraser MD FRCS FRCP assisted by mortuary technician, "Sergeant" Alfred Griffiths. Griffiths had been a police officer in the Met. but he had been discharged early on medical grounds. He then qualified as a Mortuary Technician and was posted to the Ian West Forensic Suite where the work was not as arduous as active police work. Although no longer a Sergeant he was still known as "Sergeant" Griffiths to everybody who knew him. He was always in attendance at important police cases where his previous police experience was useful to the pathologist.

On the morning of Baxter's autopsy Griffiths removed the body from the fridge, stripped off all clothing and laid it on a stainless-steel table on its back. He placed a small wooden block under the head and then covered the whole table with a white sheet for the sake of decency. The body needed a good two hours to thaw before the examination could take place. He checked that all instruments needed were placed on a small table at the side as well as several bottles, test tubes and plastic bags for specimens.

Also present was Detective Constable Sidney Fox of the Counter Terrorism Command. Although not involved directly in the investigation he had been briefed to make a note of any queries the pathologist might have. He took a seat in the viewing gallery with a speaker and microphone beside him. He recalled the first post-mortem he attended whilst under training, on a cancer patient. He had never seen a dead body before, let alone one completely naked. He almost brought up when the pathologist sliced it open. This, however, was the first case where the deceased was a victim of a crime. He was interested to see how the evidence was recovered from the body. He recognised the distinctive smell that he had noted at his first PM. The smell of death someone had called it. It wasn't unpleasant but noticeable. He always wondered what happened to bodies that were decomposing when brought in for post-mortem. Maybe the smell was a deodorant they used to camouflage the decomposition.

In the office immediately adjoining was a stenographer sitting at a computer with earphones on her head. She would record the dictation directly onto the pro-forma for the post-mortem report as the pathologist dictated it. A voice recording would also be made.

At ten o'clock Professor Fraser walked into the room, smoking a pipe.

'Are we ready Fred?' he asked.

'Yes sir.' Griffiths helped him into a green surgical gown and handed him his rubber gloves. He then clipped a microphone onto his collar.

'Can you hear me, Mavis?' to the stenographer who he could see through the connecting window. She waved her arm and nodded in reply.

The Professor took up a position by the side of the table. Griffiths removed the sheet.

'Male Adult Caucasian, age?' Querying look at Griffiths;

'54 years,' said Griffiths;

'54 years (stated),' into the mike.

'Height 1.8 metres?' Griffiths nodded.

'Weight 82 kilograms?' Griffiths nodded again.

'Date and time of death?' Griffiths held up a piece of paper, 'Friday 17th August 2012 – between 2200 and 2300 hours (stated).'

'External examination. Single gunshot wound to the head. Entry wound just left of centre of the forehead. No exit wound noted. No sign of powder or burning around the wound noted. This indicates that the shot was not fired close to the skin. No other external wounds or abnormalities noted.'

'X-ray examination of the head.' Griffiths pulled the portable X-ray over and helped the Professor position it to take a shot of the head from the top, sides and the front. These would be relayed automatically to the X-ray department in the hospital and the results sent through to the mortuary later.

The Professor then took a long thin metal rod, inserted it into the gunshot wound and pushed it in carefully until it came to stop against something solid, the bullet.

'Rod inserted into the wound indicates depth of wound 6.5 centimetres. Angle shows trajectory of bullet to be slightly from left to right and slightly downwards. This indicates that the deceased was probably seated and looking up at the assailant at the time of the shooting. It is also likely that the shooter was right-handed. Photos taken.'

Griffiths handed him a camera and he took several photos of the head with the rod sticking out.

'Specimens taken from under fingernails.' He nodded to Griffiths. This was his job. He went and sat on a bar stool at the side of the room and re-lit his pipe whilst Griffiths got on with his task.

Griffiths took each hand in turn and scraped under the fingernails, dropping the matter onto two clean pieces of white paper which he then folded over and marked left and right. Next, he took two swabs and cleaned the hands and fingers, placing the swabs into two plastic bags marked left and right. Finally, he took fingerprints from all ten digits by rolling a small rubber roller with a light film of fingerprint ink on it over the fingers and thumbs. He lifted each digit and pressed it onto a special printed form making an impression of each digit separately. Fraser had to witness all this as the report would bear his name and if there were to be a query over any of this, he would have to give the evidence in court. By being present, he maintained the chain of evidence. When Griffiths had finished, Fraser took over again.

'Internal examination of skull.'

He took a scalpel and made an incision across the top of the scalp from ear to ear. He pulled the tissue down to the front and back exposing the top of the skull. Taking a small electric circular saw he cut completely around the top of the skull. Inserting a scalpel into the cut he levered off the top exposing the brain tissue beneath.

'Brain tissue examined from top. No damage or abnormalities noted.'

Taking a wooden spatula, he probed into the tissue where the bullet was likely to be, carefully cutting away the last bit with a scalpel. This exposed the bullet.

'Small calibre bullet located in Right Cerebral Hemisphere and removed.'

Using a pair of rubber tipped forceps he carefully plucked the bullet from the brain and dropped it onto a wad of cotton wool in a kidney bowl being held by Griffiths.

'Slight haemorrhaging noted in the brain tissue around the bullet. Otherwise, brain appears normal.'

'Internal examination of cadaver.'

Taking a scalpel, he made a long incision from the base of the neck to the genitals, pulling the tissue back on either side and clamping it with clamps, exposing the internal organs. He picked up a large pair of stainless steel cutters and cut out the sternum, exposing the lungs and heart.

'Lungs have several grey black patches covering about ten percent of the surface area caused by smoking.'

Next, he probed into the centre left pushing the lung out of the way exposing the heart in its sack. He cut open the sack with a scalpel.

'Heart normal and healthy. Blood vessels into and out of heart normal and healthy. Trachea clear and healthy. Oesophagus clear and healthy.'

He pulled aside the stomach exposing blood lying at the bottom of the abdomen. Taking a small electric pump, he pumped it out into a container and measured the volume.

'Four point nine litres of blood in the cadaver.' Normal is about five litres indicating that very little blood had been lost.

Next, he cut open the stomach. 'Small quantity of undigested food in stomach. Specimen taken.' He scooped out a small quantity and put it into a test tube handed to him by Griffiths.

'Pancreas and kidneys normal and healthy.'

'Liver. Slight scarring on large lobe caused by alcohol. Not serious.'

'Small intestine. Normal and healthy.'

'Large intestine. Normal and healthy. Specimen of stool taken.' He cut into the colon and scraped out a little of the content putting it into another test tube handed to him by Griffiths.

'Bladder half full. Sample of urine taken.' He scooped out a little urine with a spoon and poured it into a bottle which Griffiths gave him.

'Death caused by a single gunshot wound to the head. Death would have been instantaneous.' Fraser took off his gloves and gown and left Griffiths to finish off.

Detective Constable Fox, who had witnessed the whole operation from the viewing gallery and heard the pathologist's dictation on his speaker, put away his notebook. The result was as expected, no surprises. Poor old Baxter was killed with a single shot. He took cold comfort from the fact that he probably had not known what hit him. He returned to his office and reported to his superior.

Meanwhile Griffiths replaced the sternum and top of skull and sewed up the incisions. As this was a murder enquiry, he slid a large white plastic tube over the whole body tying the ends up and tying a label with name and a reference number to the feet. He placed it on a tray and slid it back into the fridge. He parcelled the specimens up and sent them to forensics for checking for drugs or poisons or other foreign matter. He placed the fingerprints in an envelope for the Scenes of Crime Fingerprint department for them to check for elimination purposes.

He took great care over the bullet carefully packing it in wadding and bubble wrap to ensure it was not damaged and despatched it by secure courier to the London Hub of The National Ballistics Intelligence Service (NaBIS), the Police high tech. ballistics centre, for detailed forensic examination. It was received by Detective Chief Inspector Dave Smith.

D/C/I Smith carefully opened the parcel and removed the bullet. He examined it by eye. There was something not quite right. He placed it under his microscope and couldn't believe what he saw.

'Ere come and 'ave a shuftie at this,' he said to his colleague at the next bench. Detective Sergeant Arbuthnot went over and placed his eye on the eyepiece. 'There's no grooves,' he said. 'Where'd it come from?'

'That's what killed old Baxter.'

'What's the calibre?'

'I haven't checked yet, but it looks like a 22.'

'Do we know the weapon?'

'No.'

'Looks like a smooth bore. What smooth bore 22 weapon do we have?'

'I don't know. Could be homemade.'

'There are some marks. It has obviously been fired out of something. Looks like the barrel was dirty which has left pitting. May be difficult to match but at least there is something,' said Arbuthnot. Arbuthnot was a university graduate with a degree in physics. Smith earned his place by long service and experience.

Smith photographed the bullet on his special comparison microscope noting all the marks seen. He checked the calibre. It was ·22 but he could not identify the weapon that had fired it. He then made out his report. He removed the bullet and carefully wrapped it for storage until a test bullet was obtained. There was nothing else that could be done.

At Scenes of Crime (Fingerprint) Department, the prints taken by Griffiths were handed over to a civilian undergraduate, Cindy Cameron, for checking against the prints lifted at the scene in the hotel. Baxter's prints were clear on both the trolley handles and were eliminated. They were also found on the wine bottle and glasses together with other prints which overlaid them. Probably the MP and his friends, she thought. Their prints were not available to eliminate them. But also on the trolley handles were another set of prints that matched each other but were different to all the others. Unfortunately, they were not sufficiently clear to be good enough as evidence for court purposes but there was sufficient for her to say that the person who had made them was one and the same. She completed her report containing all this information. All the prints were carefully placed in a file and stored away until required again.

9

The phone rang as Johnson was eating his breakfast. It was Mrs B. 'Can you come in and see me this morning Number Eight. I've got something to talk to you about?'

'Yes Ma'am,' he replied, 'I'll leave right away.'

He was expecting this call. He was wearing his casual clothes as usual and collected his overalls and duffel bag from the glory hole and went to his car. He started up and using the back road to avoid the traffic, eventually arrived at his headquarters at about nine. He rode up in the lift to the second floor and walked to office 26. Sarah was not in the office. He knocked on the inner door and entered. Mrs B was sitting behind her desk as usual.

'Good morning Mrs B. Where's Sarah?'

'Good morning number eight. Sarah is on leave, getting married.'

'Sarah getting married?' he exclaimed with a surprised look on his face.

'Yes. Don't look so surprised. She is marrying her long-standing partner.' In fact, Mrs B knew she was already married and was on another job.

'Blimey!' He thought he had better say no more; wonders never cease.

Mrs B addressed him, 'I've got your computer,' she leant down and pulled up the computer in its case and placed it on her desk. 'The computer techs have checked it out. It had an Arabic password so unless Delia could speak Arabic it is unlikely that she could have opened it even if she wanted to. It contained mostly religious stuff about Islam but there was also material about the Prophet and the punishment that should be meted out to anyone who insults him. And quite a lot on the Taliban and what they stand for. It seems that Mr Raji Khan was very interested in the more extreme forms of Islam. In other words, I think we can safely assume he had been radicalized.'

Mrs B was looking directly at Johnson who was concentrating intently on what she was saying. 'Does Colonel Rutherford know about this?' he asked.

'Not yet but I intend to tell him. He has listened to the tapes you made and was very interested in what he heard. However, despite what she told you I think you have got to realize your contact is the widow of a radicalized extremist. I would be very careful how you treat her. She may not be as innocent as she appears.'

Mrs B continued. 'They have taken out the hard drive and replaced it with another one. They have also noted the code and given it a new password. The new password is "Wonder 1234". I suggest when you give it back to Delia you say the computer was broken and that our people have fixed it for her so she can use it if she wants. How far can you trust her?' she asked.

'I don't really know,' he replied. 'I haven't seen enough of her. On the face of it she seems honest, if anything, a little vague.'

'I gather she is very pretty?'

Johnson hesitated, a little embarrassed by the question. 'Yes, she is but she is pregnant,' he answered, as if pregnancy would make her less attractive, sort of exonerating him for thinking her pretty.

'Well be careful,' said Mrs B. 'Give her back her computer and say we have fixed it for her and perhaps you could suggest diplomatically that she use it to assist Mr Suleiman. She could offer to do clerical work for him.'

'I was going to ask if we could pay her a bit more because she is very hard up. She is also very lonely as most of her friends deserted her when they heard that her husband was a member of the Taliban.'

'Here give her another two hundred and fifty',taking the money from her drawer – 'and tell her we will pay her for any information she gives us. No, I'm not going to pay at a higher rate until we know more about her. Keep her hungry, that will encourage her to work for us.'

Although he was annoyed at this brutal remark, he kept quiet, his face blank. He knew that he should not get emotionally involved with an agent.

Mrs B continued, 'I've got another job for you. I want you to go to Bristol. I have an old chum there, Mrs Margaret McGregor; a very old friend – we go back to our school days. She has a son who is in his second year at Bristol University. The son, Adrian, has a close Indian friend who is also at Bristol. This chap persuaded Adrian to go with him to a meeting at the college where the speaker, a visiting Muslim whom he thought might be a cleric, gave a talk on Islam and what a wonderful world it would be if everybody was a Muslim. What concerned Adrian was that this meeting seemed to be in secret. Only invited people could attend. He felt very uneasy about the whole thing and told his mother. I would like you to go to Bristol, see Margaret and Adrian and diplomatically find out what is going on. It may or may not be connected to al-Abdullah. I'm sure you know how to handle it.'

'Can I go there in my car?' he asked, 'then I've got transport at the other end.'

'Right, and here is some money,' handing him two hundred pounds. 'You can trust Margaret. She knows what I do, but not Adrian.'

Johnson left the office. He decided that he would first return Anita's computer to her before heading for Bristol. He would not try and persuade her to use her computer for Suleiman, he would just casually mention it and see how she responded. He was fully aware that the computer whiz kids would be monitoring it and it would be an effective way to test whether she was trustworthy or not.

What Johnson did not know was that Mrs B had sent "Q" around to Anita's flat and they had secretly installed a hidden camera and microphone. He didn't realise they knew her address.

10

The following day D/Inspector Catchpole and D/Sergeant Macdonald went to the Old Plaza Hotel and asked reception if they could see the manager. They were shown into his office by his PA. They introduced themselves showing their warrant cards.

'This is Lewis,' said Mr Japour, indicating a smart young man standing next to his desk, 'he is the assistant manager. He has cleared his office for you and will help you in your work. Please be as quick as you can.' They all shook hands.

'Please follow me gentlemen,' said Lewis, as he opened the door and beckoned them out. They followed him up the stairs to the first floor, down a short passage to a small office on the right. There was a window overlooking the foyer below. There was also a door shutting off the passage.

Catchpole asked, 'Where does that door go to?'

'That leads to the Premier Suites,' said Lewis. We always keep it locked.'

'Do you know where the key is kept?'

'There,' pointing to a board hanging on the wall.

'That's very handy,' said Catchpole pointing at the window, 'you can keep an eye on all comings and goings.'

'Yes, I can,' agreed Lewis. 'Here are all the staff records you want. How do you want to work it and who would you like to see first?'

'I would like to interview them in here in private. Can we begin by going through all the names?'

Lewis took down the pile of folders and checked the names against Catchpole's list. 'Do you have the names of the agency workers?' Catchpole asked.

'Yes, but all I have is the names they give me,' answered Lewis. 'The Agency keeps all the records. We just get numbers. We had six on duty that night.'

'What duties did you give them?'

'Two were assigned to the kitchen to help the chef. The other four were waiters. We had a full dining room that night.'

'Could we start with the head chef?'

'Fine.' Lewis picked up the phone and asked for the head chef to report to his office.

After five minutes, there was a knock at the door and the head chef, Mr Imran Madoka entered. They gave him a chair to sit on.

Mr Madoka told them he was 43 years old, an immigrant from Pakistan, had been in the UK for sixteen years and had been head chef for five years. His wife worked as a receptionist.

'Were you on duty on Friday 17th August?'

'Yes sir. I remember that night very well.'

He gave a detailed account of their duties. 'We were very busy because the dining room was full.'

'Do you remember the agency workers who were there that night?'

'Yes sir. Very well. Two were in the kitchen with me.'

'Do you know their names?'

'No. One was a Pakistani. The other one was a white man. The white man said his name was "Tommy". He was quite young and he had a red beard.'

'Did the Pakistani give you his name?'

'No. He was a very quiet man.'

'What duties did you give Tommy?'

'He was a very big nuisance. He wanted to do everything himself.

If anybody wanted something he would shout, "I will do it. I will do it." I kept telling him that I tell people what to do but he would not listen to me.'

'So, what did you do to keep him quiet?'

'At about half past six he looked out of the door and saw it was getting dark so he asked me where he could go to pray.'

'Did you say "pray"?' asked Catchpole, incredulous.

'Yes. Pray. I didn't know what he meant so I said he could use my office. At least it might keep him out of the way for a while.'

'So, what happened?'

'He went to my office and shut the door. I don't know what he did but he came out after about ten minutes.'

'What happened after that?'

'He carried on as before, constantly talking and being very annoying.'

'Do you remember when the order came down for drinks and later dinner to be sent up to one of the Premier Suites?'

'Yes. Tommy said he would take the trolleys even though I said just put them in the lift.'

'And did he put them in the lift?'

'I don't know. He was away for a long time. I was very happy when he was away because he was such a nuisance when he was in the kitchen.'

'When he came back did he look or behave any differently?'

'I don't know. I tried not to look at him or talk to him. I just wanted him out of the way.'

'Was he a Muslim?'

'I don't think so. I'm a Muslim and I don't know of any Muslims that behave like him.'

'Thank you very much, Mr Madoka. If you remember anything more about Tommy will you tell us?'

'Certainly, I will. Thank you, sir,' and got up and left.

The other kitchen staff, the under-chef and two assistants, also remembered Tommy and confirmed what the head chef had said.

#

Nobody liked him.

After the kitchen staff, they went on to the receptionists. There was one lady and two men. They interviewed the lady first. She was the head chef's wife and was very nervous. Catchpole commented on this to Macdonald when she had left. Macdonald knew that she had been caught in flagrante delicto with another member of staff, one of the male receptionists and told Catchpole. He laughed. 'Alright, we won't spill the beans.'

The other male receptionist said that he came on the late shift at five pm when the other two went off. He remembered seeing a young Asian girl with a collection tin standing by the entrance. He assumed she had permission to be there. Later he noticed the tin on its own on the table by the revolving door and when people left after the meeting, many put money into it. Much later, he could not remember the time, an Asian man collected the tin. He was middle-aged with a moustache and thanked the receptionist as he left.

All the remaining members of staff were interviewed which took the rest of the day. No one had seen anything suspicious and no one had heard a gunshot. There was nothing new to add. Catchpole did all the questioning and Macdonald operated the tape recorder, making notes in a notebook about anything of importance.

Catchpole asked, 'do you notice something odd here, Luke? We have a Muslim as chief chef. I wonder what he does about cooking pork. So far as I know Muslims are not allowed to touch pork.'

'I don't know but I wouldn't rock the boat if I were you. Perhaps we could ask the manager. I don't think it has anything to do with this case.'

'We've still got to see Lewis. I think we will do it tomorrow when I have had time to digest what we have heard today. I wonder why he's called Lewis?'

They left for the police station and reported to Fitzgerald, who instructed them to go to Able Employment Agency as soon as possible now that they had something to follow up. 'We must identify

Tommy,' he said. 'I think he is our main suspect now.'

The following day Catchpole and Macdonald went to Able Employment Agency in Birmingham. On arrival, they were shown in to the manageress, Mrs Martin.

'One of your staff, Sergeant Swift, has already phoned about this case,' she said.

'Oh yes,' replied Catchpole, 'we've come instead, as we are directly involved in the investigation.'

'I've already taken out the cards of the persons we sent on that night, six of them, here they are,' handing them six index cards.

'Did you see any of them personally before you sent them?' asked Catchpole.

'No. It's all done by email. We avoid telephoning or seeing anyone we send out as it takes too long. We sent out 34 agency staff to various hotels and restaurants that night. We couldn't possibly see or speak to each one. The only thing we do is send the same persons to the same places if we can. We have a card system to enable us to do that. So far as the Plaza was concerned we could only send two, these two,' pointing out two cards, 'the other four were all new recruits, not long on our books.'

'Would we be able to contact them from the addresses we have here on the cards?'

'Well, possibly,' said Mrs Martin. 'We've found that a lot of recruits give false names and false addresses because they are on benefits and if they are found to be working, they will lose their benefits.'

'Do you report this to the authorities?'

'We did to start with,' she said, laughing, 'but we soon stopped. Not only did we not get any thanks for doing so but we very quickly got no enquiries from job seekers. Word got around on the grapevine and we were in serious trouble. It took a long time to get over it. I know you are policemen and think we should report anyone we think is moonlighting, but we are not here to police the benefits system. We are an employment agency and we rely on persons coming to us for our business. However, we always co-operate with the authorities if they have any enquiries.'

'I understand. We'll check these six out and if we need any more information can we come back to you?'

'Certainly.'

'One more thing, do you know if any of them were called "Tommy"?'

'No, they all had Asian names.'

On arrival, back at the station they had a meeting with Fitzgerald. After he had been brought up to speed with what they had found, Fitzgerald told them. 'The post-mortem has been done. Baxter was killed with a single gunshot wound to the head, much as we suspected. The pathologist says that it is likely that Baxter was seated and looking up at his assailant at the time he was shot. Ballistics report says that the weapon was ·22 calibre but interestingly there were no groove marks which indicates that it was a smooth bore weapon, possibly homemade. Fingerprints have identified Baxter's prints on the two trolleys, bottle and glasses and there were fragments of another set of prints on the two trolleys which had been overlaid by Baxter's. They state that these other prints were made by the same person. Oh, and I've sent out a bulletin to all police stations about the false number plates on the car at the Holiday Inn.'

He looked at his two assistants and saw he had their full attention.

He continued. 'From what you have just told me it seems very likely that the assassin came from the hotel, either a member of the permanent staff, or one of the agency staff. Chief suspect now is the unknown and mysterious "Tommy". We have got to identify and trace "Tommy". I think we are getting close to the stage when we could do with some help from the media. I'm thinking of Crimewatch, but we need to tie up a few loose ends first.'

'We've still got to interview Lewis,' said Catchpole, 'and we can possibly trace two of the agency staff sent on that night.'

11

Johnson had to get hold of Anita. Apart from anything else he had her computer and money for her. He decided the best way was again to arrange a meeting with Janet Butler, his old girlfriend. He put a call through to her.

'Hello Janet. Jimmy here.'

'Hello Jimmy. Funny you should call I have just been having a conversation with your friend Anita. She wants to see you urgently.'

'When did you speak to her?'

'Yesterday. I went to her shop. She is not very happy. We couldn't talk much because of other customers but she definitely wants to see you.'

'Would you ask her around to your place as before? Preferably tonight because I've got to go away for a few days. Could you ring me back to confirm? Sorry to bother you like this, but I am very busy now.'

'I'm at work so I can't use the phone. If I don't call back be at my flat at seven tonight.'

'Fine. Thanks.' Janet worked for an estate agent.

Johnson got himself ready for his trip to Bristol, filled up his car and checked it over. He did not want any breakdowns. It wasn't often that he had the chance to give his car a blast out on the motorway, so he was looking forward to the trip. As he anticipated being away for at least one night he looked up on the internet for a B&B. which he could afford and booked himself in for one night.

At six-twenty pm he set off for Tower Hamlets. He found a

parking place just around the corner and parked. It was just after seven. He took out his mobile and telephoned. Janet answered immediately.

'Is she there?' he asked.

'Yes. She has just arrived.'

'I'm parked just around the corner in Adair Road. Could you ask her to meet me at my car?'

He switched off and waited. Anita would have to come down in the lift. He estimated it would take at least ten minutes. After fifteen minutes, there was still no sign of her. After twenty minutes, he took out his phone to phone again when suddenly he saw her walking towards him along the pavement. He noticed her bump was beginning to show quite clearly, but she still looked ravishing. She spotted his car, came straight up and got into the front passenger seat without saying a word.

He started up and pulled away. He planned to drive to the car park at the swimming pool. The pool was shut now but locals had the right to park their cars there overnight. He planned to meld in amongst these parked cars where he would be unseen from the road.

He did not try to talk to Anita whilst driving because she was obviously not in a talkative mood. He arrived, found a slot and parked. The street lights, about forty yards away, gave just enough light for them to see each other.

'Something's wrong. Are you going to tell me?' he asked.

He looked at her and noticed tears in her eyes.

'Oh dear. Please tell me what's wrong because I can't help you if I don't know. Is it Suleiman?' She nodded.

'What's he done?'

She started sobbing. He pulled his handkerchief out of his pocket and gave it to her. She took it, wiped her eyes and blew her nose and then gave it back to him.

'Keep it,' he said.

'It was at Friday Prayers last week,' she said hesitantly, 'I was just leaving the mosque when he came up to me and said I must follow him. He led me back into the mosque to a small office with some chairs. We were alone and I was very frightened because of what he had done to that policeman. He then told me I was a very bad Muslim. I asked him why and he said because I had not avenged my husband's death. I didn't understand what he was talking about. He said my husband was killed by the infidels and I haven't avenged him.' She paused and then continued 'I think he's going to kill me,' and started sobbing again.

Johnson waited until she had composed herself and then asked, 'Does he go to that mosque?'

'No. I have never seen him there before but we're separated from the men so he might have been there, but I didn't see him.'

'How often do you go?'

'I only go to Friday Prayers. I thought he was going to tell me I must go more often. I didn't expect him to start talking about infidels and revenge.'

'Go on.'

'He said the worst infidels were the army and the police. And then he suddenly asked me if I had a boyfriend. I said I didn't. He repeated it, was I sure I hadn't got a boyfriend. I again denied it but I was afraid he might have seen me with you because I know you are a policeman.'

'The only time you have been with me is when we went to lunch at that pub and I am pretty sure he did not see us there. I think he is bluffing; trying to frighten you,' said Johnson.

She continued. 'Then he said the time had come for me to avenge my husband, as he put it, I must prepare myself. That really frightened me; what does he mean?' Anita then burst into tears again, 'I'm frightened, Jimmy.'

This was the first time she had called him Jimmy. He felt a surge of pity for her and desperately wanted to take her into his arms and give her a hug, but he knew he mustn't and anyway she would probably misinterpret what he meant. He put his hand on her arm.

'I want you to always remember that I will never let you come to any harm,' he said, 'but I can't do anything if you do not let me know what is going on. I assume this is why you have not been in touch with me?'

She nodded, her eyes still full of tears.

'Right. Let's work out a plan. We don't know who Suleiman is and we must know his proper name to be able to do something about him. I've got your computer here. Do you know how to use a computer?'

'Yes. We've got one at work. I put in the sales figures and can send emails. I'm not much good at anything else,' she said.

'That's fine. I suggest when you see him again say you have got a computer and ask him if you can be of any help with your computer. At least you will be showing willing so he will be unlikely to harm you. By the way it was broken, did you know that?'

'No.'

'Yes. Anyway, I have had it fixed but you've got a new password. It is "Wonder 1234". Wonder as in "Alice in Wonderland." Can you remember that?'

'Yes.'

'I've also got some more money for you. Another two hundred and fifty. My boss says again it would be dangerous for you to suddenly have a lot of cash as that would give the game away, so be careful about who knows you have it,' He handed her the envelope which she put in her bag.

'I'm going to be away for the next two or three days, but you can get me on my mobile. If you feel unsafe in your flat then you could always go to my uncle at the garage, where you took the fruit. Otherwise, I am sure Janet would help you.'

He started up the car. 'We had better get going. Remember once we have identified Suleiman our problems should be over.'

He dropped her off a block away from her flat and then drove home. She had recovered her composure a little, but he felt very unhappy having to leave her on her own.

The following morning, he got up early and went for his run. He made himself some breakfast and a large mug of coffee. He packed a small overnight bag and was ready to go.

Using back roads, he wove his way through town to the M4 avoiding the worst of the traffic. There was heavy congestion up to the Heathrow turnoff and then heavy traffic to the M25 flyover. After that the road cleared and he could put the car into sixth gear for the first time.

The car was performing beautifully. The engine was purring gently under the bonnet and responding immediately to the slightest touch on the accelerator. He pulled over to the outside lane and was quietly overtaking everything in front of him. He put on some music. He liked pop.

He was driving automatically, half concentrating on the road but also thinking of Anita and the conversation they had had last night.

Suddenly he noticed Junction 15, Swindon. 'Not bad going', he thought, 'under the hour.' Then Junction 16 flashed by. Shortly after he heard a strange noise. At first, he thought it was coming from the car so turned off the radio. Then he realised it was a siren. He looked in his rear-view mirror and there, far back were the unmistakable blue and yellow colours of a police car with flashing head lights and flashing blue light on the roof. He looked at his speedo – 103 mph.

'Bugger,' he said to himself. 'Damn and bugger.' This was the last thing he needed, to be caught up in a criminal charge. He took his foot off the accelerator and let the car coast to a slower speed. The police car drew level and indicated for him to pull over onto the hard shoulder. He did so and stopped. The police car stopped ten yards behind him. Two policemen got out, put on their caps and walked up to him. He opened the window.

'Good morning sir. Is this your car?'

'Yes officer.'

'Would you please step out of the car?' He put his hands through the open window and pulled out the ignition keys.

'Would you blow into here? One long blow.' He had a breathalyser test kit in his hand.

Johnson blew into the tube. The light stayed green.

'Do you know what speed you were driving at? We clocked you at 97 mph. You were exceeding the speed limit by 27 mph. Would you deny that speed?'

'No. If you say so. I wasn't looking at my speedo.' Silently he heaved a sigh of relief because he had heard that any speed over 100 mph resulted in instant arrest and impounding of the car.

'Can I see your driver's licence?' He pulled his licence out of his wallet and handed it over.

In the meantime, he noticed that the other policeman had been standing behind his car and was on his radio to somewhere. He assumed he was checking the registration with DVLA. Meanwhile the first officer carried out a check around the car for road-worthiness but found nothing wrong.

'I will have to issue you with a ticket for speeding,' he said handing him back his driver's licence. He pulled out his ticket pad and wrote in all the details as given by Johnson. 'You will hear in due course. You will probably have to appear before a Crown Court. The speed limit on this road is 70 mph.' The two returned to their car and drove off. Johnson sat for a while until they were out of sight. He swore again to himself. He would have to tell Mrs B. The worst thing was that his driver's licence had his real name and real address on them.

He set off, this time keeping to a steady 70 mph. He arrived at Bristol and using his satnav found the B.& B. It was too early to book in so he went and found a café and bought himself a late lunch.

After lunch, he drove off to locate Mrs McGregor's address. It was after 4.00 pm, too late to interview her. He telephoned her and made an appointment for the morning. The appointment was made for ten am.

He decided he would also telephone Mrs B in the morning and own up about his speeding ticket. He knew she would not be happy. At least he had a clean licence with no points.

12

Johnson woke at 6.00 am after a restless night in a strange bed. He got up, put on his tracksuit and trainers and went for a run to clear his head. When he got back, he had a shower in his en-suite bathroom and dressed. He had a "full English" breakfast as it was included in the price.

It was still too early for him to keep his appointment with Mrs McGregor so he drove into the town looking for the university. He located the headquarters near the town centre. At nine-thirty am he headed out to the suburbs to locate Mrs McGregor. He found her house quite easily. It was semi-detached with a small garden and parking area in the front and a well-developed garden at the rear. The parking area was empty so he drove in. He locked his car and rang the doorbell.

Mrs McGregor opened the door and greeted him with a smile.

'You must be the man from London,' she said, 'come in.' He entered. The door opened into a small vestibule where coats were hanging on hooks on the wall, and then led into the sitting room. It had a friendly cosy feel about it.

'Please sit down,' she said, 'would you like some tea?' There was a tray arranged with tea drinking paraphernalia and a plate of biscuits on a coffee table in front of the sofa. He didn't normally drink tea but he accepted a cup gratefully.

She then spent the next twenty minutes asking questions and talking about Mrs B. They had obviously been close friends at

Cheltenham Ladies College. Mrs B. he learnt, was always up to some prank or other and Mrs McGregor was constantly keeping her out of trouble.

'I don't know how she got away with it,' she said, 'but we had a lot of fun.' Somehow, he couldn't imagine Mrs B. being anything but correct.

'Well what about Adrian?' he asked. 'I gather you are worried about him?'

Her face took on a serious expression. 'He is at the university and has an Indian friend. They have been friends since school days. His friend said he had been invited to attend a secret meeting by some Asians and asked Adrian if he would like to come along. Adrian went and they had to listen to someone telling them about Allah and Islam and how it will save the world. Adrian felt very uncomfortable about what he was hearing and told me.'

'Did he know who the person was who was lecturing them?'

'I don't think so. He will be back shortly. He always comes home for lunch so you can speak to him yourself.'

'What's he reading at the university?'

'Media Studies. His Indian friend is doing Law.'

Johnson looked at his watch. It had just gone midday. To fill the time, he made small talk about her garden and the beautiful home she had made. He thought what a lovely character she was, with her gentle Scottish lilt.

At twelve-twenty Adrian arrived on a bicycle and came in through the front door. Johnson stood up and Mrs McGregor introduced him.

'I'm so sorry. I've forgotten your name'.

'Jimmy Johnson,' he said. 'I'm from the police crime prevention unit.' They shook hands and both sat down.

'Would you like some tea darling?' to her son.

'Yes please.'

'What about you, Mr Johnson. Can I refill your cup?'

'No thank you. That was lovely.'

'I've just been telling Mr Johnson about your meetings, darling, you know the ones we spoke about. He is from the Police. Could you tell him what you told me?'

'Is this going to get me into trouble? I didn't expect the police to become involved.'

'No, it won't get you into any sort of trouble,' Johnson interrupted. 'I'm from the Crime Prevention Unit. There are people going around the country holding these kinds of meetings and using them as an excuse to extract money from people. That is a crime and we are trying to stamp it out.'

'Do you think this is what he was trying to do to us?'

'I don't know. Tell me exactly what went on and I will be able to advise you.'

Adrian paused whilst he collected his thoughts. 'We were called to this meeting by one of the other Asians who told us about it. He said it must be secret and we must not talk to anyone about it.'

'Did he say what it was about?'

'No. He just said it would be a very interesting meeting.'

'So, what happened?'

'Mick and I went to the room where it was being held. It was at six o'clock in the evening when the Uni. had closed. The man was already there when we arrived. He was very friendly and pleased to see us.'

'How many were you?'

'Only six. Mick and me and four others who I didn't know.'

'I take it Mick is your Indian friend?'

'Yes, he's got an Indian name that I can't pronounce. Everybody calls him Mick.'

'So, what did this man talk about?'

'He talked about Allah and said the world needed Allah for peace. He said if everybody followed Allah there would be no trouble between people, and that sort of thing.'

'Did he ask you for any money or anything like that?'

'No. He just said we all have to give up something for Allah but did not say what.'

'So how did you feel about the meeting?'

'I wasn't very happy. I've never heard anyone saying that sort of thing before. It was peculiar.'

'What did this man look like?'

'He was an Asian, about forty years old, had black hair and a black moustache.'

'Did he speak good English?'

'Yes, but he had an accent.'

'And what did Mick think?'

'He thought it was quite interesting.'

'How many meetings have you been to?'

'Two.'

'And did he say the same things at both meetings?'

'Yes, but at the second meeting he showed us how to pray to Allah.'

'You mean he got down on his knees on the carpet.'

'Yes. He said we should do it every day and we would see how Allah works for us.'

'And have you done it every day?'

'No way,' pulling a face at the mere mention of doing such a thing.

'Are you religious, Adrian, what church do you belong to?'

'No.'

Johnson looked at Mrs McGregor. 'I'm Presbyterian,' she said as if to compensate.

'What about Mick. Is he religious?'

'He's a Hindu.'

Johnson paused to collect his thoughts. 'From what you have told me it seems this guy is trying to convert you to Islam, in other words, to become a Muslim. There is nothing illegal in that. The only thing that worries me is that the meetings are held in secret. Did this chap tell you his name?'

'He said we should call him Suleiman.'

Johnson's face did not flinch one jot although a surge of excitement went through his mind. Had he finally tracked down *the* Suleiman? He continued –

'What you've got to be careful of is that people like this persuade you to join their organisation and once you have, you are hooked. Then they rob you of everything you've got.' He paused and then continued, 'I am very glad you have told me all this. Most of the time we are only told after the person has been robbed, by that time it is too late.'

'So, what do I do now?'

'Do you want to help us track this person down and put a stop to his activities if he is trying to get money?'

'OK so long as it doesn't get me into trouble.'

'No, it won't get you into trouble. All you must do is go to some more meetings, note what he says and does and let me know. Your mother knows how to contact me.' Mrs McGregor nodded. 'At least you now know what to look out for so whatever he says, never agree to give him anything, especially money. Do you think you can do that?'

'You mean you want me to be your spy?'

'I wouldn't put it quite like that. The thing is we can only investigate crimes if people tell us about them. We can't guess what is going on. We rely on the public to tell us. Naturally whatever happens, don't tell him you are passing on what he says to the police otherwise if he is a criminal he will just vanish. Keep it to yourself and I wouldn't even tell Mick.'

'OK.' Adrian seemed quite pleased that he was becoming involved.

Johnson turned to Mrs McGregor. 'Are you happy that he should do this? If you are not, then say so.'

'No. Fine so long as you will make sure he is safe.'

'Oh, he will be safe enough. Just act normally. Don't try and do anything clever.'

Adrian had a few words with his mother. 'I'll be fine, Mum. I'll be fine. Don't worry.'

'Well, if there is nothing else,' said Johnson, 'I had better be off as I have a long way to go back to London.'

They all stood up and Johnson made his farewells. He got into his car and drove off, waving out of the window as he left. He was anxious to get back to London in case Anita wanted him. He still hadn't told Mrs B. about his speeding ticket and did not quite know how to do it.

Sticking religiously to the speed limit he arrived home at seven-thirty pm. As he had had no lunch and had nothing for his supper he stopped on the way at a MacDonald's and picked up two Big Macs to take away. There were no calls waiting for him when he reached home, so he took a beer can out of the fridge, sat down with his burgers to watch a bit of TV and when he had finished went to bed.

He awoke at six am and went for his usual 5 km run. On return he showered, dressed, had some breakfast with coffee and was ready to face Mrs B. He telephoned and was told to be at her office by nine am.

At nine on the dot he arrived at Office 26. Sarah was at her computer, looked up as he entered but said nothing, just carried on working. He went straight through to the inter-leading door, knocked and was told to enter. Mrs B. was behind her desk.

'Good morning, Number Eight. Did you have a good trip?'

'Yes, thank you. I got home last night at seven-thirty.' He paused trying to work out the best way to break the news, and then… 'Unfortunately, I picked up this on the way,' handing her the speeding ticket he had been given.

Mrs B. looked at it for some time and then looked at him. She was not smiling

'Where did you get this?'

'On the M4, Swindon.'

'Ninety-seven miles per hour. Why were you doing ninety-seven miles per hour?'

'I wasn't concentrating. I was thinking about Anita.'

'Who's Anita?'

'Sorry Delia. Anita is her proper name.'

'So, what is there about Delia that caused you to drive at ninety-seven miles per hour?'

'I had a meeting with her the night before to give her back her computer. She burst into tears. She said she is frightened. She had been told by Suleiman that she was not a good Muslim and must prepare to "avenge her husband's death" as he put it. She does not know what this might mean but since he admitted they had killed a policeman she is frightened that something unpleasant will happen to her.'

'Suleiman is the man she went to Wolverhampton with?'

'Yes.'

'So, what did you say?'

'I suggested she offer to use her computer to help with his cause. That way if he saw she was useful he wouldn't harm her. I also said that I would not let her come to any harm.'

'I think you must also find a way to contact her. I was concerned the other day when you said she could contact you, but you couldn't contact her. You must find a way to keep in touch with her, then you can reassure her and help her.

'Alright I will.'

'Did she have anything else to say about the organisation?'

'No.'

'What happened in Bristol? You saw my old friend Margaret?'

'Yes. I also saw Adrian. It seems that the meetings he is attending are just an attempt to persuade young people to convert to Islam and nothing else. The interesting thing, though, is that the person holding the meetings is named Suleiman and his description, vague as it is, is the same as the Suleiman who went to Wolverhampton.'

'So, what is he doing?'

'I warned him that people like that use their persuasive powers to get people to join them and then ask for money. So far no mention has been made of money, but they were shown how to pray to Allah.'

'Is he going to attend more meetings?'

'He said he would so I asked him to make a note of what was said and let me know via his mother.'

'Is Margaret happy about this?'

'Yes. I warned him not to do anything out of the ordinary, just to be aware that he may be asked to contribute money. He seemed quite happy to co-operate.'

'Does he know who you are?'

'I told him I was a policeman on the Crime Prevention Unit. I think it might be a good idea to get Special Branch in Bristol to follow up on the Suleiman bit. They may have some background we don't know about.'

'I will get Colonel Rutherford to look at that side.'

'Now this ticket,' handing him back his speeding ticket, 'I see it has got your proper name and address. You realise if your cover is blown you are no good to the Service?'

'Yes.'

'You are to pay any fine they impose. You are not to appear in court. I will have to report this to the Director. He may have something to say.'

'Is there any news from the team at Wolverhampton?' Johnson asked, trying to change the subject.

'I get bits and pieces from Colonel Rutherford. I gather they are not getting very far. The bullet that was recovered was apparently fired from a smooth bore weapon which they think may be homemade. Apart from that, the hotel took on six agency staff for the night, all of whom gave false names and addresses. One of them was a white convert who gave his name as "Tommy" and he made a bit of a nuisance of himself.'

'You mean a convert to Islam?'

'Yes and "Tommy" is their only suspect but I don't know that they have got any evidence against him. The only positive evidence they have is what Delia gave to you about the man admitting they had shot a policeman, so Delia is very important to the case.'

'Right then, I had better look after her.'

'You certainly must.' With nothing more to discuss, Johnson left her office and drove home. He was very worried about Anita's safety.

13

D/Inspector Catchpole and D/Sergeant Macdonald held a discussion between themselves listing things they still had to do. They were conscious they were not getting very far. The investigation seemed to have come to a halt. They realized they desperately needed a new initiative.

'We have still got to see Lewis', said Catchpole. 'I can't quite make him out. He was bloody helpful when we interviewed the staff, but I got the impression he was just a bit too co-operative, trying hard to please. What do you think?'

'He is still very young and this is possibly the first time he has been involved with the police. I don't know. I wouldn't be too hard on him. He may be our best chance of getting more information later.'

Catchpole continued. 'Anyway, we've still got the two regular agency staff to track down. We may be lucky with them. They may be able to identify the others. They may also be able to tell us more about "Tommy". Apart from that, the only other thing we must do is look for a likely weapon. I know a bit about weapons; I have never heard of a smooth bore ·22, have you?'

'No. They suggested it could be home made. I have heard,' said Macdonald, 'that some of these toy replicas that one can buy are so realistic that they can be converted into firing live ammunition. I've never seen one and can't think how anyone would go about it, but I suppose if you are desperate enough you will find a way.'

'Are you suggesting we go around all the toy shops asking if they have sold any replica guns recently?'

'No but the boss said he wanted to use Crime Watch. Maybe something could be put on there.'

'Well, I'll mention it to him, but I think we will need a bit more than mere speculation,' said Catchpole. 'Let's start with Lewis. I'll ring the manager and make an appointment.'

Catchpole telephoned and made an appointment for two pm. At two o'clock they arrived at the hotel and were shown into the manager's office.

'Are you getting anywhere?' asked Mr Japour after the usual greetings and handshakes.

'We wondered whether we could have a chat with Lewis. He was very helpful the other day when we interviewed the staff but we never had a chance to chat with him.'

'I'm afraid he's not here. He's on leave. He said his grandfather had been taken ill and was thought to be dying and asked if he could have time off. I gave him a week's compassionate leave.

'Do you know where he's gone?

'I'm afraid I have no idea. I've got a feeling he was going to London.'

Catchpole hesitated. It was annoying Lewis was not available. It would be more delay waiting for him to return. 'Could we look in his personal file, his address is bound to be there?' he asked. And then had an inspiration. Maybe Japour could answer some of the questions they wanted to ask Lewis. 'Just one thing, how much did Lewis know about the arrangements for the night of the meeting?'

'I told him the MP would be sleeping at the hotel and he would be bringing his own staff, we would not have to provide for him. I had to tell him something.'

'Yes. I fully understand. Did you tell him anything about the police arrangements?'

'No. I just said the police would be covering the meeting.'

'Did you tell him anything about numbers?'

'No.'

'Or that the waiter was in fact a policeman?'

'Certainly not!'

'Who chose Suite 113 for the MP?'

'The police Sergeant, Mr Nelson I think his name was.'

'And did Lewis know about that.'

'Oh, yes because he had to make sure the suite was made ready.'

'Thank you very much. I just wanted to get clear in my mind how things were planned on the night. Could we have a look at his file now please?'

'His file will be in his office. He handles all staff matters. I'll get my PA to accompany you.' He picked up his phone, 'Helen, could you come in here please?' A middle-aged lady opened the door and entered.

'This is Helen,' introducing her to the two policemen. 'Would you please take these two gentlemen to Lewis's office and show them the personal files. They want to see Lewis's own file.' They thanked the manager for his co-operation and accompanied by Helen went up the stairs to Lewis's office.

'I've absolutely no idea where Lewis keeps his files,' said Helen after they had entered the office, 'he does all his own filing.'

'I think they could be in the second drawer of that filing cabinet,' said Catchpole, pointing to a grey filing cabinet, 'that's where they were when we did the staff interviews the other day. Do you mind if I have a look?'

'No. Please do.'

Catchpole pulled out the drawer and saw the files. He checked through them carefully but could not find Lewis's. He checked again but still no sign of it. He checked a third time but it was not there

'That's funny,' he said, 'the file's missing.'

Helen then checked the files but could not find it either. She also checked the other three drawers but there was no sign of Lewis's personal file.

'That's very strange,' she said, 'he's normally very good with his paperwork as you can see by the way he keeps his filing cabinet. Maybe he has taken it out for some reason and put it somewhere else.' The three of them then searched all the drawers and cupboards in the office but there was no sign of the missing file.

'Whilst I'm here,' said Catchpole, 'I would like to have a look behind that door,' pointing to the door shutting off the passage. 'I think the key is up here,' indicating the board with keys on the wall. There were ten keys, nine had labels and the tenth did not. He took down this key and tried it in the door. It fitted into the lock and unlocked the door without trouble. He pulled the door open.

'I've never seen this door open before,' said Helen, 'I thought it was permanently locked and the key was lost.'

The door opened onto the passage to the three Premier Suites. Right by the door were the lifts, including the service lift. Opposite the service lift was the pantry where Baxter was shot; the scene of crime. It was only a matter of feet away from Lewis's office. Catchpole said nothing but looked at Macdonald, who just nodded his head. They both knew that if Lewis had been in his office at the time of the murder, he must have heard the shot.

The three Premier Suites were down the passage. Suite 113, where the MP was staying was at the end and the room where the police guards were stationed was directly opposite. Catchpole paced the distance from the door to the entrance to Suite 113. It was twenty-two paces.

'We would very much like to speak to Lewis,' said Catchpole to Helen, 'do you by any chance have any copies of correspondence you have had with him that is still on your computer?'

'No. Anything like that would have been printed and filed in his personal file. We changed all our computers about 6 weeks ago to install a more up to date programme and took the opportunity to clear out all old correspondence that was not wanted. We certainly did not keep any personal letters like that.'

'Well it is quite important we speak to Lewis so if you find anything could you let us know.'

'I'll have a look through my re-cycle bin and if I find anything I will certainly contact you,' promised Helen. She led the two policemen back to the manager's office. Catchpole thanked them both for their help and they returned to the station where they briefed Fitzgerald on what they had found. Fitzgerald typed the information onto his investigation diary to bring it up to date. It was a small step, but it could be important

'I think your next step must be to chase up on those two agency staff who you think you can trace. With a bit of luck, they may throw some light on the others. I particularly want to track down "Tommy". And now, of course, Lewis comes into the frame. We desperately need a break.'

'Yes sir,' agreed Catchpole, 'we certainly do.'

Catchpole and Macdonald left the office and went to Catchpole's desk. They took out the six cards they had taken from the agency and selected the two who were identified as being 'regular' agency workers. Macdonald was given the task of contacting them. He telephoned the numbers on the cards but there was no reply.

'Whatever you do don't leave a message on an answerphone,' said Catchpole. 'If they find out the police want them they'll do a runner.'

Macdonald tried and tried. He even took the cards home at night and tried after hours, but there was no reply. The next day he told Catchpole he'd had no success and suggested they visit each address. One was in Wolverhampton and the other on the far side of Birmingham.

'Ring the agency,' said Catchpole, 'they must have phoned them to get them to go to the hotel on the night.... Ah. No. Of course not; they used emails.' He thought for a moment and then, 'try composing a friendly email and see what happens.'

Macdonald was not very good at emails at the best of times, let alone friendly ones to complete strangers. 'What should I say?'

'I don't know. Offer them a job.'

'A job? What, you want me to employ them?' He couldn't believe what he was hearing.

Catchpole paused and looked at Macdonald. He was thinking and then said, 'you have just given me an idea,' with a big smile, talking to himself more than anyone else. 'Reward! We'll offer a reward.'

'You will have to put it to the boss,' said Macdonald.

'Yes. Let's go and see him.'

They went through to see Fitzgerald. 'You said we need a break, boss,' said Catchpole. 'Sergeant Macdonald here has just come up with a brilliant idea. Let's offer a reward.' Macdonald was not aware that it was his idea but said nothing.

'Not bad. Not bad,' said Fitzgerald. After a short pause whilst he was thinking. 'Yes. I'll put the idea to HQ. It can certainly do no harm.'

After they had left, Fitzgerald thought long and hard and then drew up a carefully worded email to his HQ suggesting that in view of the difficulties they were having in getting any witnesses to come forward, let alone getting any evidence, the police should offer a reward of five thousand pounds. He thought he had better not overstate the amount in view of the financial situation they were constantly being warned about.

The following day he received a reply from his HQ. They agreed to offer a reward of ten thousand pounds to any person giving information leading to the conviction of the killer of Constable Baxter. The police PR department would compose the message. In addition, they had contacted the BBC who would be sending reporters from the Crime Watch Programme. Fitzgerald and his staff were to give them full co-operation. At the next morning briefing, Fitzgerald gave his staff the news. A loud cheer went up.

PCs Butler and Stubbs from Harrow Police Station were carrying out speed checks on the A312 not far from the Police station using a laser camera. It was the afternoon on a clear sunny day and the traffic was light. They were in full uniform and with bright yellow Hi-Viz jackets over the top. The speed limit was 30 mph.

PC Stubbs, who was operating the camera, locked onto a silver/grey BMW approaching at 42 mph. He alerted PC Butler who moved out into the centre of the road holding up his right arm, signalling to the car to stop and with his left arm pointing to the curb, indicating that the car should pull over.

Instead of slowing down the car accelerated. PC Butler held his ground. At the last minute the car started to slow down but he had to jump out of its way as it just missed him; and came to a stop twenty yards up the road.

'Fuck me. Did you see that? That bloody woman nearly ran me down,' he exclaimed to Stubbs.

'Yeah. You'd better give her the gears.'

Butler ran up to it. There was only one person in the car, the driver, a middle-aged Asian woman. She sat in her seat and looked directly ahead and made no acknowledgement of his presence.

He tapped on the window signalling for her to open the window. There was no response. He tapped a second time with still no response. He then spoke asking her to open the window but there was still no reaction from her, so he opened the driver's door himself.

'Did you not see me signalling to you to stop?' he asked. She looked at him but said nothing.

'Do you not know that it is a serious offence to ignore the directions of a policeman in uniform?'

'The only reason you stopped me,' she replied, 'was because I am Asian, non-white.'

'No Madam. The reason we stopped you is because you were exceeding the speed limit. You were doing 42 mph and this is a 30-mph area.'

'I am going to report you to the Police Complaints Department for being racist,' she said.

'You are perfectly entitled to report me if you wish. We are not racist. Would you step out of the car please?' She had a very truculent manner but slowly got out of the car. He took the keys out of the ignition.

'I am going to check your vehicle. Would you please accompany me?' He opened the back door. There was nothing in the back. He went to the rear and opened the boot. It was empty apart from two number plates lying loose on the floor. They had obviously been hand painted with the number Y434HBS

'What are these number plates for?' he asked her.

'They are from a trailer,' she said

'Is it your trailer?

'Yes.'

The number meant nothing to him but he made a note to be included in their report at the end of the shift. The number plates being hand painted were the sort of plates he had often seen on small trailers and they seemed to be the correct size. There was nothing illegal about them so he left them and shut the boot. The rest of the checks confirmed that the car was in a roadworthy condition.

'There appears to be nothing wrong with your car, but I need your details and your driver's licence please. I will be writing you a ticket for exceeding the speed limit.' She gave him her name as Mrs Aisha Khalid of 44 Grenada Avenue, Barnet, North London. He checked her driver's licence. It was in the same name. He handed her the ticket.

'You will be receiving a letter in the post in due course which will inform you on what action will be taken.' She got back into her car and drove off.

At the end of the shift the two police constables returned to Harrow Police Station and completed their report. They took it to the Inspector's Office and placed it in the filing basket along with a dozen others already filed there. At the end of the month the Inspector would collate all the information for his monthly report to Police headquarters. The only thing that the two police constables failed to notice was that the car had no tow hitch.

14

At nine am on Monday morning the normal weekly briefing had started. Fitzgerald was standing by the incident board. Everyone else was sitting at their respective desks. He reminded them that they had been at this investigation for nearly a month and were not getting very far. The notice about the reward would be released to the media in the next day or so and he hoped this might produce results and the BBC would be arriving to film for the next Crime Watch programme shortly. Anybody on the team might be asked to contribute but it was decided that D/Inspector Robin Catchpole should be the main spokesperson. They discussed what information they wanted to highlight in the programme and decided that the weapon used should be made public, a smooth bore weapon that might be homemade or converted from a toy. It was agreed that before they did this they should first check with ballistics as to whether this was possible and if so, they should get hold of a sample to demonstrate.

'Is this a good idea, sir?' asked D/Sergeant Jane Smethers. 'Don't you think it might be putting ideas into peoples' heads if this is made public?'

'Good point,' replied Fitzgerald, 'anybody got any thoughts on that?' thrown to the meeting. A long discussion took place in which it was agreed that Fitzgerald should discuss the subject with ballistics and see what they said.

Next was the suspect known as "Tommy". It was agreed that

Catchpole should get a description of him from the hotel staff and this should be broadcasted as someone they wanted to interview to clear from their investigations. They would not classify him as a suspect as they did not have enough evidence.

Then there was the car with the false number plates leaving the Holiday Inn. 'You were following up on that, Jane, what is the latest?' asked Fitzgerald.

Jane Smethers referred to her notes. 'The "Y" registration came out in 2001 so it would now be quite old. It was a Ford van and owned by a small-time builder in Taunton, Somerset, A1 Home Improvements. It failed its MOT in 2009 and was scrapped. It was collected from Taunton by a car recovery firm and conveyed to Bristol Car Breakers who officially scrapped it. They completed all the paperwork with DVLA. It was then placed in their yard with hundreds of other scrapped vehicles. What they do is keep the bodies until the price of scrap metal rises when they crush them and sell the scrap. In the meantime, dozens of members of the public visit the breakers and take off bits and pieces for their own vehicles. These are recorded as cash sales. They don't keep a record of what was taken or by whom. Short of going out and checking in the yard they don't know whether the van has been crushed or not.'

'Did you ask them to check?' asked Catchpole.

'No I didn't. In fact, I said don't check. If we wanted them to check we would come back to them. I didn't know how far you wanted to take it. I also asked if anyone had ever bought number plates. They said no, they could not recollect ever selling any number plates. They get crushed up with the body.'

'I don't think we need take this any further at this stage,' said Fitzgerald, 'we will just mention in the programme that we are keen to know if anyone has seen this number on a car as part of our enquiries.'

Catchpole then explained his latest enquires at the hotel and how the under-manger Lewis had an office that was only feet away from the scene of crime. If he was in the office at the time of the murder,

#

he must have heard the shot, but made no mention of it when they were interviewing the staff. He was now absent, apparently on compassionate leave, and they could not find his file in the filing cabinet. They decided to make no mention of Lewis in the programme because if he was a suspect he would be alerted; and anyway, they had no firm evidence.

It was finally decided that Fitzgerald and Catchpole would work out the script they wanted to discuss with the BBC but if anyone had any other ideas then they should bring them up straight away.

'I think I will leave off chasing up on the two agency staff who we think we can get hold of, until the reward notice comes out,' said Catchpole. 'I feel that if they know there is money at the end of it they may magically come forward.'

'I agree,' Fitzgerald said.

Johnson felt he must speak to Anita. He had heard nothing from her since their last meeting in the car park by the swimming pool. He must work out a way for himself to contact her safely. The only thing he could do was to telephone her on her mobile in the evening. He tried that night and she answered.

'My cousin?' she queried.

'Yes. Jim'. He had to use a name she would recognise and the only one he could think of was his own.

'Oh yes. Jim,' she said in such a way that she obviously recognised his voice.

'Can we meet somewhere? I would like to give you lunch,' he said. 'Do you know a nice café or restaurant?'

'No, but I am sure you do,' she replied.

'There's a pub called the George in Hackney, near a garage. Do you know it?' It was very close to his uncle's garage.

'Yes, I do. I'll meet you there the day after tomorrow for lunch.'

'See you then,' he rang off. He hoped she did know it. It was far enough away from Tower Hamlets to ensure no-one would recognise her.

On the appointed day, he set off early to his uncle's garage. He planned to park his car there and walk the half mile to the pub. He wanted to be there in good time. when he arrived, he looked around for Anita, but she had not arrived. He went into the bar. It was almost empty. At twelve-forty pm Anita walked in. She saw him at the bar, smiled and went and stood beside him. His heart always gave a little jump whenever they met. She was just naturally attractive even though she was obviously pregnant.

'Hello cousin,' he said, 'can I get you an appletizer?'

'Thank you, yes.'

'Let's go and sit over there.' He pointed to a table in the corner where they would be alone.

'How did you come?' he asked.

'By taxi. It dropped me at the garage and I walked. I thought that would be best.'

'Absolutely perfect. I've parked my car there so I can take you back. And I'll refund the fare. How much was it?'

'Ten pounds. I had to give him a tip.'

He took ten pounds out of his pocket and gave it to her. She took it but looked a bit embarrassed.

'Don't worry. I'll claim it on expenses,' he said. 'So, have you seen Suleiman again?'

'Yes, and I told him that I had a computer and would be happy to do any work for him, as you suggested. He asked me where I had got it from. I said it belonged to Raji. He then adopted a very strange attitude. He sort of barked at me, asking if I had opened it. I said I hadn't. He then said I must give it to him. When I asked him why he would not say, only repeating I must give it to him.'

'So, what has happened to it?'

'I've still got it.'

'Well, if you don't want it, and you haven't used it at all up to now, I suggest you give it to him and see what he does with it.'

'Alright. I presume you know what you are doing?'

'Don't worry. We'll keep an eye on it but don't tell anyone. Do you know how to contact him yet?'

'No. I must wait until he contacts me. It is usually at the mosque after Friday prayers.'

'Take it with you next Friday. Don't ask him any questions otherwise he may become suspicious. Just say you want it back when he has finished.'

'OK. I'll let you know when he gets it.'

'Now, my main reason for calling you here is that I want to set up a system whereby I can contact you safely. What do you suggest?'

'Why not use my ordinary mobile number. But I suggest you use another name other than "Jim". "Jim" doesn't sound very Pakistani. Have you got a Pakistani name?'

'No, I haven't. What about "Usman"?'

'That's my boss's son's name but I suppose it is as good as any. Cousin "Usman". Sounds good,' she said.

'Before we agree to using your phone, has anybody ever checked your phone to see who you have been calling or anything, like Suleiman or any of his friends?'

'No no-one. Is he likely to do that?'

'You know that calls can be traced on a mobile. They are not in the least secure?'

'No, I didn't know that. What else do you suggest?'

'Nothing. We will use your own phone number but just be careful what we say to each other. Just pretend to be like normal relatives talking about family matters.' He continued, 'I take it you have still got the other phone I gave you?'

'Oh yes. I only use that for emergencies.'

'That's fine. Don't use it for anything else.'

They continued talking about other matters whilst they had lunch. Anita ordered a salad and he ordered a burger. At the end, they walked back to the garage and he drove her home to Tower Hamlets.

The following Friday evening he telephoned her on her phone. She confirmed that she had handed her computer to Suleiman saying she had "given her uncle his present". He immediately telephoned Mrs B. and advised her that the computer was now in Suleiman's possession.

15

Inspector Watson of Harrow Police Station knew that he was known as "Whinging Watson" by the junior ranks because he was always complaining about something but what really hurt was another story he heard was doing the rounds – "The only reason he got promoted was because he never made a mistake and he never made a mistake because he never made a decision." He had been diagnosed with a heart murmur six months ago and had a pacemaker fitted. His doctor had suggested he be taken off active police work and given sedentary duties only, so his superiors had put him in charge of admin. "Never made a decision!" It wasn't his fault that he was put onto admin duties. He had the task of collecting and collating all the statistics at the end of each month, and he hated it.

What he found so galling was that he knew the only reason these figures were recorded at all was in case an MP asked a question in Parliament and the Minister had to quote statistics to reply. All this work just in case someone asked a question? Most of the time no one ever looked at them, they just sat on file on the computer.

He had done the stop and search figures and crime statistics. Crime statistics? Every month when he submitted his schedule to his superiors it was sent back with questions as to why this or that had been included. He was constantly having to change it. He knew the final figures were often very different to the figures he originally drew up but he could say nothing. He just had to do as he was told.

Anyway, he only had a year to go until he could retire on pension, so he had to stick it out.

Whilst all these thoughts were passing though his mind, he turned his attention to the traffic figures. Every time traffic checks were made a report was completed at the end of each shift and placed in a filing basket in his office. He had to check them and collate all the figures at the end of the month. He emptied the basket onto his desk and placed the reports in date order. He went through them one by one recording the numbers onto a format he had on his computer. This report, along with all the others, would be forwarded to Police Headquarters where they would be kept. It was then that he spotted at the end of the report by PC Stubbs the comment about finding the number plates in the boot of the car. Y434HBS. He looked at the date. Eight days ago.

"Y434HBS". He paused. That number rang a bell. Where had he seen it? He thought long and hard but could not recollect where he had seen it. "Y" registrations were quite old and one did not see many on the road, which is why the number stuck in his mind. He put the report to one side and completed the rest of his return.

He printed off a hard copy of the return to send to his superiors for vetting and then turned his attention to Y434HBS. He typed the number into his search box but all he got was that it referred to a Ford Van that had been scrapped. His computer did not have all the programmes on it. He would have to go to the IT centre downstairs where they kept all the programmes.

'Can you look up Y434HBS and see if it has got anything flagged against it?' he asked the civilian clerk who operated the computer. He stood watching whilst she put in the number and clicked her mouse. After waiting what seemed an age a message appeared "Counter Terrorism Command to be advised immediately of any sighting of this number." And then he remembered – the Baxter murder. Christ. And it had been sitting in his basket for eight days!

'Thanks,' he said and went straight back to his office. He looked

up the police Internal Telephone Directory for CTC. It was part of the
Metropolitan Police Service. He telephoned the number which was
answered by a receptionist. 'I'd like to speak to anyone involved in
the PC Baxter Murder please,' he said.

'I'll put you through to Commander Birch,' she said. He flinched.
He did not want to speak to anybody quite so senior as he felt guilty
he had been sitting on the information for eight days; but he couldn't
stop the call now.

'Birch,' came the terse reply.

'Good morning, sir, this is Inspector Watson of Harrow.'

'Yes Inspector, what can I do for you?'

'The Baxter Murder, sir. I understand you are interested in a
number plate Y434HBS. One of our patrols spotted it the other day.
I understand you wanted to be advised.'

'Yes, we do. I'll send someone round to see you straight away.
Give him all the information you can. Harrow, did you say?'

'Yes sir.'

'Right. He will be with you shortly.' The phone went dead.
Watson phoned down to the Charge office and told the Sergeant in
charge that when a member from Counter Terrorist Command
arrived, he was to be shown up to his office immediately.

An hour and a half later there was a knock on his door. A Woman
Constable entered.

'Your guest has arrived sir,' she said and stood aside. A smartly
dressed man in his twenties entered, dressed in an expensive looking
pin stripe suit. He had arrogance written all over his face. 'DC Fox,
CTC,' he said.

'No handshake. No sir. No respect shown for rank,' thought
Watson. 'These plain clothes bastards think they're God's gift to
mankind.'

'I believe you've got something for us?' Fox asked.

'You wanted to know about a number plate Y434HBS,' replied
Watson. 'One of our patrols saw these plates in the boot of a car they
stopped for speeding.' He shoved Stubbs's report across the desk

towards Fox who picked it up and read it.

'Have you been sitting on this for eight days?' he asked. 'We put this notice out, what, three weeks ago. Don't you read our notices?'

'The patrol made that report and put it into that filing basket over there,' pointing to the basket on a shelf. 'No-one drew my attention to it. I saw it for the first time to-day which is when I telephoned your office.'

'I don't think the boss is going to be too pleased when he hears about the delay,' said Fox. 'Do you know this address?' pointing to the address to which the speeding ticket had been made.

'In Barnet. Yes.'

'I want to go there now. Will you give me someone to guide me?'

'I'll come with you myself,' said Watson hoping this might appease his feeling of guilt. 'Have you got transport?'

'Yes. Let's go.'

Watson telephoned the charge office and booked himself out and together they went down to the yard where Fox had parked his car, a little Nissan Micra, a bit infra-dig for a person with such a high opinion of himself thought Watson with a subdued smile.

They set off, Fox driving, Watson directing. It took him half an hour to find the address, 44 Grenada Avenue in Barnet. The house was detached in a reasonably smart area, with a small garden in the front and larger one at the back. There was no car parked in the drive. They parked in the street outside and walked to the front door. It was locked as were all the windows with curtains drawn. Judging by the amount of leaves and rubbish that had blown into the porch, the house had been locked up and left unoccupied for some time.

'Let's look around the back,' said Watson. He wanted to see if there was any sign of a trailer, but there wasn't. The back garden was completely overgrown. Obviously, these people were not gardeners. He also noticed a garage attached to the side of the house. He tested the up and over door, but it was also locked. He peered through the window at the side. There was a workbench and a variety of articles standing on the floor including a washing machine. It obviously had not been used as a garage.

'I think we had better check the neighbours,' said Fox. They walked around to No. 42 and were met by a cheery elderly man who said his name was Bert Smith, a pensioner who used to work for the Council.

'I don't know their names,' he said in answer to their questions. 'They are Asian. A middle-aged man and his wife and an elderly man who I think may be a father to one of them.' They weren't very friendly and kept very much to themselves. He had never spoken a word to them. He didn't know when they went away but it was some time ago. They had a silver car and he had never seen them with a trailer.

They thanked him for his help and then walked to the other neighbour, No. 46, but the house was locked up. The occupants were probably at work. They drove back to Harrow where Watson got out.

'Do you want me to follow up at No. 46?' he asked.

'No. We'll take over from here,' Fox said and drove away.

On arrival, back at his headquarters Fox went straight up to report to Commander Birch. He briefed him on all that had happened at Harrow and then on the visit to Barnet.

'What's the name of the people who live at Barnet?' asked Birch.

'I don't know, sir. They apparently spoke to none of their neighbours. We only spoke to one set of neighbours. The others were away.'

'Don't worry about the others. Find out from the Council who the registered owner is and then come back to me.'

'Yes sir'. Fox left the room.

Birch was not happy about the eight-day delay but decided he would not take it up directly with Inspector Watson. He would bring it up at the next Senior Officers Conference. There must be a better way of communicating between various branches of the Force. He also decided that they should keep the premises in Barnet under observation. He would give this job to Fox. DC Fox returned after twenty minutes.

'The owners of No. 44 are a Mr and Mrs Khalid. They have owned it for the past four years,' he said.

'Are they the only two registered as living there?' asked Birch.

'Yes sir'.

'I thought you said there was an old man living there as well?'

'That's what the neighbour told us, sir,' Fox replied. 'Maybe he was a visitor.'

Birch was silent as he thought for a moment, and then …. 'I think we'll keep an O.P. on that place for a while. This can be your job.'

'Yes sir'.

'Go and see Sergeant Dobson. Tell him I sent you. He will give you all the necessary equipment, binoculars, camera, etc. and arrange for the extra staff. I want twenty-four hours' observations kept for at least a week. It'll be valuable experience for you.'

'Yes sir.'

'Oh, and Fox, you can dress down.'

'Dress down sir?' Fox asked.

'Yes. You are not going to impress anyone by wearing a Saville Row suit on this type of work. Dress in the same clothes as everyone else. You have got to blend in with the crowd.'

'Yes sir,' said Fox. No-one had ever criticized his turnout before. He was very proud of his top-grade suits. They had cost him a lot of money.

'Tell Sgt Dobson to telephone me when you have spoken to him. Do as he says. He has organised numerous surveillance operations before. He is very experienced at it.' Birch continued, 'I also want you to keep a daily diary on what you do and send a copy to me every Monday morning, do you understand?'

'Yes sir. Thank you, sir.' Fox left to go and see Sgt Dobson.

When Fox was out of earshot, Birch put through a call to Fitzgerald in Wolverhampton.

'Birch here, Arthur,' he said when the phone was answered, 'I've got a bit of news for you.'

'I hope it is good news, sir. We're not getting very much here,' Fitzgerald replied.

'Uniform have found the false number plates.'

'Oh, excellent news,' said Fitzgerald, 'where did they find them?'

'In the boot of a car stopped at a speed trap eight days ago. The car was traced to an address in Barnet, North London, owned by someone called Khalid. Does that name ring a bell? The property is all locked up and appears not to have been lived in for some time.'

'Khalid? Khalid. No not now,' Fitzgerald replied. 'I'll put it to the team when I next address them.'

'I have also decided to assign you an extra man, DC. Fox. Do you know him?'

'I know of him. I've never worked with him.'

'He's all right, a bit self-opinionated. Eton, I believe but his heart is in the right place. He can be your man in London.'

'Oh, one of those!!' said Fitzgerald.

'Yes. He is the only person I've got available and it will be valuable experience for him.' He continued, 'I have also arranged for twenty-four-hour surveillance on the property in Barnet and given the job to Fox. We'll see if it brings any results.'

'Thank you, sir. I'll keep you informed if we get anything here,' and ended the call.

'Khalid. Khalid,' Fitzgerald thought. The name rang a bell but he couldn't remember why. It was a very common name, he knew. Maybe one of the others would remember.

16

Sergeant Dobson, who was in his fifties, had an office in the basement of CID headquarters where he was also in charge of a stock-room containing all the surveillance equipment. He was of the old school, from the East End and solid as a rock. He oozed confidence and reliability and obviously knew his job which was surveillance.

'Commander Birch told me to come and see you,' said Fox when he eventually found Dobson's office. 'I have to set up surveillance on a house in Barnet. He said you could tell me what to do.'

'Yes, young man, he has telephoned me. One week I believe?'

Fox felt a bit affronted at being referred to as "young man" by someone who was obviously working class, but he had to remember he was speaking to a Sergeant whereas he was only a constable.

'You're not going to go dressed like that, are you?' Dobson asked looking at Fox's suit.

'No, I'll put on casual clothes,' Fox replied.

'I will give you a pair of overalls. You'll have to look like a builder.' 'A builder!' Fox thought, 'I didn't join the CTC to be a builder.'

Sgt Dobson then went into a long briefing as to what he would have to do. He would first have to get the agreement of the neighbour to set up the Observation Post in his house. He would be given three other persons to work with. Fox was surprised to learn they were reservists, retired members of the force who were called in for special operations such as this. One was an ex-constable and the other two ex-Sergeants. They would work in pairs on twelve-hour shifts – one keeping observation while the other rested. They would be given a kettle to make themselves hot drinks, but they had to take their own food, sandwiches were recommended. They would have a pair of powerful binoculars and a camera. The others were very experienced at this type of work and knew how to operate the equipment. He must remember always that they were in someone else's home and should cause as little inconvenience to the owners as possible. They must make their own way to the premises and not leave any transport outside.

'The first thing you have got to do is get the agreement of the house owner that you can set up observations in his home. Go and visit him and select the site and explain what you are going to do. You will need a cover story. I suggest you say you are investigating benefit fraud. That always goes down well. Emphasise that he and his wife must not tell anyone. If anyone asks he is to say you are workmen doing work in his home. Any questions so far?'

'No Sarge,' Fox replied.

'Right, here's a pair of overalls for you. Try it on for size.' He handed Fox a pair of overalls covered in paint. Fox grimaced at having to put them on over his beautiful suit. Dobson noticed but said nothing.

'Right, off you go then. See the owner then come back to me and tell me what the setup is.'

By the end of the briefing Fox was impressed. His opinion of the Sergeant rose considerably, he obviously knew his job. He left Sgt Dobson and went back to his office to telephone Mr Bert Smith and make an appointment to see him. Smith was at home and said he would be happy to see him straight away. He set off for Grenada Avenue, Barnet, in the Nissan Micra.

'Thank you for seeing me, Mr Smith, at such short notice. I have a favour to ask you.' They were standing in the sitting room.

'Yes. Anything I can do,' said Smith.

'We want to keep observations on the house next door and were wondering whether we could use a room in your house?'

A surge of excitement went through Bert Smith. This was interesting. The truth was that he was becoming very bored with life in retirement. 'Of course,' he said, 'where do you want to do it from?'

'Can we go and have a look?'

They both left the sitting room and went to the side facing the house next door. Bert Smith's house was a carbon copy of number 44, and his attached garage had a window that overlooked the house and driveway. It was perfect for the job.

'This looks perfect,' said Fox, 'could we set up in here?'

'Absolutely. The toilet is just through that door on the right and there is a power point there for you to use if you want one. Can I ask what they have done?'

'We are investigating benefit fraud.'

'Oh good' said Smith, 'these foreigners. About time someone did something about that.'

'You mustn't say anything to anyone otherwise it will give the game away. We will be dressed like builders so you can say we are doing work in your home.'

'Don't worry. Mum's the word.'

'Thank you, Mr Smith. If it is alright with you, I would like to move in here tomorrow?'

'Call me Bert. What's your name?'

'Detective Constable Fox.'

'No. What's your other name?'

'Sidney.'

'Sidney. Can I call you "Sid"?'

'If you must,' Fox replied with a forced smile. He hated being called "Sid".

Fox returned to HQ and went straight to see Sgt Dobson. He briefed him on the arrangements he had made with Bert Smith.

'Perfect. A garage is fine because it means you are not getting in the way of the owners. Report here tomorrow at eight o'clock and you will meet with the other members of the team. You can work out your shift times together and then get going.'

Fox left and returned to his office. This was the first responsible   job he had been given since he joined the CTC and he did not want to make a mess of it.

17

Mrs B. was worried. She did not like what she had heard from Johnson about Delia. If she had been told to "prepare herself for revenge" it sounded as if something was being cooked up: And as for being told she was a "bad Muslim!" No. Something's not right. Also, the organisation "al-Abdullah". It was strange that no-one else seemed to have heard of it; and what were they supposed to be doing? If they were just converting people to Islam why were they so secretive? There were too many unanswered questions. She decided she would send Johnson back to Bristol to see Adrian McGregor and whilst there he could also see someone in Special Branch. She would arrange a meeting through Colonel Rutherford. She was also worried about Johnson. Picking up that speeding ticket and having to disclose his real name and address was not clever even though he said he was a welder. Also, it was obvious that he had gone soft on his agent, Delia. Not good. She wondered whether she should take him off the case and hand Delia over to someone else, but she knew that agents tended to build up a rapport with their handlers and did not take kindly to being chopped and changed around. Delia was the only contact they had so far so she would leave things as they were and just keep a careful watch.

Having made the arrangements with Colonel Rutherford about a meeting with Special Branch she put a call through to Johnson telling him to report to her office in the morning.

Johnson arrived at exactly nine am and went straight up to her office. Sarah was not at her desk so he knocked and went in.

'Good morning, Mrs B.'

'Good morning, No. 8. Take a seat.' Johnson sat down opposite her, wondering what was coming up.

'Firstly, have you heard anything more from Delia?'

'I contacted her two nights ago. She has not seen or heard from Suleiman since she gave him the computer. She has nothing to report. Have IT Department got anything from her computer?'

'Apparently not. It seems as if he has not used it.'

'Didn't you say they changed the hard drive and gave it a new password?'

'Apparently so, yes.' she replied.

'Well I am pretty sure Delia did not give him the password.'

Mrs B. paused and thought for a moment. 'There is nothing she can do now. If she suddenly tells him there is a new password having told him she has never used it he will become suspicious. If he is clever he can bypass the password and get a new one. We'll just have to leave it and keep watch.'

She continued, 'I've got another job for you. I want you to return to Bristol. See Adrian McGregor and find out if he has heard anything more from Suleiman. Then I want you to go to Special Branch. See Detective Inspector Hobbs and ask him what he knows about the university. Presumably he knows about these secret meetings. Perhaps he knows something which to him is unimportant but may be of importance to us. We must find out who Suleiman is. I have a feeling that our case hangs on that. Hobbs knows you're coming. You can be open with him. Colonel Rutherford says he is a very good man. I have also told Margaret McGregor to expect you.'

'I'll leave first thing in the morning. Can I use my car again?'

'Yes, but don't pick up any more speeding tickets.'

Johnson went home to prepare for his trip to Bristol. He left at five the following morning to get onto the M4 before the rush hour traffic started. He arrived in Bristol at eight-thirty; too early for Mrs McGregor so he went to the Central Police Station. It took him nearly an hour negotiating himself through the rush hour traffic before he found it. After enquiring at the reception, he was directed to Special Branch and to Inspector Hobbs's office. 'Crikey. Don't you people sleep? I've only just arrived,' complained Hobbs after Johnson introduced himself. He thought to himself that half past nine was not too early for the police unless Special Branch were different.

'I left early to miss the rush-hour traffic,' he explained.

'You on the Baxter case?' asked Hobbs.

'Yes. Sort of.'

'How is Bristol involved?'

'Apparently, they found some number plates in a car which was traced to a Ford van that was scrapped in Bristol and a Muslim has been holding meetings at the university trying to convert people to Islam.'

'I don't know about the Ford van but I do know about the meetings. A Pakistani, middle-aged man has paid a couple of visits and tried to persuade some of the graduates to adopt Islam but without much success. I don't know of a single person who was converted so we weren't interested. He wasn't breaking any laws.'

'Do you know when he was last here?' Johnson asked.

'Yes. About six weeks ago. He addressed six people, but no takers.'

'However,' Hobbs continued, 'there was one odd case about two years ago. The bursar's son, name David White. He suffers from Asperger's Syndrome and suddenly started calling himself "Tommy" and prattling on about Allah, falling to the ground to pray, and so on. It was very strange behaviour even for him. We saw him but couldn't get anything out of him. I put it down to his condition. Apart from the fact he never stops talking, he is quite harmless. His father was and still is very concerned, but his mother is very protective, as mothers are in these cases.'

'Do you know where he is now?'

'No. He comes and goes all the time. I think that half the time even his parents don't know where he is.'

'Do you know who tried to convert him? Was it this Muslim person?'

'I don't think so. I think it could have been one of the other students, probably as some sort of prank. He is quite harmless. I wouldn't get too worked up about him.'

'Are there any other subversive activities going on at the university?'

'No. Nothing at all that we know of.'

'I don't suppose you know the name of this Muslim person?'

'No I don't. As I said we did not put much into this enquiry as he wasn't breaking any laws and wasn't getting any converts. We were a bit suspicious that they were being held in secret, but we presumed it was to avoid any racist reaction from other students.'

They chatted generally about various things, London, the latest rumours about changes to Police conditions of service. He wasn't sure if Hobbs knew he was not a policeman so said nothing about conditions of service. Hobbs did not offer any refreshments and at five to eleven Johnson took his leave.

'Well thank very much. You have been an immense help.' He deliberately did not tell Hobbs that someone called "Tommy" was in fact a suspect in the murder because he did not know just how much of a suspect he was or whether, in fact, it was the same "Tommy".

Johnson went down to his car and drove off. It was now eleven o'clock so he made his way to Mrs McGregor, arriving half an hour later. He parked in front of her house and knocked on the front door.

'Hello Mr Johnson, have you just driven all the way from London?'

'Yes. I left early this morning.'

They made small talk about the weather, her garden, the traffic on the road, and he was offered and accepted a cup of tea and biscuits.

'I would actually like to see Adrian if he's around,' Johnson said.

'Yes, he is in fact, but he's just popped into town on his bicycle. I'm expecting him back any moment now. He has some project which he is doing at home.'

'Do you know if he has attended any more meetings, or if anyone is trying to get money out of him?' He had to keep up the pretence that he was still investigating organisations trying to extort money out of people.

'No, or at least he has said nothing to me,' Mrs McGregor replied. They continued making small talk when suddenly there was a crash of a bicycle in the porch. Adrian appeared through the front door.

'Hello darling. Mr Johnson is here to see you.' They shook hands. Adrian poured himself a cup of tea, took three biscuits off the plate, and sat down.

'I was speaking to your mother to find out whether you have had any more meetings or contact with that man who we spoke about last time?' Johnson asked.

'No, absolutely nothing.'

'Has anyone become a Muslim that you know of?'

'Not as far as I know. The subject is never mentioned.'

'Have you ever heard of anybody called "Tommy"?' asked Johnson.

'Tommy! Yes. Everybody knows Tommy. He's mad.'

'How do you know him?'

'He's the Bursar's son. He used to be here but left some time ago. He comes back occasionally. But everybody knows he's mad. He never stops talking,' said Adrian.

'Have you ever met him?'

'No. I've seen him around but kept out of the way. Why are you interested in Tommy?'

'Only that I have heard a rumour that he converted to Islam.'

'Well it could be true. I've heard he is always talking about Allah, but we just put this down to his madness.'

Johnson realised he was not going to get anything more out of

Adrian. He decided that whilst in Bristol he should go and see Tommy's parents. He chatted to Adrian for a short while about his course and the project he was doing and then took his leave. He drove to the university and was directed to the bursar's home, situated in the grounds. He knocked on the door which was opened by an elderly lady who he assumed was Mrs White.

'Mrs White? Good afternoon. I'm James Johnson from the Police Crime Prevention Unit. I wonder if I could have a quick word with you about your son, David?'

Mrs White caught her breath and appeared very apprehensive about speaking to Johnson, especially when he said he was from the police.

'Oh no, what has he done now?' she wailed. Johnson thought for a moment she was going to burst into tears.

'Nothing. Nothing,' he assured her, 'it's just that I would like to speak to him as I think he can help me in our investigations.' He deliberately did not say what sort of investigations. 'Do you know where I can find him?'

'He's not in any trouble then?' she asked.

'Absolutely not. I just want to talk to him about a case we are investigating. He may be a witness.'

Mrs White appeared reassured and relaxed a bit. 'I don't know where he is,' she said, 'he never lets us know. The last I heard he was somewhere in the Midlands working as a waiter.'

Johnson decided that in view of what he had heard about "Tommy" and what he had just seen of his mother he had better not mention anything about Islam because he was sure she would not know anything and it would just upset her. He went on, 'do you know when you will see him again?'

'No I don't. As I said, he never tells us. He just pitches up.'

'Thank you very much. I'm sorry to have disturbed you,' said Johnson. He decided that they would need a bit more evidence about "Tommy" before questioning his parents and it would be better to speak to his father rather than his mother.

He took his leave of Mrs White and set off back to London.

He arrived home after dark, stopping at his favourite McDonalds to pick up a couple of burgers. He had his supper followed by a mug of his special coffee and went to bed.

The following morning, he awoke and went for a 5-km run after which he showered, ate some cereals for breakfast and then rang Mrs B. to make an appointment to see her. She told him to come in right away. On arrival, he noticed that Sarah was still not in her office but made no comment. He knocked and went in. Colonel Rutherford was there as well.

'Ah number eight.'

'Good morning, Colonel.' Rutherford grunted something which could have been an acknowledgment.

Johnson briefed them in detail on everything that had happened in Bristol. The three of them discussed all facts they had and concluded that firstly the man they knew as Suleiman had apparently gone to ground and secondly the suspect in Wolverhampton, "Tommy", was likely to be the Bristol University Bursar's son David, and was a very unlikely murderer, especially one who used a firearm. Johnson was dismissed.

'Well progress of a sort, I suppose,' said Mrs B. addressing Colonel Rutherford after Johnson had left. 'I hoped we might get more.'

'I'm disappointed in Hobbs. I thought he would have more,' Rutherford replied. 'We can write off "Tommy" as a suspect.'

'I can't understand why Suleiman has gone to ground. What have we done to frighten him?'

'Nothing. Certainly, on my side we have been very discreet. It would help if we knew his proper name,' said the Colonel.

'Yes,' said Mrs B. 'We are going to have to do something to draw him out. I will put on my thinking cap and let you know.'

18

Detective Constable Fox had been carrying out surveillance on No. 44 Grenada Avenue for four days and three nights and was getting very bored as nothing interesting had happened. On the fourth night, he was on duty with his co-observer, ex-Sergeant Jefferies. It was a miserable night, pouring with rain. At five past eleven, Fox, who was on duty at the window, suddenly saw car lights turn into the driveway from the main road. He immediately alerted Jefferies who got up and came to the window. Together they watched.

The car drove up to the front of the house and then went behind towards the garage where it was lost to sight. Jefferies said they must log everything they saw. A notebook and pencil was there for that purpose.

'Did you get the registration number?' asked Jefferies.

'No. I couldn't see because of the glare of the lights and the rain.' Fox replied.

At eleven-twelve a light came on in the ground floor window facing them, the sitting room. They could not see in because the curtains were drawn. They could identify the rooms because the house layout was the same at Bert Smith's house.

At eleven twenty-three the sitting room light went off. They could not see the kitchen or garage because they were on the opposite side to where they were. They could, however, see a slight glow coming from the far side of the house.

'Do you think I should sneak out and see if I can get the registration number?' asked Fox.

'No. Never. If you are seen that will be the end. You have no idea who might be keeping a lookout over there. You have just got to be patient. This is a waiting game,' Jefferies replied with emphasis.

At three twenty-seven in the morning the car lights came on and they heard the engine start up. They could see the red glow of the rear lights. The car reversed all the way down the drive onto the road, turned to its left and dove away. Again, they were unable to see the registration number because of the glare from the headlights.

'From what I could see it looked like a silver or light coloured BMW,' said Jefferies, 'put that down on the log.'

'I'll take your word for it. I'm no good at identifying car makes,' said Fox.

'When you knock off, go and see Sgt Dobson and give him the details. He knows what to do with it.'

There was no further movement for the rest of the night. At eight-thirty am they were relieved by the incoming pair. Fox went to CID Headquarters, to Sgt Dobson's office. Sgt Dobson was sitting at his desk reading a newspaper. 'You got something for me young man?' he asked as Fox put his head round the door.

'Yes Sarge. A car arrived late last night and left at half past three this morning.'

'You got the log?'

'Yes Sarge.' He handed over the page from the log book.

'Good. Keep it up,' and carried on reading his newspaper. He wasn't in the least bit excited or, apparently, interested.

As soon as Fox had left and shut the door, Dobson put away his newspaper and telephoned Commander Birch, giving him all the details.

'Good,' said Birch, 'I had a feeling something might happen there. Are they continuing with the surveillance?'

'Yes sir. I told him to keep up the good work.'

Birch decided there was enough evidence now to warrant a clandestine search of the house to check what was there. He telephoned his deputy and instructed him to apply for a search warrant and arrange the search with forensics. He also decided that he would get DC Fox to be present when the search was carried out to give him the experience. The warrant was delivered later that day and the search was arranged for the following morning.

Birch contacted Fox, who was resting at home. 'Sorry to disturb you. We will be carrying out a search of No. 44 first thing tomorrow morning. I want you to be present. You may lose a bit of sleep but I am sure you can make it up later.'

'Yes sir. Thank you, sir.' Fox knew he would be on duty that night so he would just stay at the premises when the shift changed and join in the search. He was beginning to enjoy this CTC work.

Meanwhile, back at Wolverhampton, Fitzgerald was addressing the routine morning meeting.

'Morning everybody. Is everyone here? – Right, we have had a few new developments. Firstly, we have found the false number plates used on the car which left the Holiday Inn the morning after the murder. They were found in the boot of a car in Harrow. The car has been traced to an address in Barnet, London in the name of a Mr and Mrs Khalid. Does that name ring a bell with anybody?' He waited for a reply.

'Yes,' exclaimed Sgt Macdonald, 'that's Lewis's name. The manager of the hotel said Lewis was his nickname. His proper name is Khalid. I am sure he said Khalid, I'll check again.'

'Good. Do we know his other name?'

'No. The only other name we have is Lewis.'

'Fine. Follow that up. The next development is that we have identified "Tommy".' There was a surge of excitement amongst his listeners … 'but don't get excited. He is not our suspect. He is the son of the bursar of Bristol University and suffers from Asperger's

Syndrome. There is no doubt that Tommy is the same person as the one described by the kitchen staff at the hotel. His behaviour is the same. So, we can strike him off as a suspect.' A feeling of gloom descended on his listeners. 'That leaves us with only Lewis as a possible suspect and we really have no proper evidence against him, only suspicion.'

'What about the other man, Suleiman I think was the name given?' asked Joe Swift.

'Nothing. Vanished. Gone to ground,' said Fitzgerald. He continued, 'we've got the Crime Watch programme being broadcast tonight when they will also announce the reward. Now, this is our only hope. The contact number being given is this one here. I want the telephones manned twenty-four hours for the next seventy-two hours. Sgt Macdonald will work out a shift system. If we need any more persons, the station say they can call up some reservists for us. There will be a camera present for tonight so you will be live on TV. Don't make any cock-ups. I'm determined we are going to crack this case. Remember one of our own was the victim.' Fitzgerald left the room and went back to his office.

At eight-thirty pm Fox made his way to No. 42 with Jefferies to continue their observation duties. He told Jefferies that they would be doing a search the following morning.

'I thought they would,' Jefferies said, 'it's the usual procedure.'

Fox couldn't wait for the night to pass. He was very excited. Things were happening. He tried to get as much sleep as possible when it was his turn to rest but found it difficult. Eventually the morning dawned. Jefferies made them both coffee whilst waiting for the relief crew to turn up. When they arrived and took over observations, Jefferies left to go off duty. Fox remained until the search party arrived at nine-thirty in a white van. It consisted of a Detective Sergeant and a civilian. Fox walked over to them.

'You Fox?' asked the Sergeant. 'Yes,' replied Fox.

'Here, put this on,' and threw him some white overalls. Fox took off his builder's overalls and put on the white ones.

'Right, you're here to watch us,' said the Sergeant, 'just watch and don't touch a thing.'

'Yes Sergeant,' promised Fox.

'I gather the premises are empty?'

'Yes Sarge.'

'Good. That makes life easier.'

They went over to the garage door. The Sergeant pulled some keys out of his pocket and after a little fiddling unlocked and opened the up and over door. They went in. The garage was very untidy. There were workbenches around two walls with a variety of tools lying on them, including an electric hand drill and some long high-speed drill bits of assorted sizes. On the floor was an old washing machine, not connected, and various cartons. They looked inside the cartons and found varieties of sweets and biscuits, some open. On the floor was a plastic fertilizer bag marked "Ammonium Nitrate. For Healthy Plants and Vegetables". The Sergeant took several photographs of the garage as they found it.

The fertilizer bag was open and about half full. They took a sample and placed it in an exhibit bag. Sealed and marked it. On the workbench were several long slender sausage-like plastic bags. 'What do you think these are?' asked the civilian, 'condoms?'

'I dun-no.' replied the Sergeant, 'take some anyway.' The civilian took a dozen and put them in an exhibit bag, sealed and marked it.

Also on the workbench was a two-litre tin can. The Sergeant opened it. It contained diesel. He poured a sample into a jar and placed it in another exhibit bag and marked it.

'You know ammonium nitrate and diesel is what they use to make explosives, don't you?' he said to the civilian.

'Yes, and these condoms could be what they put them into.'

Fox was fascinated by what he saw. He was impressed by the way they always put what they wanted into special plastic bags and carefully marked and sealed them. 'Can I ask a question Sarge?' he asked.

'Ask away.'

'Why do you put everything into separate plastic bags?'

'It is to maintain the chain of evidence and keep them safe. If any of these are produced in court, we must prove that they are the ones we took away from this garage and not planted ones, and have not been contaminated; and you will be our witness.'

He didn't know that. They carried on searching and checking. Under the workbenches was a lot of dirt and leaves which had blown in when the door was open. Suddenly Fox saw a piece of electric wire poking out from under some leaves. He pointed it out to the Sergeant. The Sergeant gently pulled it out. On the end was another piece of wire and a small aluminium tube.

'That looks like an electronic detonator. I think we're on to something here, Dave,' he said to his colleague.

They carefully pulled out all the dirt from under the workbenches and checked if there were any more interesting items, but found nothing else. The detonator was also carefully put into a bag and marked. They then replaced the leaves and dirt as they had found them.

Having finished in the garage they went through the connecting door, which was unlocked, into the house. They checked the sitting room, kitchen and all the upstairs rooms but found nothing of interest. In the hall on a table they found some letters. Three of them were addressed to "Patel's Provisions" at 44 Grenada Avenue. 'Is Patel the name of the people who live here?' the Sergeant asked Fox.

'No. I thought it was Khalid.'

'Yes, some of these letters are addressed to Khalid but these three are to Patel's Provisions. I think we had better take them.' They were placed into an exhibit bag and marked.

They had now finished the search. They both carefully checked with the photos taken at the start of the search, that the premises were as far as possible as they had found them; and left by the garage door shutting and locking it behind them.

It was now mid-afternoon and Fox was exhausted having been awake all night and he knew he had to go on duty again at eight-thirty tonight. He asked if they could give him a lift to headquarters.

19

Fitzgerald had just arrived at his office. It was the morning after the Crime Watch programme had been broadcasted when the telephone rang. It was Commander Birch.

'Morning Arthur. I wanted to catch you early.'

'You have sir, I've just arrived.'

'We have some more developments. You know we put a surveillance team on that house in Grenada Avenue?'

'Yes.'

'We've had success. A car came in late at night two nights ago and remained for about four hours and then left. Unfortunately, they couldn't get the number because of the glare of the lights and it was raining. Anyway, yesterday I authorised a search and they found some fertilizer and diesel in the garage and an electronic detonator on the floor, hidden under some leaves. Forensics say that these are ingredients to make explosives. The name of the owner is Khalid but they also found some correspondence addressed to Patel's Provisions, of the same address. So, it looks as if the Khalid's are shop owners and this is borne out by some cartons of sweets and biscuits also in the garage. I'll put Fox onto following up Patel's Provisions.'

'That's very interesting, sir,' said Fitzgerald.

'Any information on the name Khalid?'

'Yes. It is the surname of the under manager of the Plaza who was given compassionate leave and has still not returned, but we don't know, of course, if it is the same Khalid.'

'Anything interesting happen after the Crime Watch programme? I thought it was very good.'

'We were inundated with calls, over a hundred. Most were rubbish but half a dozen or so could be interesting.'

'Did the reward bring in any response?'

'Yes. Most of the rubbish calls were people asking what they had to do to get the reward. Or they gave us some implausible story and then asked if that qualified them for the reward. We had to politely but firmly put them right,' Fitzgerald explained.

'Unfortunately, when there is money in the offing this is what you must expect, but in amongst the rubbish there may be something useful.'

'Yes sir, this is how we're treating it.'

'OK. Keep me in the picture.'

'Thank you, sir. Goodbye.' Fitzgerald hung up.

Two days later the internal telephone in Fitzgerald's office rang. He answered 'Fitzgerald!' It was the receptionist downstairs. 'Call for you sir. Manager of the Plaza Hotel.'

'Put him on.' There was some clicking and then he was put through. 'Good morning, Mr Japour.'

'Good morning. I think I might have some news for you. Could you come and see me?'

'Can you tell me what it is about?'

'It's about Lewis. I don't want to talk on the telephone.'

'I'll be with you right away.' He put the phone down and called Catchpole. 'Robin. Drop everything. We're going out.' Catchpole left his desk and went to Fitzgerald with an enquiring look on his face. 'Lewis,' said Fitzgerald. 'The manager wants to see us. He won't say why.'

They went downstairs, got into a car and drove straight to the hotel. On arrival, they were shown into the manager's office.

'I brought Inspector Catchpole with me because he is the main investigating officer on this case,' said Fitzgerald after the usual greetings on entering the manager's office and being shown to chairs.

'That's fine,' said Japour, 'it's about Lewis. He is still not back from leave. He should have been back two days ago but I have heard nothing from him.' He paused and then went on ... 'This morning, one of the barmen, the one who serves in the cocktail bar next to the dining room, came to me out of the blue. He said he shares a flat with Lewis and he thinks Lewis is a Jihadist. I asked him why and he said because he hates the police. He calls them "*kuffars*" and he hated having to help you when you were interviewing the staff the other day. In fact, he said, he did not like anyone who was not a Muslim, calling them all "*kuffars*" – that means non-believer if you didn't know.'

'Can I have his name?' asked Fitzgerald.

'Ahmed Mustafa. He's been here just over a year. Quite reliable. Good worker.'

'Can we see him?'

'Yes. You can use Lewis's office. You know where it is,' looking at Catchpole. Catchpole nodded. 'I'll send him to you.'

Fitzgerald and Catchpole left the manager's office and went upstairs to Lewis's office. 'Interesting,' said Fitzgerald, 'did he give any indication of this when you first interviewed him?'

'No. None,' Catchpole replied.

After a wait of ten minutes a young Asian man arrived at the door. 'Are you Mr Mustafa?' Fitzgerald asked.

'Yes sir.'

'Please come in and take a seat.' Mustafa sat down in the chair indicated. 'I believe you had a meeting with the manager this morning?'

'Yes sir.'

'Would you please tell us what you told the manager?'

'Yes sir.' Mustafa then went on and repeated exactly what the manager had told them earlier. When he had finished, Fitzgerald asked, 'how long has he held these thoughts?'

'For a long time, sir, ever since I have known him.'

'Are you a Muslim?'

'Yes sir.'

'Do you have the same thoughts towards non-Muslims?'

'No sir. I was born here.'

'Where were you on the night the policeman was killed?'

'In the bar sir, over there,' pointing to the cocktail bar on the far side of the stairs by the entrance to the ding room.

'Do you know where Lewis was?'

'I think he was in his office, here, sir.'

'Do you think he killed the policeman?'

'I don't know sir.'

'Have you ever seen him with a gun?'

'No sir.'

'Did you hear a bang or anything that sounded like a shot that night?'

'No sir but there was a lot of noise coming from the dining room.'

Catchpole interrupted the questioning. 'Why did you not tell me all this when I first saw you?'

'I was afraid sir.'

'What, afraid of Lewis?'

'Yes sir. We're all afraid of him.'

'You mean all the staff who work here?'

'Yes sir.'

Catchpole and Fitzgerald looked at each other. They said nothing. They didn't have to. This would explain why the staff were so reticent when questioned. Fitzgerald then asked, 'do you mind if we have a look at your flat and Lewis's room?'

'No sir.' The three of them got up and went downstairs to the car.

'We don't have to drive, sir, it is just over there,' pointing to a row of two storey flats on the other side of the road. In fact, they had about two hundred yards to walk as it was at the end of the road. Their flat was on the second floor. It consisted of two bedrooms, a small living room, small kitchen and bathroom. Mustafa pointed out Lewis's room.

'This is Lewis's room,' said Mustafa pointing into one of the bedrooms. It was very sparsely furnished; a single bed, neatly made, a chair next to the bed and a built-in wardrobe and that was it. Catchpole opened the wardrobe doors. It had hanging space one side and shelves on the other. There were a few clothes, the ones on the shelves neatly folded. Also on one of the shelves he saw a flat file and picked it up. It was Lewis's personal file missing from the office. He showed it to Fitzgerald who nodded. They said nothing whilst Mustafa was standing by the door watching.

'I would like to take this file with me,' said Catchpole to Mustafa. Mustafa just nodded.

'Do you know what his proper name is?'

'Khalid sir, Rahna Khalid.'

'Do you know why he is called Lewis?'

'No sir. He wouldn't tell me. He said it was a joke.'

They checked the rest of the flat but found nothing of interest. They left and walked back to the hotel.

'Do you know there is a reward out for this case?' asked Fitzgerald when they reached the hotel.

'Yes' Mustafa replied.

'Are you telling us all this because you want the reward?'

'No sir,' he emphasised, 'I was not happy when he didn't come back from his leave so I thought I should tell the manager.'

'Well you did the right thing. Thank you,' Fitzgerald replied. With that they bade him farewell, got into their car and drove back to the police station.

On the way back, they discussed the meeting with Mustafa. 'It looks as if Lewis needs further investigation,' Fitzgerald said.

Mrs B. was feeling very uneasy at the lack of developments. She had just heard about the finding of possible explosive making materials in the garage in Barnet and the letters with two names, Khalid and Patel. She knew that the name "Khalid" was the name of the under-manager of the hotel, who had gone missing. "Patel" was a very common name and there had been no mention of it in this case so far.

She was also suspicious that al-Abdullah had gone quiet. These extremist organisations don't normally just stop operating for no reason so what had made them go to ground? The only contact MI5 had was Delia but she was proving to be a bit of a dead loss, and to make matters worse her handler seemed to have fallen for her; but she had been threatened by being told "she must avenge her husband's death". She wondered what they had in mind. MI5 had put a camera in her flat, which Delia knew nothing about, and, so far, she had had very few visitors, certainly no-one who looked like a middle-aged Asian with a moustache. She was also pleased to see there were no visits by Johnson. She read through her notes noting the salient points that were recorded. Suddenly a pattern started to appear. It all hinged around finding those false number plates.

The numbers first came to light in the register of the Holiday Inn in Wolverhampton the morning after the murder. Checks revealed they referred to a Ford van that had been scrapped. But the number plates themselves were found in the boot of a car in Harrow. The car was registered to an address in Barnet owned by a Mr Khalid. Khalid is the name of the missing under manager of the hotel. Search of the garage at the Barnet address produced some possible bomb making materials. Possible conclusion is that Mr Khalid of Barnet is involved with explosives? The only link is the agent Delia to whom the owner of the car admitted "killing a policeman". His name in the hotel register was S. Khan from Edinburgh, but it was a false name. So, is S. Khan really Mr Khalid; and is Mr Khalid of Barnet the under manager of the hotel, or a relation?

She decided it was time to start a new line of investigation. So far there had been nothing to directly link al-Abdullah with explosives but maybe this was about to change. She would put another agent onto checking out the explosives side. There might be some connection or they might be onto a completely different case.

Her explosives expert was 04. She would put her in the picture and let her get on with it. She wanted her to operate separately from Number 8 and to keep him in the dark. She particularly did not want Delia to know.

20

Commander Birch put a call through to D/Constable Fox. Fox had finished his surveillance duties and was back in his office.

'Come and see me when you have a moment, Fox' he said.

'Yes sir, I'll come right away.' Ten minutes later Fox appeared in Birch's office.

'Sit down.'

'You have done a decent job on that surveillance. I want you now to do the follow up.'

'Yes sir,' said Fox with emphasis.

'As you know they found some fertilizer that could be made into explosives. But it could also be quite innocent and just be for use in the garden. I want you to check that out. Check if the house owners have an allotment or are keen gardeners, or something. We would have egg on our faces if we accuse them of making explosives and they show us a beautiful garden full of flowers or vegetables.'

'Yes sir.'

'The next thing is the name of the people in that house. We have the name "Khalid", but you also found letters addressed to "Patel's Provisions". Find out who or what "Patel's Provisions" is. Maybe Mr Khalid owns a business by that name. He produced the letters they had taken from the house.

'Right sir,' said Fox.

'Keep me informed and put the details in your diary.'

'Yes sir.' Fox got up and left. He was delighted to be given more responsibility in this case. He had visions of grandeur, of even being promoted. This could be his chance to make a breakthrough.

He returned to his office and started work immediately. He decided to start with checking allotments first as he thought this would be the easiest task. He telephoned Barnet Borough Council and asked to speak to whoever held the list of allotment holders.

'Which allotment sir?' asked the receptionist.

'All of them.'

'But there are forty-nine allotments sir. I must know which one you are looking for.'

'Well forty-nine is not much. Can you send me the list of holders?'

'There are forty-nine allotment sites all over the borough. Each one with several separate plots, probably hundreds of plot holders.'

He hadn't realized that. He thought for a while and then decided he would have to plan it a bit more carefully. This was going to be a bigger job than he had realised. He thanked the receptionist and terminated the call.

After much thought, he decided the best way would be to go personally to the Council headquarters and show his identity card. Tell them he was investigating a serious case and ask them to check their records for any plot holder with the name Khalid. He didn't have to go into details but if they asked what case he would just say murder. They probably had all the names on computer so it should be easy.

Next, he tried "Patel's Provisions". He put the name into Google but drew a blank. No record. What a disappointment. He hoped the council would have some information in their records and would check whilst he was at the Council Office. He decided it was too late to do all this now so he would come prepared tomorrow.

Fitzgerald planned to have a meeting with Robin Catchpole after the nine o'clock briefing the next morning. In the meantime, he read through his investigation diary from the beginning, making notes of anything of importance that he wanted checked out. If Lewis was indeed their man, he wanted to work out exactly what evidence they had against him. He was very knowledgeable of the law and knew Catchpole also knew his law. They had to prove their case "beyond reasonable doubt" and now all they had was nothing but "doubt".

He started looking through Lewis's file. Whilst he was doing this the telephone rang. It was Commander Birch. 'Good morning Arthur. I've got a bit more information for you.'

'Yes sir,' he replied, 'we've also had some developments here. You go first.'

'You know we found some fertilizer and diesel at that property in Barnet?'

'Yes sir.'

'And some letters addressed to Patel's Provisions?'

'Yes sir.'

'And the name "Khalid" is on some correspondence?'

'Yes sir. That name also applies to the under manager at the hotel whom we know as "Lewis",' said Fitzgerald.

'Is that a coincidence or do you think they are connected?'

'I don't know. His personal file, which was missing from the office, has been found at his flat. I am just looking through it now. Apart from his name being Khalid there is nothing to indicate where he came from, which is very strange.'

'Is that because of incompetence by the manager or do you think certain details have been removed?'

'It is unlikely to be incompetence because Lewis is responsible for all personnel records. His contract of service is here but it only has his name, no address.'

'So, are you saying he took his file home to remove any reference to an address?'

'Yes, that's what it is looks like. There is one other thing – he did his training at Bristol University.'

'And isn't that where "Tommy" comes from. It gets more and more intriguing by the day. Maybe he originates from Bristol.'

'Yes. Could be,' agreed Fitzgerald. He continued, 'he also won a shooting prize at the Bristol gun club. There's a certificate in his file.'

'What sort of prize? It seems strange that someone like him, should be a member of a gun club.'

'Looks like small arms.'

'Could be pertinent. Anyway, I have put young Fox onto checking out the Khalid name and Patel's Provisions. He did a very decent job on the surveillance. I am making him give me a diary on everything he does. I think he will be alright.'

'Thank you, sir. I'm sitting down with Catchpole tomorrow morning and going through all we've got with a fine toothcomb. I'm worried we've got lots of suspicions but very little actual evidence. No witnesses.'

'OK. Well best of luck. Keep me informed.' Fitzgerald knew Commander Birch very well. Birch had been the senior investigating officer on several cases he was involved with when he first joined the department. They were familiar with each other's strengths and weaknesses. Fitzgerald knew he could rely on Birch absolutely for anything he wanted and Birch knew Fitzgerald would leave no stone unturned to solve this case.

The following morning after the briefing he and Catchpole retired to his office carrying their mugs of coffee. He arranged for all telephone calls to be put through to the enquiry room. He did not want to be disturbed.

'Right, Robin. I hope you have got your legal hat on. I have been through my diary and made a few notes. I want to list our suspects and the evidence we have against them, and then note what more evidence we need.'

'Right sir.'

'First I think we can write off Tommy. We never had any factual evidence against him and now we know he is the bursar's son and a bit loopy, he is a most unlikely murderer, especially with a gun.'

'I agree.'

'That leaves us Suleiman and maybe Lewis. Let's start with Suleiman. How did he become a suspect in the first place?'

'He first came to light when he took that MI5 agent to Wolverhampton and booked into the Holiday Inn under a false name and address and gave a false registration number for his car. They attended the meeting at the Plaza and afterwards he admitted to the MI5 agent that they had shot a policeman.'

'So, we are relying on the MI5 agent for the evidence?'

'No. We've got the hotel register and records show that the vehicle number refers to a Ford van belonging to a builder in Taunton which has been scrapped, and the number plates were seen in a car, registered in his name, stopped in a speed trap in Harrow.'

'That just proves he was dishonest. It doesn't prove he is a murderer.'

'Agreed. The only evidence that connects him directly to the murder is the statement he made to the MI5 agent and I doubt if MI5 will agree to one of their spies being a witness in court.' Fitzgerald paused whilst he thought. 'I'll speak to Mr Birch. Maybe he has some idea how we can get around that problem. Do we know Suleiman's proper name yet?'

'We think it's Khalid. That's the name on the registration of the car stopped in Harrow. The address was in Barnet registered under the same name,' said Catchpole.

'Oh, yes and that is the address where the OP was carried out and where they found the detonator and possibly bomb making equipment.'

'… and letters addressed to "Patel" so he may also be using the name "Patel".

'OK. What about Lewis?'

'Lewis has only just become a suspect due to the statement made by his flat mate Mustafa. Until then we thought he was a nice, pleasant, helpful young man. Funnily enough I always had a feeling he was trying to be too helpful – if you know what I mean.'

'Yes. I've not met him, but I know what you mean. We must not forget he overstayed his leave. OK, assuming his flatmate is correct, what have we got on him?' Fitzgerald asked.

'Quite a lot, mostly circumstantial. His office is situated right next to the scene of crime, separated only by a locked door to which he had the key; his flatmate said he thinks he is a Jihadist as he expresses pro-jihadist sentiments; he knew that Baxter was not a hotel employee, because he organised the room, therefore he must have guessed that he was a policeman; If he did hold pro-Jihadist sentiments then he would have been very anti the MP's speech which was based on Muslim fundamentalism; finally he taught himself to shoot by joining the Bristol Gun Club and won a prize.' Catchpole paused.

'So, what you are saying is that he had opportunity, motive and ability. Unfortunately, all those points could be explained away by a clever defence lawyer. His office was established before the pantry next door became a crime scene; he had the key because he was the assistant manager and had all the keys; he was told about the MP and his entourage by the police, Sgt Nelson no less, as he had to get the rooms ready; his flatmate was his junior and may have held a personal grudge against him; and anybody can join a gun club and win a prize. It doesn't make them a murderer plus the fact no-one has ever seen him with a gun.

'Yes. You're right but I think we should treat him as a suspect for now until we can prove otherwise,' Catchpole added.

'OK. What I would like you to do is go to Bristol yourself and follow up on these points as far as you can. Before you do that, can you check with DVLA as to what happened to the van before it was bought by the builder in Taunton.'

Catchpole left to go to his desk where he telephoned DVLA. Thirty minutes later he was back in Fitzgerald's office. 'You'd better listen to this, boss,' he said. 'Y434HSB was first registered on 8th September 2001 in the name of a Mr S. Patel of 21 Wayfare Street, Pinner.'

'Where's Pinner?'

'Near Harrow' said Catchpole triumphantly, 'which is not far from Barnet.'

'Nothing about Patel's Provisions?'

'No. It was sold by Patel in 2006 when it was bought by the builder in Taunton.'

'Lovely,' said Fitzgerald. 'I have a funny feeling we're getting somewhere. I'll get onto Fox and he can check 21 Wayfare Street.'

21

Johnson's phone rang. He switched to Receive and looked at his watch. It was one-twenty in the morning. It could only be Anita.

'Yes,' he said, trying to sound friendly.

'It's me'. He recognised her voice. 'I know.' he replied.

'Suleiman saw me this evening after prayers,' she said. 'He said he has got something for me next Saturday and I am to make sure I am free.'

'Did he say what or where?'

'No. He just said I must be free and I must not take any bags.'

'What did he mean by that?'

'I don't know. I presume he means suitcase because we won't be sleeping in a hotel.'

'Very strange. What else did he say?'

'He said my computer doesn't work.'

'He probably doesn't know the password. Did you tell him the password?'

'No.'

'Well he's obviously not very experienced with computers because he could get around the password by just setting a new one. Anyway, don't worry. If he can't work it out, tough.'

'If he takes me away again will you be there with me?' She asked.

'If I know where you will be, yes, of course I will be there.'

'Good, because I will only feel safe if I know you will be around.'

'Don't worry. I said I would look after you and I will. Just keep me informed.'

'OK. Good night.' She ended the call.

Johnson had been contacting Anita at least once a week since his last meeting with Mrs B. pretending to be her cousin Usman and since these calls, she had become much more confident and secure in her attitude. She expressed no anxiety tonight about Suleiman's proposal. He would brief Mrs B. first thing in the morning. He went back to sleep.

At six am he woke, got up and went for his usual run, showered, had breakfast and coffee and at eight-thirty am telephoned Mrs B.

'Good morning, Mrs B.'

'Good morning, Number 8.' She was always very prim and proper about greeting people especially first thing in the morning.

'I got a call from Delia this morning,' he said. 'She's been contacted by Suleiman. He says he wants her to be free next Saturday for something. He did not say what.'

'Did she say anything else?'

'Yes. She mustn't take any bags and he said her computer doesn't work.'

'The man's a fool,' said Mrs B. 'He isn't computer literate obviously. Never mind. Now he probably has in mind another meeting being organised by the MP Robertson. It is scheduled for next Saturday afternoon in Nottingham in one of the community centres. I don't have too much information now but you had better make sure you are free to attend.'

'Delia will confirm the venue and date later I'm sure,' Johnson said.

'Are you keeping in regular contact with her?' asked Mrs B.

'Yes, I ring her at least once a week. I telephone in the evenings when she is back from work and usually alone.'

'Do you ever visit her?'

'No. I have never been into her flat,' Johnson replied. He knew what she was fishing for. He continued. 'As you pointed out, she is much more self-assured since I have been in contact with her.'

'Is it safe you are telephoning her?'

'It's as safe as anything else. We've worked out a system.

'Well look after her because she is still our only contact.' She ended the call and immediately contacted agent 04 who was investigating the explosives side. She had previously briefed her on the result of the search in Barnet but so far nothing had turned up. She now passed on the information that Johnson had just given her.

At eight-thirty in the morning Fitzgerald telephoned his HQ in London. He asked to be put through to D/Constable Fox.

'Good morning,' he said when Fox answered. 'This is Chief Superintendent Fitzgerald. I don't think we've met.'

'No sir,' Fox replied, 'but I know who you are.'

'Good, because I have been told you've been put onto our case and are looking after the London side.'

'Yes sir. Commander Birch is telling me what to do.'

'Fine. I've got two jobs I want you to do. Have you got a paper and pencil handy?'

'Yes sir.'

'Go to Harrow Police Station. I understand you know about the discovery of the number plates in the boot of the car?'

'Yes sir.'

'I want you to see the PC who stopped and searched the car and found the number plates and take a detailed statement from him. Do you think you can do that?'

'Yes sir.'

'He should have made notes in his notebook. Seize his notebook. We want it as an exhibit.'

'Yes sir.'

'The next thing I want you to do is a bit more complicated. I understand you are checking allotments for anyone named Khalid?'

'Yes sir.'

I want you also to check out an address in Pinner, 21 Wayfare Street, Pinner. Do you know where Pinner is?

'I'll find out.'

'Somewhere near Harrow. I want you to just check the address and let me know what it is. It may be owned by someone called Patel. Be discreet. Don't blow it and let them know you are a policeman. All I want to know at this stage is what is there. When you have done that ring me here at Wolverhampton.'

'Yes sir. Thank you, sir,' Fox replied. Fitzgerald terminated the call.

Fox was elated. Things were really getting interesting and he had been briefed by the great man himself. He knew Fitzgerald's reputation. He was determined he was not going to make a mess of what he had been told to do. He thought out his plan.

He first telephoned Barnet Council and made an appointment to see the person who dealt with allotments. Next, he telephoned Harrow Police Station and asked to be put through to Inspector Watson.

'Oh hello,' he said when Watson answered, 'DC Fox here. Do you remember I came and visited you and we went out to Barnet together?'

'Yes,' said Watson. Still no "sir" but at least Fox sounded a little more courteous. Someone must have spoken to him, Watson thought.

'I need to take a statement from the PC who stopped and searched the car and found the number plates. I also need his notebook in which he recorded this. We need it as an exhibit. Could you arrange for me to see him tomorrow morning?'

'I'll just check when he is on duty,' Watson replied. He put the phone down and shuffled through some papers on his desk looking for the time sheets. 'He's on nights tomorrow,' he said, 'he comes on at six pm.'

'Damn,' Fox thought. It would mean his having to wait around until the PC came on duty, but it had to be done. 'OK I'll be there at six if you could ask him not to go out until I have seen him. What's his name again?'

'PC Stubbs and PC Butler.'

'Two? Will they both be on duty then?'

'Yes. They work as a team. You will need to take statements from both.'

Fox felt a bit resentful that Watson should be telling him what to do, but made no comment. 'Thanks, I will see them both then.' With that the call ended.

The following morning Fox went to work wearing a suit. He also took his briefcase. He had bought the briefcase when he joined the CTC. He thought all detectives used briefcases when they were on a case and was surprised to find that very few did. Anyway, he thought, he would appear far more business-like with a briefcase. All it had in it was a clipboard, notepad, biro pen and pencil, but it was appearances that mattered.

His appointment was with Mrs Jones and was not until two pm so he spent the morning going through his paperwork and mulling over in his mind exactly what he wanted to find out and what questions to ask. He did not want to have a situation where, when he returned to his office, he realised he had forgotten to ask some vital question. He made notes on his notepad. At one-thirty pm he got into his car and set off for Barnet Council Headquarters.

He arrived just after two pm and went into reception. This was a large room with a counter at the far end. He marched up to the counter and deliberately adopting his public school upper crust manner, announced to the receptionist, "Fox. Metropolitan Police Service. I have an appointment with Mrs Jones.'

His attitude certainly had the desired effect upon the receptionist who was new to the job and seemed intimidated by his attitude. 'I'll telephone Mrs Jones,' she said and picked up the phone. After a pause she said, 'Mrs Jones said she will be with you as soon as possible. Would you like to take a seat?' pointing to some chairs under a window on the far side of the reception area. Fox didn't reply or take a seat. Instead, he wandered around the reception area reading the notices that were pinned to the wall.

After ten minutes, a middle-aged lady appeared through a door. 'Mr Fox?' she enquired wearing a warm smile and looking at Fox, 'I'm Ann Jones.' Fox went towards her and offered his hand for a handshake. 'Here is someone I can do business with,' he thought. He was impressed by her demeanour.

'Shall we go in here?' said Mrs Jones opening a side door into an office. They both went in.

The office was an interview room furnished with a desk with a computer and telephone and four chairs. She indicated to Fox to take one of the chairs whilst she sat behind the computer. 'How can I help?' she asked.

Fox took his notepad out of the briefcase. 'I'm investigating a serious case,' he said, 'and I need to know if you have a Mr Khalid who is an allotment holder on one of your allotment sites.'

'How do you spell his name?' she asked.

'I'm not sure. It could be K.H.A.L.I.D. or K.A.L.H.I.D.

'Do you know his initials?

'The only one I know is "S".'

'Which allotment is his?'

'I have no idea. Can you check them all?' he asked.

'We have forty-nine sites and about a thousand plot holders,' she replied. 'Anyway, I'll do what I can.' She switched on the computer. Whilst it was warming up she asked, 'am I allowed to know what the case is?'

'Murder,' he replied.

'Oh dear. Well I hope you catch him.' After a short wait, she said the computer was now up and running. 'I'll try both names,' she said, 'it could take time as I will have to go through each site individually. Would you rather leave it with me and I can let you know the result or do you want to wait?'

'I'll wait if that is OK with you, in case some other queries crop up.' Then he suddenly remembered "Patel's Provisions". It's a long shot but you never know. 'There is another name I want to check as well,' he said. 'Can you check it at the same time?'

She had already started checking, 'What name?' she asked.

'Patel. Patel's Provisions. I don't know any initial. He replied.

'Patel is a very common name,' she said, 'We've got lots of Patels living in the area.' With that she opened a drawer in the desk and pulled out a writing pad and pencil. 'The best thing I can do is note down any sites where any of these names crop up.'

It took over an hour for her to check all the forty-nine sites for any of the three names he had given her. All he could do was sit in his chair and watch her. He was impressed by her efficiency and the speed with which she worked the computer. At the end of it all she looked at her pad. 'No Khalids in either spelling have a plot. There are four Patels.' She handed him her notes on the writing pad.

He looked at her notes. 'And these are all Barnet sites?' he asked. 'Do you cover Pinner at all?'

'Yes, they are all Barnet sites and no we don't cover Pinner. That comes under Harrow.'

'Final question,' he said. 'Do you have any business registered under the name "Patel's Provisions"?'

'No. There is no business registered under that name on our records. Of course, if they are registered under another name, the official name as shown on the deeds, then it would not be on our records.'

'Thank you very much,' said Fox. 'You have been an immense help.' They stood up and shook hands. Fox left and went back to his car. He had learnt something new which he did not know before, businesses could be officially registered with the council under one name and trading under another. He looked at his watch. It was nearly four o'clock and he had two hours to kill before he was due at Harrow police Station, so he decided he would try and find Pinner and look for No.21 Wayfare Street.

He found Pinner without too much trouble. It was part of the Borough of Harrow. Wayfare Street, he discovered, was a busy road to the South of the main shopping centre. It seemed to be mainly residential properties on one side of the road and businesses on the other. After driving slowly for fifteen minutes, he found a short stay car park so he drove in and parked. He paid for half an hour and then walked down the street checking the property numbers. Most did not have a number displayed but he was able to work out the numbers by counting from where he did find a number.

Number 21 was not showing but he calculated where it was and saw it was a small groceries shop. He looked through the window and saw groceries and vegetables, newspapers, drinks, chocolates and cigarettes. A typical corner shop. Above the shop window was a sign reading "THE CORNER SHOP". Over the door was another sign reading in small print "Proprietor Mr S. E. Patel". Judging by the state of the paint, that sign had been there some time. He looked again at the sign over the window. The paint was in much better condition, probably recently painted.

He then walked up and down the road from this shop checking all the signs but there were no premises with a sign reading "Patel's Provisions". The only conclusion, he decided, was that "The Corner Shop" is or was "Patel's Provisions". Anyway, he decided, he had enough information to be able to give C/Superintendent Fitzgerald a pretty accurate description of the premises.

He also noted that the car park where he had parked was not very far away and that if anyone wanted to carry out observations on the shop, it would be a good place to do it from. He made up his mind, though, that before he spoke to Fitzgerald, he would check with the Borough Council to see if they had any information on Patel's Provisions.

It was now five-forty pm so he got into his car and drove to Harrow Police station. PCs Stubbs and Butler were waiting for him. He was shown to an interview room and the two PCs handed him their statements. They also gave him their notebooks. He didn't expect this. He thought he was supposed to record the statements himself. He wondered if they knew how a statement should be recorded. After all he was supposed to be the expert. He sat down with them and read through the statements. They seemed to have covered everything and, indeed, had been beautifully typed.

'Who typed these?' He asked.

'The civy typist,' said Stubbs.

'They seem fine. Thanks. You have saved me a job,' he said. He left the station and drove back to his headquarters.

22

It was half past eight on Tuesday evening when Johnson telephoned Anita for his weekly chat. He looked forward to his weekly contact with her. She always sounded cheerful when he rang and seemed to enjoy their little chats making small talk about all sorts of topics.

'Hello,' he said, 'it's me.'

'Hello,' she replied. She was not her usual chirpy self.

'Is something wrong?' he asked sounding genuinely concerned; and then continued. 'Are you alone? Is there anyone with you?'

'No.'

'What's the problem?'

'I got a huge fright this morning,' she said, 'Suleiman walked into the shop.'

'Suleiman! What did he want?' This *was* a surprise.

'He brought in some boxes of vegetables.'

'What for?'

'He was selling them to my boss.'

'Has he ever done this before?'

'No. Well I've never seen him, but I am not there every day.'

'So, what did he do?'

'He was arguing with my boss, presumably about the price but they were speaking Urdu which I don't understand. Anyway, after a while my boss opened the cash till and gave him some money.'

'And then what?'

'He walked towards the door then stopped and looked at me, tossed his head indicating he wanted me to follow him.'

'Did you go out?'

'Yes. I waited a minute and then went out. He was waiting on the pavement just outside.'

'Did he seem pleased to see you, or greet you?'

'No. He just said he would pick me up outside my flat at six o'clock on Saturday morning.'

'Did he say where you were going?'

'I asked him if I should bring a suitcase and he said, "no, come as you are". I then asked where we were going and he told me it was to Nottingham.'

'Is that all?'

'Yes. Then he walked off down the pavement. I didn't know he knew I worked there. He frightens me. I don't like him.' He could tell by the sound of her voice that she was very concerned.

'Going back to the vegetables, what were they like?' asked Johnson.

'They were beautiful. There was one box of carrots, all made up into bunches and another box containing ten cabbages and ten cauliflowers. My boss told me to put them out on the shelves which I did and people came in and bought them.'

'Did any paperwork change hands?'

'No. It was just cash'. Johnson hoped there might have been an invoice or something to get a name from.

'He's not a farmer, is he?' he asked. He was fishing, hoping to get something to identify him by.

'I don't know. He doesn't look like a farmer. I have no idea where he comes from. He has never told me anything about himself.'

'OK. Anita; don't worry about Nottingham. I will be there. Also, Anita, be careful what you say on this line.' A bit late now, he thought. He just hoped no-one was listening in. He rang off and immediately telephoned Mrs B.

Mrs B. answered straight away. 'Good evening, Mrs B,' said Johnson, 'I'm sorry to bother you now.'

'No bother. That's why I'm here,' she replied.

'I've just had a long chat with Delia,' he said. 'She saw Suleiman this morning and he told her to be ready to go to Nottingham with him on Saturday morning.' He repeated to her all that he had been told by Delia.

'Yes, this fits in with what I have heard,' Mrs B. replied. 'The MP Robinson is holding another public meeting at the Central Community Hall in Nottingham on Saturday afternoon. I gather it will follow the same procedure as the one at Wolverhampton except he will not be staying the night. I want you to attend but I will have some more information for you before you go. I will contact you later.'

'Thank you,' he replied.

The following morning Mrs B. called in agent 04. She briefed her on what Johnson had told her. 'The public meeting is being held in Nottingham and I'm pretty sure that is where they will be going. We've got until Friday to come up with something. Are you getting anywhere?'

'Yes, we have had some success though not in the way you want. You gave me the address No. 44 Grenada Avenue in Barnet. Well, I put a watch on those premises and on Saturday afternoon a car drove into the driveway, a silver BMW registration number WS04NFX which is registered in the name of Khalid. An Asian man got out and went into the house through the front door. He came out shortly afterwards carrying some mail in his hand and got back into his car. He was very obviously the owner as he had a key to unlock the door.'

My agent tailed him when he drove off and he drove to Pinner near Harrow. There he stopped outside a shop in Wayfare Street and went inside. My agent, who is a woman, watched for a while and when he did not come out, went in herself. The shop was called THE CORNER SHOP. Inside it was very well stocked with all the usual items you would expect to find in a corner shop and there was a middle-aged Asian woman behind the counter but no sign of the man. The shopkeeper was very pleasant and spoke perfect English and asked if she could help. To mark time the agent pretended she wanted some chocolates. She checked the shelves and saw boxes of chocolates but no tins, so she asked if they had any tins, naming some brand she knew of but was not displayed. The woman apologised saying they didn't stock that brand. The agent sounded very disappointed and asked if she would check in her stock-room in case they had something similar. The Asian woman said they did not have a stock-room. My agent knew that was not true as she owns a retail business herself and recognised some of the stock that came from a wholesaler in the Midlands. One could only buy these products in standard large cartons so they must have a stock-room somewhere. Also, there was too much stock in that shop for there not to be a stock-room.'

'Did you get a name?' asked Mrs B.

'There is a name "S. B. Patel" painted on a board over the main entrance. That is the only clue.'

'So, what are you doing now?'

'We are keeping a watch on the shop hoping that someone will lead us to their stock-room.'

'And then what?'

'We'll go in and have a good look around. But there is more.'

'Go on.'

'As you know I live in Barnet and I have a close friend who works for the Council. Her name is Ann Jones and she is a senior Admin. Officer in the Council Offices. The other day a member of the CID, a Mr Fox, came and interviewed her. He was interested in a Mr Khalid and wanted to know if he had a plot in an allotment. She said the Council knows Mr Khalid very well. They are always having trouble getting his rates off him. They believe he owns a business but do not have his business address. He is apparently very cagey about disclosing his business address. She did not tell Mr Fox this. He said he was investigating a murder case so why he was interested in allotment plots is not clear. However, I think we might have tracked Mr Khalid's business to Pinner in Harrow. That's as far as I have got.'

Mrs B. thanked her and ended the meeting. If nothing else there seemed to be a definite link between 44 Grenada Avenue and the shop in Pinner.

23

D/Constable Fox was at his desk early. He was dressed in a suit again and had his briefcase with him. He was determined to crack the "Patel's Provisions" mystery. There had obviously been some organisation of that name otherwise why would anyone address mail to it. He had the three unopened letters they had found in the house. He had a good look at them. He noted that the post mark on one was over six months old and that it had been opened and then re-sealed. The post mark on another was three months old but had apparently not been opened. He was unable to determine the date on the third letter but it had not been opened either.

He first opened the oldest one and pulled out a leaflet advertising satchels. 'Satchels,' he thought, 'why would anyone with a corner shop want satchels.' The leaflet was from a company called "Mr Right's Satchels" of Loughborough in the Midlands. The photos were of various satchels in pastel colours and said they were suitable for women, men and children. Some had shoulder straps, some had carrying handles and some had no handles at all. There were photos of them being carried by various people. They were all the same size, namely 38cm x 25cm x 5cm and made from simulated leather dyed in a variety of colours.

He then opened the second letter. It was an invoice from Mr Right's Satchels to Patel's Provisions for ten satchels with shoulder straps @ £9.99 each plus delivery £5.00 plus VAT @ 20%, total

£125.88.

He opened the third letter. It was dated three weeks ago and was a Final Demand from Mr Right's Satchels for the sum of £125.88.

'Well,' thought Fox, 'I've learnt something I didn't know before. Mr Patel's Provisions, whoever he is, obviously deals in satchels so is presumably not a corner shop dealing in groceries.' But what connection it had to Khalid of 44 Grenada Avenue was still a mystery.

He put the letters back into their envelopes and into his file and then turned his attention to what he really had in mind, to check whether anyone by the name of Khalid or Patel had an allotment in Harrow. He put a call through to the Borough Headquarters and asked to speak to the business rates section. He was eventually put through to a Mr Martin Franklin. 'Good morning, Mr Franklin. My name is Fox from Metropolitan Police Service. I'm on quite a sensitive investigation and would like to discuss something with you about businesses. May I make an appointment for a meeting with you?'

'Can you tell me what it is about?'

'I can't talk on the telephone.'

'When would you like to meet?'

'As soon as possible. It is quite urgent.'

'What about eleven o'clock this morning? I am in meetings all afternoon.'

'Eleven o'clock is fine. I'll meet you then and thank you,' Fox replied. He was beginning to realise that if you spoke civilly to people, especially government officials, you normally got what you wanted. 'I must stop trying to show off,' he said to himself. Nobody seemed to know he'd been to Eton, and if they did, they were not particularly impressed by the fact.

At ten o'clock he went down to the yard to get his car and set off for Harrow. He found the Borough Headquarters quite easily, parked and went into reception. 'Good morning. My name is Fox. I have an appointment with Mr Franklin,' he said to the receptionist. She looked at her pad and replied. 'Oh yes. Please take a seat. I'll telephone Mr Franklin and tell him you are here.' Fox went in and sat down in one of the padded chairs by a window.

After about five minutes a young lady walked across the foyer to Fox. 'Are you Mr Fox?' she asked.

'Yes,' he replied.

'Would you follow me. I'll take you to Mr Franklin.' This is not what he expected. They walked across the foyer and through a door to a lift. She pressed the button and the doors opened. She stood back whilst he entered. She followed and pressed the button for the third floor. They got out and walked down a short, carpeted passage to an oak door. She knocked and entered. Fox followed. It was a large well-furnished office with an impressive mahogany desk in front of the window. Mr Franklin was sitting in a comfortable looking office chair. He rose and came around the desk to shake Fox's hand. Fox was very glad he was wearing his suit and not jeans.

'Let's sit here,' indicating a couple of easy chairs by the side with a coffee table between them. 'Can I offer you some tea or coffee?' he asked.

'Coffee would be fine thanks. White, no sugar.'

Franklin looked at the young lady who was standing beside the chair, 'and I will have black as usual. Thanks Ruby.' Ruby left the office.

'How can I help?' Franklin asked.

Fox decided to come straight to the point with Franklin. He was obviously in a very senior position so there was no need to beat about the bush, as it were. 'I'm on a sensitive murder case,' he said, 'and I'm interested in tracking down two people, both Asians I assume. One is named Khalid and the other Patel. To be quite honest with you I am not sure whether it is two people or one person using two names.'

'They are both very common Asian names,' said Franklin. 'Can you give me anything more to work on?'

'I wondered whether you could check your business rates schedule to see if either person has a business and whether either has an allotment.

'What kind of business? We have thousands of businesses.'

'I think it is some kind of grocery business, maybe a corner shop, or one that deals with leather goods, like satchels or cases.'

'Do you mean travel goods?'

'Yes, travel goods would be a good start. I'm sorry to be so vague but we get a lot of small clues and I am trying to put them together.'

'This is not the murder of that policeman in the Midlands, is it?' asked Franklin.

'Yes, it is,' Fox replied. 'Our enquiries have led us to London.'

'Nasty business. I read about it in the press. Let's go to my desk and I will fire up the computer for the business rates. I'll get my PA to check the allotments. Will it be alright if she knows why?'

'As long as she doesn't go telling anybody that we are looking for these people.'

'No. She's pretty discreet. I trust her.' With that he picked up a telephone. 'Could you come through Doris?'

The door opened and an elderly lady appeared with notebook in hand. 'This is Doris. Doris this is Mr Fox from the Metropolitan Police Service.' To Fox, 'will you tell her what you want?'

Fox explained as clearly as he could that he was looking for one or two people who had an allotment. 'The only other piece of information I can give you is a shop called THE CORNER SHOP at 21 Wayfare Street in Pinner. I know that shop does exist but I am not sure if it is connected or not. The owner's name is above the door as "S. B. Patel". I don't know whether he is still there so anything you can find on that would be helpful.'

'Doris. This is a sensitive murder case so please no talking to anyone,' said Franklin.

'I know Mr Franklin. Don't worry no one will know.' With that she left.

Franklin turned to his computer. 'Let's start off with the Corner Shop in Pinner because we know it exists. After five minutes of clicking, 'yes,' he said, 'S. B. Patel of THE CORNER SHOP, 21

Wayfare Street, Pinner – been there for years and still there apparently. Nothing flagged up against them. They appear to be good honest citizens.'

'Do you know what "S. B." stands for?'

'It says here "Salim Binyamin".

'What about other businesses?' asked Fox.

'We've got dozens and dozens of businesses with the name Patel in them. I think you had better get a bit more background information. I can give you a print-out if you want, but it will take you ages to check them all out.'

'What about Khalid?'

After another ten minutes, 'not so many Khalids. There is a lawyer...... a doctor.... a general dealer, doesn't say what he is dealing in....... I can't see any that indicate anything like a corner shop or grocery. I'll print out the general dealer for you.' With that he printed the details for Fox.

Whilst the printer was running Doris appeared with a piece of paper in her hand. 'I have found Patel of Wayfare Street. He's had an allotment for years.' She handed Fox the piece of paper with the details.

'You have given me something to work on. Thank you very much. If I get any more information, can I come back to you?' Fox asked.

'Of course, you can. We would be glad to assist,' said Franklin. Fox shook his hand and took his leave. Doris accompanied him back to the foyer where he thanked her again and left.

Before he drove off, he looked at the two pieces of paper he had been given. The general dealer did not look very promising. It seemed to be located on the High Street. He decided to leave it for the moment. The allotment though did look promising. It was in Pinner, at Brightwell, not too far from the shop, so he decided to go there and have a look.

He found the allotments quite easily and parked his car on the side of the road. He took his clipboard and a pencil from his briefcase. If anybody asked him he would say he was from the council. He opened the gate and went in. He was looking for plot No. 16, but he had no idea where to start. It was quite a big site with, he guessed, 50 or so plots and there were a few people working on them. He went up to the nearest person, an elderly woman, whose plot was near the entrance gate.

'Hello,' he said in the friendliest tone he could muster, 'you look very busy.'

'Preparing for cauliflowers for winter,' she replied.

'What number is this, then?' he asked.

'Six' she said.

'It looks like arduous work,' he said to make conversation.

'It is but it gives me exercise. If I didn't do this I would just be sitting at home watching the telly.'

'I quite agree. I should do more gardening myself, but I am tied up with this,' waving his clipboard at her. They continued discussing the merits of gardening with him praising her for what she had grown in hers, most of which he did not recognise. Whilst talking to her his eye was caught by the plot next to hers which looked like a show garden.

'Whose plot is that?' he asked pointing to it.'

'I don't know. An elderly Asian gentleman comes here and works on his own nearly every day.'

'Do you know his name?'

'No. I've tried talking to him but he ignores me. I don't think he speaks English.'

'Do you know where he comes from?'

'I've no idea. It must be somewhere local because he always walks here.'

'I've never seen anything so neat. I wonder what he does with his produce.' There were rows of carrots, cabbages, cauliflowers, beetroot and at the end, four ridges with potatoes. The lines were dead straight and the soil between them completely clear of weeds.

'Rumour has it that he sells them to a shop. Probably the way he earns extra money.'

'Is that his shed?' pointing to a small wooden shed in the corner. It looked old but had been patched up.

'Yes. He does everything by hand,' she replied.

'Well thank you. I'm impressed. I had better get on.' He waved his clipboard again and started walking up and down the plots as if checking them all to give the impression that he was not just interested in plot No. 16. The plots varied completely. Most had vegetables growing in them. A few had flowers. Some were neat and tidy, even to the extent of having the grass surrounding them mowed. Some were very unkempt. None came up to the standard of No. 16.

When he had finished, he made his way back to his car, waving at his new-found friend still working on her plot. He decided he would go to Wayfare Street and this time he'd have a look inside the shop.

He parked in the car park and walked across the road to the shop. He went straight in and immediately saw the vegetables on a shelf. There were carrots tied in bunches, cabbages and cauliflowers neatly trimmed, beetroot also in bunches, potatoes all clean and healthy looking. A middle-aged Asian woman was behind the counter. 'Can I help you?' she asked in perfect English.

'I'm admiring your vegetables,' he said, 'where do you get them from?'

'We buy them from plot holders,' she replied. 'That way we know they are fresh.'

'Could I have one bunch of carrots and half a kg of potatoes?' he asked. She came around the counter, prepared his order, placing it into a paper bag for him. Whilst she was getting his order ready, he had a good look around the shop. It was very well stocked with groceries and confectionary items but no sign of any satchels. He paid and left the shop. At least he felt he now had something to tell C/Superintendent Fitzgerald and to put in his diary for Commander Birch.

On Wednesday morning Mrs B was at her desk as usual digesting a report she had just received from Colonel Rutherford confirming that the political meeting was going ahead on Saturday at Nottingham. The MP would be protected by two police VIP protection officers and he would be sending Sergeant Nelson and his team as normal. Mrs B was thinking about Number 8 and his contact, Delia. Delia was not bringing in much information. She had hoped to get a lot more from her but this was not happening. Still Delia was the only contact they had, unsatisfactory though it was.

She was also concerned about the lack of information on al-Abdullah. So far, they had found nothing new but the fact that Delia had been told to "prepare herself to avenge her husband's death" would seem to indicate they had something planned.

Suddenly there was a knock on the door and Agent 04 entered. 'We've found it.' She said.

Mrs B. looked up 'Found what?'

'The stock-room.'

'Oh sorry, I was miles away,' said Mrs B. 'Where is it?'

'In a private garage two blocks away from the shop,' 04 replied. She continued. 'It is in a cul-de-sac at the end of a road with a whole batch of other garages. I think they are assigned to a row of council houses in the next street.'

'So, did you find anything?' asked Mrs B.

'We went in in the early hours of this morning. It had a normal up-and-over-door, but he had fitted an extra padlock to give it more security. Luckily it was a common make, so it presented no problem. The garage was chock-a-block full of cartons, boxes, bundles, batches of sweets, biscuits, cleaning material, toilet rolls and everything you would expect to find in a corner shop. Down one wall was a row of shelves stacked with items they had unpacked. We didn't find anything suspicious, certainly nothing that looked like explosives. However, on the top shelf there was a small pile of what looked like shoulder bags. They were brand new, still in their plastic wrapping. They were pastel coloured. I couldn't recognise what they were. The nearest description is ladies shoulder bags but they were pretty awful, I certainly would not want one and they don't seem the sort of thing you would expect to find in a corner shop.'

'What about satchels?' asked Mrs B.

'Satchels? ... Could be. I think they were a bit small to be satchels, but I suppose small satchels do exist.'

'The reason I suggested satchels is, as you know, the police carried out a search at Grenada Avenue and found three unopened letters addressed to Patel's Provisions. Well, they opened these letters and found that they contained literature from a firm in the Midlands that makes satchels and Patel's had apparently bought some but had not paid for them. Would they be big enough to take a bomb?'

'Oh yes – a small one.'

'Well, they ordered ten of them. How many were on the shelf?'

'I don't know. I didn't count them.'

'We've also got the warning made to the agent Delia to "avenge her husband's death". This could be what they are planning,' said Mrs B. She continued. 'There's a public meeting on Saturday in Nottingham which would be an ideal time to strike, so we haven't got much time.'

'Right then, we will go back tonight and this time take a sniffer dog,' said O4. 'If we find anything, what do you want us to do?'

'Neutralize it.' Mrs B said emphatically.

24

D/Inspector Catchpole arrived at Bristol Temple Meads Station mid-morning having caught the early morning train from Birmingham. He had previously made an appointment to see the bursar, Mr White, at the university. He caught a taxi to take him there.

On arrival, he was shown straight into the bursar's office. After the usual greetings and offer of coffee which he gladly accepted, he took a seat.

'I take it you are on the murder of the policeman case?' asked White.

'Yes. I hope you can help us clear up a few outstanding queries that I have.'

'I also believe my son David was at the hotel. Is this why you are here?'

'Not entirely, but I would like to talk about him,' said Catchpole.

'One of your colleagues was here the other day and spoke to my wife. I have to say she was very upset about it.'

'Oh. I'm sorry to hear that. I do apologise. Your son's name cropped up with several witnesses so we have to make enquiries to clear him – eliminate him from our enquiries is the term used.'

'So, he's not a suspect then?'

'No and we have no reason to think he will be,' said Catchpole. He would not normally go as far as this with an outsider when investigating a case. The normal procedure is to be as non-committal as possible but, in this case, he felt White would be more use to them if he didn't have to worry about his son. He continued. 'Do you know how he got the name "Tommy"?'

'Hm.' White paused and then, 'he was given it by a young Asian student we had here at the time called Rhana Khalid. David befriended him for some reason which I have never understood. You know David was caught stealing money in the changing room?'

'Yes. I had heard something about it but don't know the details.' In fact, he knew exactly what had happened but wanted to hear it again from White.

'It happened about three years ago. Rhana went into a changing room and caught David red handed with his hand in someone else's trouser pocket. David said he was taking the money because he wanted to give it to him, Rhana. Why he wanted to give him money I am afraid I don't know. Anyway, Rhana stopped him. There was very little money involved, less than twenty quid, which was given back to the owners and that was it. No complaint was made but I got to hear about it and was very embarrassed. David, as you probably know, suffers from Asperger's Syndrome and occasionally does strange things. However, in view of my position here I decided to report the matter to the police just to cover myself as these things have a habit of emerging later. I know Inspector Munro at Police Headquarters. We frequently meet on various conferences that take place. He said I had done the right thing and he would take care of it for me. Well, he came out here and interviewed David on his own. He then took him back to the Police Station for about three hours after which he brought him back. He said there should be no more trouble, and there hasn't been. What he said to David I am afraid I don't know. David wouldn't tell me.'

'Do you think David learnt his lesson?'

'No. I think David thought it was a great adventure. I don't think he understood that what he had done was wrong. Anyway, he has never done anything like that before and never done it since so maybe I'm wrong.'

'So how did the name "Tommy" come up?'

'He said Rhana called him "Tommy". He liked the name and said we must always call him "Tommy" and not David. There is something else. Rhana is a Muslim and one day David suddenly said he must pray to Allah and got down on his knees and banged his head on the floor, as Muslims do, though I don't think Muslims bang their heads as David did. My wife and I discussed what we should do and decided to ignore it. He was not doing anyone any harm so we left him alone, presuming he would eventually get bored and stop.' He paused and then continued ... 'Can you tell me how he is involved with the murder case?'

'He's not actually involved,' said Catchpole. 'He was at the hotel as a temporary waiter on the night of the murder and we have to interview everyone who was there. No-one interviewed David as he had left by the time the Police arrived. But we know enough about his movements not to have to interview him yet. If circumstances change I will let you know.'

'That will be a great relief for my wife. She gets very emotional about David as you can imagine.'

'What happened to Rhana? Is this the person who was called Lewis?'

'He was a student studying Tourist Management and then branched out into Hotel Management. He did two years here and then left for some hotel. I have no idea where he is now. He was given the name Lewis by the other students after the TV Detective because of the money incident.'

'Do you have his home address?'

'Yes. Somewhere in London. Do you want his actual address?'

'Yes please, if you have got it.

'I'll have to get my PA to look it up.' He picked up his telephone, 'Betty. Do you remember that Asian student who was here about three years ago, the one called Lewis? ... That's him .... Would you look up his file and get me his home address ... Yes. It was somewhere in London as far as I can remember ... Thanks.' To Catchpole, smiling, 'she remembers him because of the money incident. Everybody remembers the money incident. She'll phone it through when she finds it.'

Catchpole didn't want to leave until he had this vital bit of information but he didn't want to sound desperate. He and White chatted about a variety of matters to pass the time. After ten minutes, the phone rang. White answered. He took a piece of paper and started writing. He then handed it to Catchpole. On it he had written "44 Grenada Avenue. Barnet. London," with a telephone number.

'Thank you very much Mr White. You have been a great help. Please convey our apologies to your wife. We did not want to upset her.'

'I will indeed. Good bye, Mr Catchpole'.

Whilst Catchpole was waiting for the taxi to pick him up he started thinking about the meeting he had just had. 'Why did I not think about asking the university for this address before?' he asked himself. Then he remembered that Lewis had only recently become a suspect and anyway the university was hardly likely to give out someone's address to a stranger even if the individual identified himself as a policeman. Lewis had been considered an obliging young man who had helped them interview the hotel staff. In fact, it was only recently that they associated him with the case at all. Now they had his home address and providing it was correct, he was linked to the person who was high on their list, the mysterious "Suleiman". The boss will be pleased to hear that. The taxi arrived. 'Police Headquarters please,' he said to the driver.

Catchpole asked the receptionist if Inspector Munro was in. He was. After identifying himself, he was directed to Munro's office. On entering he was surprised at how old Munro was. He must be well past his retirement age, in fact if someone said he was seventy I would not be surprised, Catchpole thought.

He introduced himself and proffered his hand for a handshake, but

Munro did not respond. 'Sit down,' was the only response he got. Catchpole sat.

'I'm always suspicious when the big boys from London pay us plebs in the provinces a visit,' said Munro. 'What do you want from me?'

Catchpole ignored the abrupt manner. 'I've just come from seeing the bursar at the university. I gather you know him?'

'Yes. We meet at various conferences and meetings. Not a bad chap.'

'He told me you investigated a theft case his son David was involved in.'

'Yes. He stole some money from the changing room – about twenty quid. It was returned to the complainants.'

'What happened to the case?'

'The CPS declined to prosecute. Said it was not in the public interest. He's mad.   They say he has got Asperger's but I think it is far worse. In fact, I think he should be locked up in a loony bin but of course, no-one would agree with me.'

'Did you interview him?'

'I tried. It was impossible to get through to him. As I recall he said he wanted to give the money to an Asian friend. In fact, it was the Asian who reported him. It was all very odd.'

'I desperately want to get a set of his prints. He was at the hotel where a murder which I am investigating, took place. I need the prints to see if they match some found at the scene. Did you by any chance take any?' Catchpole was hoping that he would be able to get a reference so that they could be traced.

'Is this the Baxter murder?'

'Yes.'

'Well you're in luck. I did take his prints and I've still got them.'

Catchpole was stunned. This must be at least three years ago. Hesitantly he asked, 'how come?'

'When the CPS said they were not going to prosecute I closed the docket off and filed it away with the prints inside. I presume they are still in the file.'

Catchpole racked his brains. He seemed to remember an order came out from the Home Office some time ago saying that all prints and DNA samples in cases that were not going to court had to be destroyed. He didn't want to upset this crusty old man so hesitantly asked, 'is that according to the rules?' He had visions of a judge in the High Court blowing his top if a set of prints that were illegal were produced.

'Rules, rules, bloody rules,' Munro erupted. 'We're plagued by rules. Rules are for idiots and nincompoops who can't think for themselves. I work to the principle of common sense.'

Catchpole was flabbergasted by this outburst but was sympathetic to the principle.

Munro continued. 'If I had conformed to your bloody rules you would not be able to clear your case and another murder would go unsolved. Do you want them?'

'Well I need to send them to the fingerprint department at the Met. Can you send them electronically?'

'Oh, I don't have anything to do with all this electronic whiz-kidery. If you want them, I will get them out of the file and you can do what you like with them.'

'Right. Thanks, I will,' said Catchpole.

'It will take me some time. If you like, make yourself some tea or coffee and make me some as well. I'll have tea.' He pointed to a kettle and mugs standing on the top of a filing cabinet. He then disappeared through the door. Catchpole wondered why he did not get a junior to get the file for him, but then realised that the man was obviously very set in his ways. He had not had any lunch and was feeling a bit peckish so made himself a mug of coffee and put a tea bag in another mug for Munro.

After nearly half an hour Munro returned carrying a docket in his hand. It was very slim and looked very dusty. He blew the dust off and opened it on his desk. He took out a set of prints marked, "David

White" and in red across the top "NOT FOR COURT USE". Catchpole had never seen that before and assumed it was another "Munro" method. Munro handed the prints to him without a word.

'Do you want them back?' Catchpole asked.

'No. You had better stick to your bloody rules,' he replied. 'Anything else?' he asked.

'Yes. I want to contact the Bristol Gun Club. Any idea who I should contact?'

'Mrs Judith Morris is the secretary. She lives at Knowle. I do the registration of their guns,' he added.

'Where's Knowle?'

'It's a suburb to the South of the City. You got any transport?'

'No.'

'I'll get a patrol car to take you there.' He telephoned down to the front office. 'See the constable on duty and tell him I sent you.'

Catchpole got up and this time they shook hands. 'He wasn't such a bad chap,' he thought, 'once you get used to his abrupt manner.' He bade farewell and went downstairs.

The patrol car was waiting for him, driven by a woman constable. 'You know where to go?' he asked. She nodded. 'Knowle,' she said. They set off. The traffic in Bristol was congested and it took them some time to get onto the A37 and head South. After five miles, she turned off onto a side road and after a short distance stopped in front of a smart looking detached home.

'Is this Mrs Morris's house?' He asked. She nodded. 'Not very communicative,' he thought.

'Wait here while I see if she is in?' He rang the doorbell and waited and waited. No-one seemed to be in. He was just about to leave when a pleasant looking middle-aged woman opened the door. 'Can I help you?' she asked.

'Good afternoon,' he replied. 'I'm Inspector Catchpole from the Police. Inspector Munro said I should come and see you.'

'Bert. Oh yes. Please come in.' She opened the door wide and stood to one side.

'Can I just give instructions to my driver?' he said and went to the car. 'When I am finished, I'll telephone the charge office for you to pick me up and take me to the station.'

'I'll tell the Sergeant,' she replied and drove off.

Once inside Mrs Morris's home and seated in her conservatory he explained, 'I'm making enquiries about someone who was a member of your club. I was wondering if you could tell me anything about him?'

'Who is it?'

'A young Asian. A student at the university named Rhana Khalid.'

'Rhana! Oh yes. I remember him very well. He was last here, when ... about two years ago. He was a very good shot.'

'I believe he won a prize?'

'Yes. He won a club competition. We gave him a certificate.'

'How did he become a member?'

'He just pitched up one day and said he wanted to learn how to shoot and could he join us and be taught.'

'Just like that. Is that usual?'

'No not at all usual. Most of our members come from other clubs and have moved into the area.'

'Do many students join?'

'No. He was the only one, which is why I remember him. He was a very pleasant young man.'

'Had he had any experience in shooting before?'

'He said he had only fired a pellet gun.'

'Is that an air gun?'

'Yes.'

'So, what did you teach him?'

'We have tutors who are club members. We put him onto small bore, Point two-two. He didn't have his own weapon, so he borrowed one from the club.'

'Is that a rifle? What about handguns?'

'We're not allowed handguns, but we have air operated ones

which are quite good over short distances. They work off a small gas cylinder, you know, compressed air, fire a ball bearing.'

Catchpole didn't know but pretended he did. 'Was he any good with that?'

'Oh yes. That is where he won his certificate.'

'What about with a rifle?'

'Yes, he was good with that as well.'

'What do you do about ammunition?'

'They have to be a club member and we issue out whatever rounds are needed for the particular shoot that they are going to do. Then we mark it in the register. Most members also want a few extra rounds to practice with and to adjust the sights.'

'Do you have the register for when Rhana was here?'

'I don't know. I'll have to check.' She got up and went into the house. Five minutes later she was back with two hard covered A4 size registers. She looked at the first and immediately put it away. 'That's no good. It is the current one,' she opened the second. 'This one starts at August 2010,' she said. 'Yes. Here we are. R. Khalid. 15 rounds on 27th August. Again, on 26th September 27 rounds.... That seems to be the last entry. I presume he left after that.'

'So, of the rounds he took, can you say how many were for the competition and how many for practice?'

'No. Most of the shoots are ten shots so my guess is that he would have had five practice rounds in the first shoot and seven on the next one.'

'Does anyone check that all the rounds issued are used? Does anyone ever hand any back?'

'No-one ever hands any rounds back. I am sure they are all used.'

'What happens to all the expended cases?'

'We sweep them up and they are sold for scrap metal to give us a little extra income.'

'And nobody checks the expended cases against the ones that are issued?'

'I'm afraid not. No. No ... You're making me feel guilty of something,' she said.

'I think that what you have here is a very easy way for someone to steal your ammunition without you knowing.'

'So, you think we should be taking tighter control on the ammunition we give out to members.'

'Yes. I would say it is vital that you account for all the ammunition you issue.'

She looked aghast. 'Right. I'll bring it up with the committee. Is this what Rhana is involved in and why you are asking all these questions? We've never had any problems.'

'I can't say why I am interested in Rhana, but I suggest that due to the current security situation, we should all be taking tight control over arms and ammunition.'

'Thank you. I shall certainly mention all the points you have raised to the committee.'

'You have been very helpful,' he said. 'May I telephone the charge office for someone to come and pick me up?'

'Please do. Do you want to use my phone?'

'No, I've got them on my mobile phone,' he replied waving his phone in the air. He left the conservatory to make his call and then returned. Whilst waiting for the patrol car they made small talk, mostly about gun crime and trouble in London with armed gangs. He thought this would go some way to camouflage the reason for his questions.

When the patrol car arrived, he bade farewell and left. He asked the driver to drop him at Temple Meads station. He thanked the woman constable and went in to buy his ticket to London. It was after six pm, and the station was heaving. He had had a very long day and was now feeling very tired, added to which he had not had a proper meal all day. He bought a first-class ticket and then found a restaurant and ordered a full blown mixed grille, something he had not had for years.

There was still time to kill until the train left so he first telephoned his wife to tell her he would be home that night. She was delighted and promised him an intimate reception. Next, he telephoned Fitzgerald, who had gone off duty but was very pleased to get his call. He filled him in on all that he had learnt; getting Lewis's home address; getting hold of Tommy's fingerprints and the situation at the gun club. Lewis was not only taught how to use a weapon but had ready access to free ammunition. Fitzgerald was astounded that they had not followed up this route earlier.

'I'm going back to London tonight and will be at home,' Catchpole said. 'I can't remember when I last saw my home.'

'That's fine,' Fitzgerald replied, 'and take tomorrow off. You know the meeting is going ahead on Saturday. I want you to be there.'

'Right. I'll go straight from home. Can I use my car and claim mileage?'

'OK. Don't overdo it.' He continued, 'I am closing down here on Saturday. There is nothing happening here. All the action seems to be in London so I will set up a new incident room in London next week. I'll hand over here to the local CID and they can keep it running, so when you finish at Nottingham, return to London and I will see you on Monday.'

'OK Boss,' he said and boarded the train, finding a seat in a corner where he settled down to make himself comfortable. He was hoping to get some peace and quiet.

His mind drifted to Elizabeth, his wife. They had been married twelve years but had no children. It was not for lack of trying. They had had tests to discover if there was anything wrong, but these had been inconclusive. They had discussed adoption and even IVF but Elizabeth said, 'No. It is the will of God and it would be wrong to challenge the will of God.' She was a devout Catholic. He was not a member of any church, however he accompanied Elizabeth to church every Sunday because she liked the company. Anyway, he thought, 'we are praying to the same God so what does it matter what church you belong to.' Their passion was visiting exotic places around the world when he took leave. It helped that Elizabeth worked for a travel agent and could get good deals. With the movement of the train he soon dozed off dreaming about their last holiday in Croatia.

25

On Thursday morning Mrs B. arrived at her office at eight and found 04 waiting for her. She was resting in an easy chair looking very tired.

'You haven't been waiting for me all night, have you?' she asked.

In fact, she had been there since five am. They had returned from their search in the stock-room and had had a positive result. She had to speak to Mrs B. face to face straight away and by the time they arrived back from their search it was too late for her to go home. 'We found one,' she said.

'I had a feeling you would,' said Mrs B. 'It was just too much to expect the organisation would just fade away. Where was it?'

'In one of those satchels, as you said, a pale blue one buried in a pack of toilet rolls. We would not have found it if it hadn't been for the dog.'

'Go on.'

'There were three packs of toilet rolls, each holding about 50 rolls packed into what looked like large plastic sacks. They had slit one open and removed some of the rolls making a space into which they stuffed the satchel. They then replaced the rolls and re-sealed the pack.

'And what was the device?'

'Two phials of fertilizer explosive in long slim plastic tubes with an electronic detonator stuffed into a golf ball size slug of P4 plastic explosive as an accelerant. The detonator was wired to a standard mobile phone. Very simple but, according to Dave the explosive expert, could cause a devastating explosion in a confined space.'

'So, what did you do?'

'Dave said the P4 looked very old, possibly more than 20 years old, and may not be viable. However, we couldn't take the chance. We neutralized the whole thing. We removed the detonator and replaced it with one of our own dummies and re-connected it to the phone; and substituted the explosives with sand. We then put the whole thing back into the sack, replaced the toilet rolls to cover it and re-sealed it with their own tape which they had conveniently left on the shelf. I don't think anyone would know that anything had been tampered with,' she said.

'And where is the detonator now?'

'Dave dismantled it as he was not sure how safe it was. I took a photo on my mobile.' She opened her phone and showed Mrs B the photo.

'Good. Keep that in case we need it as evidence. What are you doing now?' asked Mrs B.

'I haven't slept for two nights so I want to go home, have a hot bath and a good long sleep.'

'Fine. Take the rest of today off and tomorrow. I would like you, though, to go to the meeting in Nottingham on Saturday, just to keep watch on what happens, if anything.'

'Yes, I was going to ask you if I should go. I'll be in on Monday.'

'You can contact me on my mobile if anything happens. Keep me informed,' Mrs B. said as 04 got up to leave.

Mrs B. was delighted with the latest news. She did not like it when there was a vacuum with nothing happening. She now had to brief Number 8, but she felt she should also keep Rutherford in the picture. She decided to telephone him first. She looked at her watch, eight-forty am. She put through the call straight away.

'Hello Colonel Rutherford. Can you scramble?' She heard some clicking and then he answered. She continued, 'just letting you know that we are setting up a trap for the meeting in Nottingham on

Saturday.'

He was too experienced to ask for details, but he asked, 'are you using your Number 8 and that girl?'

'Yes.'

'Alright I will tell Nelson to keep out of the way.' With that he terminated the call. Doesn't waste time on words, she thought. She then put a call through to Johnson.

Johnson had just finished his breakfast, having gone for a much longer run than usual as he was beginning to feel lethargic. He answered immediately and saw Mrs B.'s name on the display. 'Good morning Mrs B,' he said.

'Good morning Number 8. Can you come in and see me please?'

'I'll leave right away,' he replied. He knew that when Mrs B. summoned him like that it meant she had something for him to do. Due to heavy traffic slowing him up, it took him an hour to reach the office. Sarah was still not at her desk. He knocked and went straight into Mrs B.'s office.

'Take a seat Number 8,' she said. When he had settled, she asked, 'when did you last talk to Delia?'

'I spoke to her two nights ago.'

'Did she have anything to say?'

'Nothing new only that she is afraid of what will happen to her on Saturday.'

'So, she hasn't been told why she is going?'

'No, just that she has to be ready early in the morning and he will pick her up.'

'What do you think?'

'To be frank with you I am worried. I don't trust the man. He admitted to her that he had shot a policeman and threatened that she must avenge her husband's death. I've got an uncomfortable feeling about him.'

Mrs B. was silent. She just sat and looked at him, wondering whether she should tell him or not. If they wanted to trap Suleiman it was vital that Delia acted perfectly normally. She did not know how much she could trust Johnson not to act impulsively if he thought she was in danger. In the end, she decided it would be better to inform him and warn him not to do anything stupid to spoil the trap than keep him in the dark. 'You are nearly right', she said. 'They have found a bomb.'

Johnson's heart missed a beat. There was no need to ask who "They" were. He knew that Mrs B. had several agents who specialised in various skills and one never asked who these people were unless you were working with them. The principle of "Need to Know" was rigidly applied. Instead he asked, 'can you give me any more details?'

'An explosive device was found made up inside a pale blue lady's shoulder bag. It was wired to a mobile telephone and could be detonated remotely. We think he is intending to sacrifice Delia and kill the MP at the same time.'

Johnson's heart missed two more beats. He couldn't believe that Mrs B. was going to let Delia be sacrificed. This was just too much. No. He was getting emotional.

Mrs B. carried on, 'it won't happen. They have neutralized the device and substituted a dummy detonator.' Mrs B. continued, 'this is for your information only. We want Suleiman to do whatever he has in mind. We want to put him away for a very long time, but we have very little evidence against him. This way we can trap him. It is vital that Delia does not know anything. She must act absolutely normally and whatever happens you must not interfere.'

'But she is pregnant,' said Johnson. Won't this be bad for her pregnancy?' He knew nothing about pregnancies but guessed acting as a decoy in a trap like this couldn't be very good for her health.

'I don't think it should have any effect on her pregnancy. She is not going to do anything physical or exert any effort. She will just be holding the bag and when Suleiman tries to detonate it nothing will happen. My guess is that he won't tell her she is holding is a bomb. He will give her some other explanation. In other words, she will not know.'

Johnson was not convinced. 'Do you think she should see her doctor first?'

'Absolutely not. You are not listening to me. It is vital that Delia acts normally otherwise Suleiman will get suspicious and the whole thing will be blown. I don't have to remind you that she volunteered to help us and we are paying this young lady a lot of money. So far the amount of information she has given us is very disappointing.'

That was cruel, he thought. Anita had told him all she could. She did not know Suleiman's proper name or even where he lived so how could she be expected to get more information. He said nothing. He knew better than to try and argue with Mrs B.

Mrs B. continued. 'My guess is that when Suleiman sees that his device does not explode, he will do a runner. That's the normal procedure. They are not very brave, these people. If anything goes wrong they run to save their hides. I want you to be there and keep an eye on him. If he does a runner you can chase after him and arrest him. Do you still have your police warrant card?'

'Yes.'

'Good. Take it with you and if there are any questions from the police on duty show them your card. Sergeant Nelson and his team will also be there but they will not know about the explosive device. The only person who knows is you. Any more questions?'

'No.'

'Right. Keep me informed ... Oh. You can use your car to get there and claim mileage,' she added.

'Thank you,' he said, got up and left.

As he was driving home his mind wandered to what was planned for Nottingham. It was not the first time he had been involved in an operation of this sort so he knew the score but it was the first time he had had to "use" a pregnant woman. And, yes, he had to admit that the feelings he had for Anita were very different to how he usually felt about his agents. He was attracted by her demeanour and her stunning good looks. He suspected she had similar feelings towards him. He was unhappy that she was going to be used as a decoy in the trap, but at least she would not come to any harm. He made up his mind that if he thought she was likely to be harmed in any way he would intervene directly and to hell with the consequences.

26

Robinson's meeting was scheduled to be held in the Central Community Centre in Nottingham. It was an ideal venue with a car park attached and with large metal framed windows to let in the light. The hall could hold about 250 people and had a stage at one end. It was used for school plays and by the local amateur dramatic society. The local party officials had laid out all the chairs and placed a table and lectern on the stage. Robinson had listened to Police advice after the experience at Wolverhampton. The meeting would be held on a Saturday afternoon from 3.00 pm and he would not be staying the night. However, he insisted that he be allowed to mix with the audience at the end of the meeting. The two police protection officers would be sitting on the stage concealed behind the curtains.

Sergeant Nelson was again in charge of security on the floor. As in Wolverhampton he had five persons mingling with the audience, one a bomb disposal expert. He himself sat at a table at the front next to the stage. There were additional uniformed policemen in the car park and by the front door to marshal the people arriving for the meeting.

From 2.30 pm people started to arrive. They were mostly white but also a few Asians, more than at Wolverhampton, males and females. Some of the women were wearing hijabs. Nelson and two assistants were the ushers and guided people to their seats. By 3.00 pm the hall was full.

Johnson had arrived early at 2.30 pm before the main crowd. He introduced himself to Nelson. 'Will your spook be here to-day?' Nelson asked.

'Yes, I think so,' Johnson replied, 'when I see her, I will point her out to you.' He found himself a seat at the rear of the hall so he could observe everybody in the hall in front of him. He made no mention of the trap.

At five minutes to three he saw Anita arrive. She was accompanied by a middle-aged Asian male whom he assumed was Suleiman. They were mingling with the crowd entering the hall and taking their seats. Anita was wearing Western style clothes and had a pale blue shoulder bag over her shoulder. He suspected that this was the bag which contained the explosives. Although Anita was apparently not aware of what was in the bag, the expression on her face indicated she was not happy, and her pregnancy was very apparent. Because of her pregnant state, she was being given preferential treatment by one of the ushers who asked her where she wanted to sit. He noticed they were given seats at the side, five rows from the front.

D/Inspector Catchpole had travelled from London and mingled with the crowd. He took a seat at the rear. He did not introduce himself to any other police details. He wanted to be incognito.

At five past three the speaker, Mr David Robinson MP, accompanied by the local Party chairman arrived. They made their way down the side to the stage. As they mounted the stage there was a round of applause. The MP took his seat whilst the chairman stood up and introduced the speaker. More applause. Eventually everyone went quiet and Mr Robinson started to speak.

His speech was about the problems with mass immigration and the strains on local services in the area. This received enthusiastic applause from the audience. He then went on to the problem with immigration of people from the Middle East, especially Muslims. Whilst the clear majority were making a very positive contribution to society and the economy, unfortunately there were others who were not. He talked about the wars in Iraq and Afghanistan and how some British Muslims were fighting with the enemy against British soldiers. He questioned why such persons could live in Britain and how this question had been brought up by Muslims themselves who felt their reputation was being damaged. This remark received prolonged applause, but Johnson noticed that no Asians were applauding; indeed, their expressions were non-committal.

He then went on to say that it should be the duty of everyone to assist the intelligence and security services in their tasks and not make trivial complaints about their rights being breached, resulting in lengthy and expensive tribunals. He continued by suggesting ways and means by which people could assist, He suggested everyone should be able to live together as one nation following British culture because this is Britain. Again, loud applause but no response from the Asians.

After one hour of talking, the meeting finally came to an end and was thrown open to questions. This went on for about twenty minutes after which the chairman brought it to an end. He and the speaker descended from the stage into the auditorium and many in the audience gathered around them, shaking hands and engaging in general discussion.

Johnson, who had no political opinions of his own, could see how such a speech could be considered provocative to Asians, especially Muslims. It was not his job to make any judgement, he was only interested in security and making sure there were no violent incidents.

Meanwhile when the meeting ended Johnson saw Suleiman and Anita get up from their seats and make their way forward to the people gathered around the speaker. He could see they were speaking to each other but was too far away to hear what was being said. He tried to make his way forward to get closer but was hampered by the crowd.

Suleiman and Anita were in the side aisle, blending in with the people gathered around Robinson and about four feet away. Suleiman was gesturing with his arm and appeared to be having an agitated conversation with Anita who was answering back. Johnson could see by the expression on her face that she was very unhappy. Then suddenly Suleiman walked away making his way up the side aisle towards the exit door, leaving Anita standing on her own. Johnson was by this time about six feet away from her and he could see her face had gone completely white. Suddenly and without warning she collapsed onto the floor in a dead faint. Many people who were standing by her exclaimed as they saw this pretty young pregnant girl lying on the floor. One woman knelt and was patting her face to try and bring her round.

Johnson rushed forward forcing his way through the crowd. 'It's all right. I'm her brother. I'm her brother,' he shouted. He knelt beside her. 'It's all right, Anita, it's me,' he kept repeating. Then he noticed her bag had slipped off her shoulder and was lying on the floor next to her. He picked it up and hurled it at the window, breaking the glass, which shattered outwards as the bag went flying through the window and landed in the road outside. A stunned silence fell on those who saw him do this. Even the MP and Chairman were silent, completely taken by surprise with what had happened.

Johnson looked up and saw a Muslim woman dressed in black with a black hijab and thick framed black spectacles standing watching him. She was carrying a black leather shoulder bag very like the one he had hurled out of the window.

'Get rid of it.' He shouted at her, 'it's a bomb'. The woman ignored him. She stood watching him for a while and then quietly turned and walked away towards the exit. No-one seemed to have heard him say it was a bomb because there was no reaction from anyone standing nearby. Everyone was more interested in Anita and what had happened to her.

It flashed through his mind that the Muslim woman might be another terrorist with a bomb. He just hoped that it had been made safe.

Johnson turned his attention to Anita who was groaning and

clutching her stomach. Someone had obviously rung for an ambulance because a few minutes later he heard the siren and paramedics forced their way through the crowd. The woman medic who appeared to be in charge asked him, 'are you related?' 'I'm her brother,' he replied. She turned to her colleague and told him to bring a stretcher. Anita was loaded onto the stretcher and carried out to the ambulance. Johnson accompanied her in the ambulance as she was driven away to hospital.

The two police protection officers who were guarding Robinson ushered him speedily away and out of the building by a back door.

Mrs B. was at home waiting for a call when her phone rang. After scrambling O4 identified herself. 'Drama at the meeting,' she said. 'The girl fainted and has been taken to hospital.'

'Oh my God. Where is number 8?'

'He's gone to hospital with her.'

'What happened to her accomplice?'

'He's done a runner. He bolted through the exit door so God knows where he's gone.'

'Anybody chasing after him?'

'No.'

'Alright. Thanks. Stay there for a while and keep observations. If nothing else happens come home.'

Mrs B. immediately telephoned Colonel Rutherford and gave him the news. 'That bloody girl again. I knew we could not trust her,' was his only comment and then, 'I'll tell Birch.'

Meanwhile D/Inspector Catchpole, who had been sitting towards the back of the hall, made his way forward when the meeting ended and took up a position by the exit to watch who was leaving in case he recognised anyone. He saw the woman faint near the front of the hall and saw the shenanigans that this caused but decided it was nothing to do with him; this diverted his attention for a while. When he looked back he saw a young man in the crowd forcing his way to the exit door who looked familiar. He suddenly realised it was Lewis. What was he doing here? At the same time, Lewis recognised Catchpole and made a dash for the door pushing his way through the crowd. He rushed through the door and ran across the road towards some vehicles parked on the far side of the road.

Catchpole tried to follow him but was held up by the crowd leaving the hall. He eventually forced his way through and saw Lewis making for a Peugeot 205 car.

'Get that man. Get that man,' he shouted at some uniformed policemen standing on the road, one of whom was examining the bag that Johnson had thrown through the window. 'He's wanted for murder.'

PC Blackford, who had been on duty by the front door, saw the young man rush out of the hall. The haste and way he forced his way through the crowd raised his suspicions and when he heard Catchpole shouting, wasted no time. He ran towards the car as Lewis was putting the keys into the door and tackled him to the ground. Blackford, who weighed 16 stone and played lock forward for the local rugby club, had no difficulty in restraining him. He put him in handcuffs and pulled him to his feet. Catchpole caught up, out of breath.

'Well done. Good work,' he said, 'make sure you keep tight hold of him. He is a suspect for murder.'

Blackford did not know who Catchpole was but could see by his manner and the way he spoke that he was obviously someone senior and anyway this was the most exciting thing that had happened since he had joined the force. He was not going to let his quarry go. He was holding him by the handcuffs behind his back.

'DI Catchpole, C.I.D,' said Catchpole, puffing as he introduced himself to Blackford. 'I want to check this car.' Turning to Lewis, 'is this your car?' Lewis was silent. He had a very arrogant and truculent expression on his face. Not at all the co-operative young man who had helped them when they were interviewing the staff at the hotel in Wolverhampton.

Using the keys that were sticking out of the car door Catchpole opened the door and looked inside. There was nothing in the front or back. He opened the boot. Again empty. He then opened the front passenger door and the glove box. Inside he saw a towel. He pulled at it and could feel that it was heavy and obviously had something wrapped inside. He gently pulled it out and unwrapped it. A short barrelled stumpy revolver was exposed. Catchpole had never seen anything like it before and did not recognise it.

'That looks like a starter gun sir,' said Blackford who was watching the proceedings with interest. He was an athlete and was familiar with starter guns.

Catchpole broke open the cylinder. He noticed it held seven rounds and it was fully charged. He pulled one round out and saw it was in fact a live ·22 short bullet.

'I didn't know that starter guns could fire live rounds,' he said to Blackford.

'Neither did I but this one obviously does.'

He replaced the bullet, snapped shut the cylinder and carefully wrapped the weapon in its towel.

Turning to Lewis he said, 'I'm arresting you on a charge of Murder. You do not have to say anything but it may harm your defence if you do not mention when questioned anything that you later rely on in court. Anything you do say may be given in evidence.' Lewis again said nothing.

Catchpole turned to Blackford, 'I haven't got a radio. Can you call up for transport and escort him back to the station and lock him up. It is important that you escort him all the time as you were the arresting officer. Don't let him out of your sight until he is safely locked into a cell and don't talk to him or ask him any questions. I will come back to the station later. Oh, also tell the Charge Office Sergeant that he must be checked by a doctor because you tackled him to the ground. Very important.'

'Yes sir.' Blackford had never been given such a responsible job before. Arresting a real live murderer? He felt very important.

Catchpole made his way to his car which was parked in the car park, carrying the weapon in its towel. He opened the boot and took out a plastic exhibits bag. He placed the weapon in the bag and sealed it shut and locked it in the boot. On the road, nearby was a uniformed constable. 'Keep an eye on this car, Constable, it has got some valuable items in it.' He assumed the constable would realise by now that he was a senior police officer; anyway, he must have witnessed the arrest that had occurred on the other side of the road.

'Yes sir,' said the constable. Catchpole went back into the hall. It was nearly empty. No policemen were present. The only police he could see were uniformed members outside marshalling and directing traffic as people left the meeting. He did not know or recognise Sgt Nelson and he was completely ignorant of what the plans had been for the meeting, but he was feeling elated that Lewis had been arrested and that what he hoped was the murder weapon had been recovered. He put a call through to Fitzgerald who was on his way to London. Catchpole gave him as much detail as possible. 'Brilliant, brilliant,' Fitzgerald said. 'I knew we would break it eventually. Where is he now?'

'In the nick back at the station, I hope, under guard. I'm going there now and will arrange for him to be transferred to Paddington Green tonight.'

'Yes, that's fine. I'll come in tomorrow morning and I think you should be there as well. Have you told Mr Birch?'

'No, only you.'

'Right, I'll phone him. I'll see you tomorrow.'

Catchpole went out to the car park to retrieve his car. He opened the boot to check that the weapon was still there. He then asked a uniformed constable for directions to Police Headquarters and drove out. On arrival, he went into the Charge Office, showed his identity to the Constable on duty behind the counter and asked where the cells were. The constable pointed to a door and pressed a button under the counter to unlock the security lock. He went through to a Sergeant at a desk. Again, showed his identity and asked the whereabouts of the prisoner brought in by PC Blackford.

'In cell No,1,' pointing to a door that led to the cells.

'Is he under guard?'

'PC Blackford is sitting outside the door. He said you told him he was not to let him out of his sight.'

'I didn't mean that. Still at least he's keen. Has he said anything, the prisoner I mean?'

'Not a word. Very sulky young man.'

'Good. I've got to get him transferred to London. Who do I see about that?'

'You had better see the Deputy Chief Constable. He is in his office.'

Having got directions Catchpole went up to see the Deputy Chief Constable, Mr Yeoman. He identified himself and explained why he was there.

'What happened about the bomb?' Yeoman asked.

'Bomb? I know nothing about a bomb,' said Catchpole.

'I was told there was a bomb at the meeting.'

'Well I was at that meeting and there was certainly no bomb. A woman fainted and was taken off to hospital. That's all I saw.'

'So how can I help you?'

'The person arrested is the murderer of PC Baxter and must be transferred to London, Paddington Green, as soon as possible, like tonight. He is a suspected jihadist and we don't know how many others there may be who might try and spring him.'

'Who made the arrest and when?'

'Your PC Blackford about an hour ago. He's in your cells now.' He added to make more emphasis, 'he is to be interviewed tomorrow morning by Chief Superintendent Fitzgerald, who is leading the investigation.'

'Blackford. Good man Blackford. Alright I will organise an armed escort tonight. Do Paddington Green know he is coming?'

'No. I'll warn them,' Catchpole answered, he thanked Yeoman

and left.

He next telephoned the CID twenty-four-hour incident room in London and asked them to warn Paddington Green and complete any paperwork necessary.

He was tired and wanted to get home. He finally telephoned Elizabeth, his wife, and told her he hoped to be home shortly after nine, adding that they had had success. He did not go into details but she knew why he was in Nottingham. 'Well done darling,' she said, 'I will prepare your favourite dinner to celebrate.' He set off for the long trip back with a smile on his face. It had been a good day and he reckoned it was to get even better.

It was the rush hour and Nottingham was heavily congested with traffic. It took him some time to get onto the M1 but eventually he did and settled down, doing a steady 70 mph. His mind started to wander thinking about the dinner Elizabeth would now be preparing for him; his favourite meal - prawn thermidor with new potatoes tossed in olive oil and herbs with a crisp green salad washed down with a lovely bottle of cha....

'BLOODY HELL!' he shouted as he jammed on the brakes. 'Phew!' His heart was in his mouth as he nearly went straight into the rear of the car in front of him which had suddenly slowed down. That was too close for comfort he thought to himself. He pulled out slightly to see what had happened and saw that he was at the rear of a lengthy line of vehicles that had all slowed down for some unknown reason. Then, again for no reason, everybody suddenly speeded up. Mysteries of the motorway, he thought. I had better concentrate on driving and not on food otherwise I will not get home at all.

27

In the ambulance on the way to the hospital Johnson was sitting on a seat beside Anita holding her hand. She looked awful, badly traumatised and obviously in pain. The medics had inserted a drip and were making soothing comments to encourage her but she did not seem to hear. After a while she opened her eyes and saw him.

'Please don't leave me,' she said. It sounded so pathetic, so pleading. She was obviously frightened.

'I'll never leave you,' he replied, and he meant it.

They soon arrived at the hospital. Anita was wheeled out on the stretcher, with one of the medics holding the drip up above her, and into A. & E. Johnson followed. They spoke to a doctor who was attending to another patient. He left his patient and looked at Anita. After just a moment he said something to the medics and they started off again accompanied by a nurse, through some double doors and into a lift. Johnson squeezed in. The medics left them.

On the way, he asked 'Where are we going?'

'She's going to theatre,' said the nurse, 'she must be seen by a specialist.'

Theatre, he thought. Must be serious but said nothing.

They got out at the fourth floor and went charging down a passage. They go at a hell of a lick, he thought. He had trouble keeping up. When they arrived at another set of double doors the nurse stopped and told Johnson that he would have to wait there. He noticed a row of chairs against the wall. Anita was pushed through the doors which shut behind her.

He sat down in one of the chairs to wait. There was no-one else in this waiting area. He started thinking. I've got to retrieve my car, still in the car park. Probably be clamped or at least have a ticket. She is bound to be admitted for the night. I'll have to spend the night.

After about twenty minutes the door opened and another nurse dressed in a surgical gown came out with a clipboard and came over to him.

'Are you her partner?' she asked.

'Yes,' he replied. Brother, partner, what does it matter, he thought.

'Could you give me her name.'

He had to think quickly. He decided to give her correct name. It could be tricky with a false name in these circumstances. 'Anita Hussein,' he said.

'With an "a" or an "e".'

He wasn't sure. 'E,' he guessed. She wrote it down.

'And her address?'

Again, he wasn't sure. He knew she had a flat in Mandela house but did not know the street or post code. He decided to give his own address. She wrote it all down.

'Can you tell me what's happening?' he asked.

'She is being seen by Mr Parker, a specialist. He will come out and tell you when he has finished.'

'Any idea how long that might be?'

'I can't say. Mr Parker will come out when he has finished,' and with that she disappeared through the doors. He resumed his seat to wait.

He saw some magazines on a table and picked one up, flipping through the pages but could not concentrate. He ran over in his mind the build-up to this incident. He felt resentment towards Mrs B. She had said that they could not tell Anita that the bombs had been made safe. 'She has to think they are real otherwise she won't act the part properly,' she had warned. He had pointed out that she was pregnant, but this was ignored. It was Colonel Rutherford who had made the comment that annoyed him. 'Let her earn her money,' he said. If he says anything like that again, Johnson thought, I'll thump him, colonel or no bloody colonel.

He looked at his watch. It was five minutes to six. He wondered if they had a list of B. & B's at reception so he could phone around to find a bed. Suddenly the doors at the end of the passage opened and Sergeant Nelson appeared. He came up and sat down next to Johnson.

'They told me you were up here,' he said, 'I take it she was your spook?' Johnson nodded.

'Why didn't you tell me?'

'I didn't have a chance. They only arrived just before the meeting started. You were at the front and I was at the back and we had no means of communication.'

'Is she going to be OK?'

'I don't know. She is being examined by a specialist.' He paused, wondering whether he should tell but decided it wouldn't do any harm. 'She is pregnant.'

'What? pregnant!' Nelson exclaimed. 'Do you mean they are using pregnant females to do their dirty work for them? Whatever next?' He continued, 'I take it that bag you threw out of the window was meant to be a bomb?'

'Yes, but it had been made safe,' Johnson replied.

'It wasn't a bomb at all?' Nelson enquired.

'What do you mean?' Johnson answered.

'I was suspicious when there was no explosion so I told my bomb man to go and retrieve it. It was lying in the street with two uniform bods poking at it with a stick. It contained a few plastic sausage shaped bags full of sand and the detonator was a piece of aluminium tubing with a few electric wires stuck in at one end.'

'They told me that all they had done was change the detonator for a dummy.'

'No. It was never going to explode and if she had looked inside the bag she would have seen for herself.'

Anita would never have known the difference, Johnson thought, but said nothing. He changed the subject.

'She is obviously going to be admitted and she should have a guard and I don't know what to do.'

'They will have to come from the local cop shop.' After a pause, 'I'll arrange it,' Nelson said. 'What's her name?'

'Anita Hussein'

'Is that her real name or an alibi?'

'Her real name.'

'Is that safe?' asked Nelson looking surprised.

'It could get complicated if we used a false name, what with medical records etc. etc. You never know what could happen.'

'Well, she is your agent. You know best. Do you know they arrested the chap who murdered that police constable in Wolverhampton?' Nelson asked.

'No!'

'Yeah. A young Asian chap. He had a weapon in his car apparently.'

'Who was he?'

'Someone who worked at the hotel I believe.'

'Who made the arrest?'

'A uniformed constable. Saw him running across the road and rugby tackled him.'

'Excellent. He'll probably get a medal,' said Johnson. Nelson smiled.

'Right. I'll leave you to it. I'll go and arrange that guard.' Nelson got up and left. He seemed quite friendly for a change.

At ten to seven the door opened and a middle-aged man came out wearing a surgical gown and a face mask hanging around his neck. He had a solemn look on his face. 'Are you Mr Hussein?' he asked. Johnson nodded. 'We've done what we can for her,' he said, 'she has been badly traumatised and I am worried about her baby. She is stable now and if she can get through the night she should be OK. She will have to be admitted so we can keep an eye on her. I'm sorry I can't give you better news.'

'Thank you, sir,' said Johnson, 'I'm sure you've done the best you can. Can I go and see her?'

'Yes of course. She has been admitted to Queen's Ward, the next floor up. She is heavily sedated so I don't think she will be saying much, but yes, please go and see her.'

'Thank you again sir,' and with that he made his way to the lift doors at the end of the passage. He quickly found Queen's Ward and went to the nurse's station. 'Could you tell me where I can find Miss Hussein?' he asked.

'Follow me', said the nurse who came out from behind her desk and walked off down the passage. She stopped at the door to a private room, opened the door and went in. Anita was asleep in the bed with a drip on a stand beside her. 'She's been heavily sedated. Sleep is the best thing for her now.' She smiled at Johnson and went out, leaving him standing beside the bed.

Johnson sat on a chair and gazed at her. She looked very comfortable. He sat there for ten minutes, deciding not to wake her up and then left the room quietly and returned to the nurse's station.

'Do you know that she is an important witness in a criminal case?' he asked the nurse.

'No, I didn't. Nobody tells me a thing here.'

'There will be a police guard coming to protect her for tonight. I'll stay with her until he arrives. If she wakes up in the night, would you tell her I came to see her.'

'Yes of course. Who are you?'

'I'm her ... (he thought quickly) partner,' he said.

He went back to Anita's room and sat on the chair again. Forty-five minutes later a uniformed constable knocked on the door.

'Mr Hussein?' he asked, 'I'm the guard for the night.'

'Thanks. I'll leave you to it,' and with that he left.

28

Commander Birch received his call at 7.30 pm. He was at home and digested what he had just heard. 'I'm going to have to go back to the office,' he said to his wife. 'Something has just come in.' His long-suffering wife was used to this sort of thing but thought that now he had reached a senior rank, he could pass this call to a junior to deal with. Obviously not, but she said nothing.

Whilst on the road he was thinking about what he had just heard and making plans in his mind. This was not the development he was expecting. He would have liked to hand over the issue to Fitzgerald but he knew Fitzgerald was at present on his way down from Wolverhampton. He could take over tomorrow. In the meantime, he would call in Inspector Barlow who was working with Customs on drugs. He was a solid, reliable old timer, who could take over until Fitzgerald was available.

He had been told by Colonel Rutherford that the man on the run was a middle-aged Asian whom he knew as Suleiman. It must be the same person at 21 Wayfare Street, Pinner, whom he thought was called Khalid or Patel. He decided it was far too late to put up road blocks. He could go anywhere but the most likely place was home because the Police had taken no overt action to frighten him off. All their activities in Pinner had been covert. The best plan, he decided, was to give him time to get home and then carry out a raid on the premises. Four am would be just the right time.

When he arrived at his office he telephoned D/Inspector Barlow who answered the phone himself. 'Birch here Mr Barlow. Could you come in and see me please.'

'What now?'

'Yes now.'

Barlow knew that you only got calls like this if there was something urgent. 'I'll be with you as soon as I can sir,' he replied.

Birch next telephoned the CID twenty-four-hour incident room. 'Can you lend me a telephonist for a couple of hours?'

'Yes sir, who would you like?'

'Somebody reliable.'

'We've got Mrs May. She's the wife of Sergeant May in traffic. She is a reservist and very reliable.'

'Mrs May sounds fine. Please send her up to me straight away.' Fifteen minutes later Mrs May arrived, a middle-aged lady who looked and spoke like a school mistress. She looked and breathed reliability. 'Hello Mrs May. Thanks for coming up at short notice. Would you work here?' pointing to a desk in an adjoining office. 'Please phone Detective Constable Fox on this number,' handing her a piece of paper with the number written on it – 'and put him through to me in my office.' Five minutes later his phone rang. 'Fox this is Commander Birch. I want you in my office as soon as possible. Have you got transport?'

'No sir.'

'Then call a taxi. Come as you are.'

Half an hour later Fox arrived followed shortly by Inspector Barlow. Birch took them both into his office and shut the door. They sat down and he explained all that he had heard from Colonel Rutherford about the meeting in Nottingham. 'I have decided that the best action for us is an early morning raid on 21 Wayfare Street. You're in charge, Mr Barlow, until Mr Fitzgerald is back in action. I take it you have done these raids before.'

'Oh, yes sir. We do them all the time in drugs.'

'Fox here knows the premises and can guide you there. Here is a road map of the area. You see there is a service lane at the back of the premises where I gather the suspect parks his car. I will leave you to choose your team. You know the best people and Mrs May can do any telephoning you want,' pointing to the office next door. 'Work out your plan and let me know. I would like you to go in no later than four am.'

Barlow and Fox moved to another office with the street map. 'You done one of these before?' Barlow asked Fox.

'No sir. This is the first time.'

'How many people live there?'

'So far as I know only two, a man and his wife. I've never seen the man but his wife runs the shop below the flat.'

'What's she like?'

'I've only been in once to buy some vegetables and have a look around. She seems very pleasant. Speaks good English. It is a well-stocked shop. I can't say much more.'

'That's fine. We need some uniform bods with us. I will try and get the ones I normally use on drugs. They are good chaps and know the ropes. I will put you with Sergeant Kirkwood and you can go to the back door. We will put two uniformed men at the junction of the service lane and Wayfare Street, here,' pointing to the map, 'and two more down the street here,' pointing to the map again. 'When everybody is in place you radio me and I with two other uniformed members will knock on the front door and demand entry. It is essential that everyone moves quietly into place so as not to wake them. OK so far?'

'Yes sir.'

He continued. 'Now it is quite likely that when I knock on the front door he will try and escape through the back door, if he is there. That's what you and Sergeant Kirkwood are there for. Arrest anyone who tries to come out no matter who. On the other hand, there may be some other way out which is why we have the long stops on the road at either end. OK?'

'Yes sir.' Fox's attitude had completely changed since he had been working on this case and he realised just how inexperienced he was. Although he had done all this in training it was completely different doing it for real.

'I will just go and see the boss. If he has nothing for you, go home and get your head down. Be here at three am. Have some food before you leave home as we may have a long day. Come in casual clothes. I will have a flak jacket for you just in case there are any firearms or knives.' Barlow knocked and went into Birch's office. A minute later he signalled to Fox that he could go. He then ran over the plan with Commander Birch. After that he spent the next hour with Mrs May telephoning his team telling them to report at three am. He did not go home. His home was too far away to go there and be back at the office before three am. He busied himself getting his kit together, flak jackets, torches, notebooks, battering ram and transport. He then found an easy chair to settle down and rest.   Commander Birch decided there was nothing more he could do and went home at midnight.

At two-fifty Fox arrived at the office. He hadn't slept a wink as he was too frightened of not waking up in time to get to the office. He had had breakfast of a fried egg sandwich. Barlow was already up and about and soon the rest of the team arrived, all uniformed men. Everybody seemed to know exactly what needed to be done. They all wore flak jackets and Barlow threw one to Fox to put on. There was very little talking. Eventually Barlow got everybody together in the meeting room and briefed them as to what was going to happen. Fox was introduced to Sergeant Kirkwood. He liked him immediately.

'Is this your case?' Kirkwood asked.

'No. Mr Fitzgerald's,' Fox replied.

'But you're working on it?'

'Yes.'

'Right. If we make any arrest, you can do it. You know how?'

'Yes. I think so.'

On the orders from Barlow everybody em-bussed into the transport that he had organised and was in the yard. There was a car for Barlow which Fox drove as he knew the way. They headed off to Pinner in convoy, the car followed by a people carrier. Barlow stopped the convoy half a mile away. Fox told him that there was a car park nearby which they should be able to go to without being seen from the shop. They got out and walked to check. Barlow agreed and sent Fox back to drive the car and lead the people carrier into the carpark. Everybody de-bussed from the transport. Not a word was spoken by anyone. The only light was from street lamps.

Barlow pointed out the premises across the road and using hand signals despatched them to their allotted places as previously planned. Fox and Kirkwood set off up the road to the service lane and then down the service lane to the rear of the shop. Light came from a single street lamp.

As they were approaching the shop Fox saw a silver BMW parked on the side of the road. He signalled to Kirkwood that that was the car. Kirkwood signalled with his thumb that he understood. They reached the back door and Kirkwood signalled that Fox should stand on one side of the door and he on the other. Kirkwood then signalled on his radio by pressing a button and they waited.

They waited and waited hearing nothing. After ten minutes which felt like an hour, Fox looked at Kirkwood and shrugged his shoulders holding his hands sideways trying to ask if anything would happen. Kirkwood placed his finger across his lips indicating silence.

When Barlow received confirmation that all persons were in position, he went to the front door with his two uniformed officers and knocked loudly. He continued knocking, shouting, "Police. Open up," several times.

Inside Mrs Khalid heard the noise, scrambled out of bed and looked out of the window. She saw the uniformed officers and realised immediately what the situation was. 'Papa hide,' she shouted to her father-in-law who was sleeping in the next room. Her husband Usman had only got in from Nottingham at half past one and was fast asleep. She shook him violently to wake him up. 'Quick. Police', she said. This woke Usman with a start. He leapt out of bed and fiddled around looking for some clothes. He found a sports shirt and jeans and pulled them on over his pyjamas. He couldn't find his car keys and fumbled around in his trouser pocket eventually dropping them on the floor. He picked them up and collected a pair of slip-on canvas shoes which he carried. His wife, in the meantime, was waiting impatiently signalling for him to hurry up. The banging and noise continued from the front door. He had to precede her down the stairs and then sneak through the shop to the back door. She decided to delay opening the front door to give him time to get into his car and drive away.

Meanwhile Papa, on hearing her call, woke up immediately. He jumped out of bed and scrambled into the loft, pulling the ladder up after him and shutting the trap door. He had prepared for this eventuality some time ago and had a mattress, blankets and pillow in the loft together with a small supply of provisions. He even had a bucket to use as a latrine. He was prepared for an extended stay.

Mrs Khalid had by this time reached the bottom of the stairs. She had seen her husband carefully open the side door into the shop and creep through. She shut it and went to the front door. Barlow was now shouting that he would break the door down if it was not opened.

'Alright, alright,' she shouted back, 'I'm here.' She then unlocked and re-locked the mortice lock in the door several times to make it appear that she was unlocking multiple locks on the door. She engaged the door chain and opened the door to the extent of the chain and peered through the gap. All this was designed to delay opening the door so her husband could get away. 'Yes?' she said to Barlow on the outside.

'Police,' he said showing his warrant card. 'Would you open the door please.'

'Why?' she asked.

'We want to speak to your husband,' he replied.

'He's not here,' she said.

'Please open the door otherwise I will have to break it down.'

She shut the door, disconnected the chain and opened it fully.

Usman crept through the shop in his bare feet carrying his shoes in his hand. He made sure no-one was looking through the shop window and anyway it was still too dark for anyone to see him. He reached the back door and inserted the key, unlocked it and seeing no-one outside, went out, making straight for his car which was parked immediately opposite.

Kirkwood and Fox heard the door being unlocked. Kirkwood signalled to Fox to remain still. As soon as he saw Usman trying to put the key into the car door he stepped forward. 'Not so fast Sunshine,' he said. 'We want to talk to you,' and snapped a handcuff over his wrist.

Fox came up from the other side. 'Are you Mr Khalid?' he asked. 'Patel. Patel,' Usman shouted. 'My name is Patel'. He kept repeating it.

'Mr Patel I am arresting you for the crime of Murder. You do not have to say anything but if you do it will harm your defence.' He was trying to remember the format. He had gone over it time and again in his head but felt he had got it wrong.

Kirkwood had heard the wrong wording being used and glanced heavenwards. Anyway, he thought, Patel or Khalid had obviously not been listening as he was still crying out that his name was Patel. He placed the other cuff on his wrist and said they should take him through the shop to the front.

When they got to the front door Mrs Khalid was still talking to Barlow. She turned and saw her husband with the two policemen. She rushed to him and threw her arms around his neck 'Usman. Usman,' she sobbed, 'Oh Usman.' Barlow came in and gently prized her away.

'Load up,' he said to everyone. 'Let's get going.' Usman was placed in the back of the car with a uniformed detail sitting next to him. Mrs Khalid was put in the people carrier with the rest of the team. He turned to Fox, 'Paddington Green. Know the way?'

29

The following morning at ten am Johnson arrived at the hospital. He had found a B. & B. with a spare room easily enough but had trouble explaining why he had no luggage. He explained that his partner had been taken ill suddenly and admitted to hospital. He had just come from the hospital and had not had time to get anything, which was not far from the truth. He was given a room but had to pay in advance.

He went up to Queen's Ward and to Anita's room. She was lying in bed, awake, but had clearly been crying. Tears were running down her cheeks.

'What's the matter?' he asked, alarmed at the sight of her. 'What's happened?'

'I lost my baby,' she sobbed.

'Oh no. I am sorry,' he took both her hands in his, looking directly into her eyes.

'She was a little girl,' she sobbed. 'I so wanted a little girl.'

'I am sorry. I'm really sorry for you.' He did not know what else to say.

At this moment, a nurse came in pushing an instrument to record blood pressure. 'How are we doing darling?' she asked in a cheery voice. Quite the opposite to Anita's mood but it seemed to buck her up a little. She took the blood pressure and temperature and made an entry in the file at the end of the bed.

'Do you want me to phone anybody?' asked Johnson, 'your parents for example?'

'No' said Anita decisively. 'I'll tell them myself when I get out.'

'Anybody else?' He knew she had very few friends because of what her husband had done.

'No. Nobody,' said Anita.

'Now you are not to worry. I will be staying here until you are well enough to go home and then I will take you back to London. Do you know there is a police guard sitting outside your door?'

'No,' said Anita, amazed, 'why?'

'Because you are a very important person which is why I am staying here to look after you.' Anita was relieved to hear it.

He stayed with her until lunchtime. Anita was brought a plate of soup with bread and ice cream for pudding, all of which she ate. After lunch, a nurse came in with some pills. 'I think it is time you had a sleep,' she said implying it was time for Johnson to leave. Johnson took the hint. 'I'll be back this evening,' he said and left, blowing her a kiss which she blew back. She smiled. His visit had cheered her up considerably.

Anita was kept in hospital another three days during which time she made excellent progress. Johnson visited her every day. On the third day matron called Johnson aside and said that Anita could go home but warned him to beware of depression. 'She will be given some pills and she must take them every day, even if she feels alright. She will be checked out by a doctor tomorrow and if she is pronounced fit, you can collect her,' she said. Anita was delighted.

At ten am Johnson arrived at the hospital. Anita had been checked and pronounced fit to travel. Like Johnson she had no luggage so there was nothing to pack. She had a plastic carrier bag with some pills in it and that was all. They both bade farewell to the nurses who had been so good to them.

On the journey, back to London Anita recovered her composure and got back to being her old self. No mention was made of the miscarriage she had suffered and there was no sign of depression. They chatted amicably without mentioning Suleiman or the experience in the community hall. It was as if it had never happened. Anita was just happy to be in his company, alone.

Johnson, however, was worried about his job. No-one had tried to contact him whilst he was in Northampton and he wondered why.

30

Fitzgerald arrived home just after six pm on Saturday having first called in at his office to drop off some papers he had brought from Wolverhampton. It was his first visit home for ten days when he had last taken a mini-break. He was given a rapturous welcome by his wife, Isobel, and two young sons, Simon and Christopher.

He told his wife the good news he had received from Catchpole on the journey down. They all knew he was investigating the murder of PC Baxter and when his sons heard him tell Isobel of the arrest, they bombarded him with questions. 'Is he the murderer Dad?' 'Did he kill Mr Baxter?' 'Dad what does he look like?' 'Was he covered in blood?' 'Young minds,' he thought, 'where do they get these ideas from?'

Isobel suggested they go out to celebrate but Fitzgerald declined tactfully. He said he was very tired after the long drive down from Wolverhampton and would far rather she cooked him her popular fry-up of bacon, eggs, tomatoes and beans washed down with his favourite tea, blend of Earl Grey in his own favourite over-sized mug. He had missed his home comforts. After tea, he had an early night and went to bed.

The following morning at eight forty-five he was sitting up in bed with Isobel, drinking tea. His two sons were playing an energetic game of hide and seek diving under the duvet one end and emerging at the other. This was home and what he had missed all the time he had been at Wolverhampton. Fitzgerald was very much a family man. The phone rang. He answered and recognised the voice. 'The Boss,' he mouthed to Isobel placing his finger in front of his lips for silence. 'Good morning, Sir.'

'Good morning, Arthur' said Birch, 'You heard the good news?'

'About Lewis. Yes. Catchpole telephoned me on my way down yesterday.'

'Well, I've got some more good news for you. Suleiman has been arrested.'

'Suleiman!' Fitzgerald exclaimed, 'When?'

'This morning. I organised an early raid on his home. He was caught trying to get away in his car.'

'Who arrested him?'

'Fox.'

'Fox!' Fitzgerald was astonished.

'Yes. He's done very well these last two weeks and completely changed. Are you coming in to-day?'

'I'm meeting Catchpole at Paddington Green this morning to interview Lewis. We had better interview Suleiman at the same time.'

'His wife has also been brought in but not arrested. Apparently, she delayed opening her door to give Suleiman time to escape.'

'Sounds a bit like attempting to pervert the course of justice?'

'Could be but at this stage she is just being treated as a witness. She is also at Paddington Green so you could see her as well.'

'Right sir, I will.'

'OK. Bring me up to speed on Monday.'

'Thank you, sir. Goodbye,' Fitzgerald terminated the call. He immediately telephoned Catchpole. 'Heard the news, Robin?'

'No. What?'

'Suleiman's been picked up.'

'Who by?'

'Fox.'

'Fox!' He exclaimed – bloody hell, 'I thought he was nothing but a self-opinionated toff.'

'So did I. Apparently he's improved. Suleiman's at Paddington Green as well. I'll meet you there at ten-thirty.'

'OK Boss.'

Fitzgerald got dressed and had a quick breakfast. He kissed his wife goodbye and said he hoped to be back for a late lunch. Isobel knew better. She thought she would be lucky if he got back before dark.

The traffic was light, being Sunday, and Fitzgerald arrived at the station before ten-thirty to find that Catchpole was already there. 'She's in that interview room with a woman constable,' he said referring to Mrs Khalid.

'Have you spoken to her?'

'No. I haven't spoken to anyone.'

'We'll speak to her first, then the old man and then Lewis. I don't want to go into a long-detailed interrogation until we have all the facts. We'll keep this brief, tell them why they are here and that they could be here for twenty-eight days.'

'And that could be shorter if they co-operate with us,' said Catchpole.

'No. No. No. Don't mention that otherwise a defence barrister will accuse us of coercing them into making statements. Make no mention of co-operating or say anything that could be taken as a threat.'

'OK Boss. You're the boss.' They went to the interview room, knocked and entered. Mrs Khalid was sitting on a chair with the W.P.C. sitting opposite. On the table was a tea cup and plate with crumbs. Fitzgerald introduced himself and Catchpole. He switched on the tape and did the normal introduction. The W.P.C. asked if she should leave but he told her to stay.

'I see they have been looking after you and you've had some tea and a sandwich. Do you know why you are here?'

'Because they arrested my husband,' she replied.

'No. You are not here because of that. You are here for another reason. Before I go any further do you want a lawyer to be present whilst we ask you some questions?'

'Will I need one?'

'It is up to you. You're not being charged with anything, but we would like to ask you some questions. We are recording this interview and you are not obliged to say anything that might incriminate you. Do you understand?'

'Alright.'

'Firstly, what is your proper name?'

There was a long pause and then, 'Mrs Ayisha Khalid.'

'Do you use the name "Patel"?'

'That is my parent's name.'

'Who owns the shop?'

'My husband and I own it.'

'Did it belong to your parents before?'

'Yes. They gave it to us when they retired about three years ago.'

'Do you know the name "Patel's Provisions"?'

There was another long pause.

'Mrs Khalid?' Fitzgerald enquired.

'We were going to change the name to that, but our friends said it would confuse customers, so we didn't.'

'Have you ever used that name?'

'No.'

'Do you also own a house in Barnet?'

Again, a long pause, longer this time.

'Mrs Khalid? Would you like me to repeat the question?'

'Yes,' she said.

'You mean "Yes" you do own a house in Barnet or you want me to repeat the question?'

'Yes, we do own a house in Barnet.'

'Then why aren't you living in it now?'

There was another long pause. Her demeanour was changing. She was becoming more agitated with the questions. Fitzgerald spotted the change and knew he must be careful not to get her to admit anything that could be criminal as there was no legal representative present.

'My husband decided that we should move to the flat because it is over the shop.'

'Is that the only reason?'

'Yes.'

'One final question. Do you know anyone called Rhana Khalid?'

Her manner changed completely. She looked as if she was about to burst into tears.

'Are you alright Mrs Khalid?' Fitzgerald asked.

She looked at him and then whispered, 'he's my son.'

Fitzgerald and Catchpole looked at each other. This confirmed what they had suspected after learning about his home address. However, their expressions did not change. 'Do you know where he is now?'

'No,' she whispered again.

'He's here. He was arrested for murder yesterday afternoon.'

Mrs Khalid collapsed and dropped her head onto the table, weeping.

The W.P.C. got up and placed her arms around her shoulders to console her. Fitzgerald just sat there and looked at her. There were so many more questions he wanted to ask her. What did she know about the number plates in the boot of her car; what did she know about her husband's trips to Wolverhampton and Nottingham; what time did her husband get home last night; why had she delayed opening her door this morning; but he couldn't make out if this woman was a witness or an accomplice. He was beginning to think it was more likely to be the latter, in which case he would have to be careful how he interrogated her. In the circumstances if she said anything incriminating it would not be admissible as evidence because she was unrepresented, even though he had warned her not to say anything that would incriminate her. Anyway, he remembered he had told her she would not be charged. They could always get her back later when they had more facts at their disposal.

'Interview terminated,' Fitzgerald said and switched off the tape. They waited a while for Mrs Khalid to compose herself.

'Thank you, Mrs Khalid. We may need to ask you further questions later but in the meantime you can go home. Please do not try to leave the country. I suggest you get hold of a lawyer for your husband and your son.' They signalled to the W.P.C. to take care of Mrs Khalid and left the interview room.

'What do you make of that?' asked Fitzgerald when they were outside.

'I wondered what Lewis was doing at that meeting yesterday. Now it all makes sense.'

'When we've got all our facts together, I think we might well be having another chat with Mrs Khalid and we will ensure she has a lawyer present. I think she knows more than she is telling us ... Let's see if we can find a cup of tea and then have a chat with Mr Khalid, or is it Patel?'

Whilst drinking their tea, before they questioned the two Khalids, they discussed exactly what charges they had against them. It seemed they had a pretty good case of murder of PC Baxter against Rhana Khalid and a pretty good case of attempted murder of the MP Robinson against the father but were they acting together or individually? It was clear that the father was at the hotel at the time PC Baxter was shot and now they knew that Rhana was in the hall at Nottingham. Why were they there if they were not actively involved together in the commission of these crimes? They decided that at this stage they would question them as acting together. The Prosecutor would make the final decision when all the evidence was available.

To interview the Khalids they were directed to another interview room in the secure custody section of the station. There they saw a middle-aged Asian male seated at a table with a young white male sitting next to him. The young man introduced himself as the duty solicitor called by the police station. Neither Fitzgerald nor Catchpole had met Khalid before. Indeed, up till recently they only knew him as

Suleiman. Fitzgerald introduced himself and Catchpole. He started the tape and made the introductory statement identifying the defendant as "Mr. Khalid".

He addressed himself to Khalid. 'I assume you have had your rights explained to you by your solicitor?' Khalid nodded.

'First, what is your proper name?'

'Patel.'

'What is your forename, or other name?'

'Usman.'

'Are you sure your name is not "Khalid"?'

'That is my old name. I changed it to "Patel".'

'Did you change it by deed poll?' Khalid looked nonplussed. His solicitor leant over and whispered in his ear. The solicitor said, 'my client is happy to be called "Usman Khalid" for the purposes of this case.'

'Do you know Rhana Khalid?'

There was a long pause. The solicitor again whispered into Khalid's ear. They whispered to each other for a few minutes and then after another short pause Khalid said, 'he is my son.'

'Do you know where he is?'

Another pause and then 'Yes. He's here.'

'He was arrested for murder yesterday, at Northampton. Do you know why you are here?'

'No comment,' Khalid answered. He had obviously been briefed to say this so as not to incriminate himself.

Fitzgerald continued. He knew from experience that in interviews of this nature a straightforward assertive approach without showing any emotion is always the best. Never react to any statement made by a defendant. 'Inspector Catchpole and I are investigating two cases. The first is the murder of a police constable at the Old Plaza Hotel in Wolverhampton on the night of the 17th August and the second is the attempted murder of a Member of Parliament, Mr David Robinson, in the community centre in Northampton yesterday afternoon. We believe you and your son are related to both these cases. Is there anything you wish to say?'

'No comment.'

'Do you admit or deny that you were at these places at the times mentioned?'

'No comment.'

There did not seem any point in continuing the interview as he was obviously going to block all their questions, so Fitzgerald moved to end it. He would arrange another interview when he had all the facts at his fingertips. 'I wish to inform you that I have to-day interviewed your wife about these cases. She has not been detained.'

Khalid had nothing to say. He knew his wife had been brought in this morning with him.

'We will also be interviewing your son.' Khalid was silent.

'You will be detained in custody whilst these cases are being investigated.'

'What about bail?' Khalid asked.

'We will oppose any application for bail,' Fitzgerald replied. 'Interview terminated' and switched off the tape. Catchpole opened the door and a constable came in to escort Khalid to the cells.

When Khalid had gone, Fitzgerald turned to the solicitor and asked if he was representing the young Khalid as well. He said he was. Fitzgerald said he would give him ten minutes to speak to his client before the interview. He and Catchpole left the room and went back to the office.

'How do you think that went?' Catchpole asked when they were in the office.

'More or less what I expected. These solicitors usually tell their clients never to answer questions. Just say "No Comment" and it keeps them out of trouble.'

'Exactly. I suspect we will get the same response from Lewis ... I wonder if we can get another cup of tea?' It was past lunchtime and they had had nothing to eat. I'll go and see what I can find.' He returned five minutes later with two mugs of tea and two sandwiches.

'Excellent work!' Fitzgerald said as he accepted his sandwich.

They returned to the interview room. Lewis was now sitting at the table with the same solicitor sitting next to him. Fitzgerald placed a new tape into the machine and did the normal introductory statement. Lewis gave no indication that he knew either of them.

'I believe you have met Inspector Catchpole before, but we have never met. I oversee these investigations.'

'No comment,' he replied.

'Do you know why you are here?'

'No comment.'

'We are investigating two cases,' and he repeated exactly what he had said to the father.

'No comment.'

This interview was also going much as he predicted. Lewis had also obviously been advised not to answer any questions, so Fitzgerald moved to terminate. 'I have to inform you that we have already interviewed your father and your mother.' There was a slight look of surprise on his face at the mention of his mother.

Fitzgerald continued, 'you will be detained in custody whilst these cases are investigated.' There was no mention made of bail. Catchpole went to the door and the constable entered and escorted Lewis back to the cells.

When Lewis had left, they shook hands with the solicitor. 'Will you or your firm be representing them in these cases?'

'No. At least they haven't asked yet.'

Fitzgerald smiled. When the solicitor had gone, he said to Catchpole 'Now the work really starts!'

'Yes Boss. I'll see you tomorrow.'

31

Johnson and Anita arrived back in London at two-thirty pm having stopped at a service area for a sandwich and cup of tea on the way. Johnson found a parking spot near Mandela House and parked. They got out and went up to Anita's flat on the second floor. It was the first time he had been into her flat.

Anita's flat was very small, one bedroom, a small living room, kitchenette and bathroom. Basic but adequate for a single person, he thought.

'I have got to phone my boss,' he said, 'do you mind?'

'Of course not. I am feeling tired so I think I will go and lie on my bed and leave you to it. If you want anything please help yourself.' With that Anita went to her bedroom and shut the door.

Johnson telephoned Mrs B. on his mobile, 'Number Eight, Mrs. B. I'm back in London.'

'I want to see you as soon as possible, can you come around now?' She didn't sound too friendly. He felt there could be trouble. He just hoped Colonel Rutherford wouldn't be there as well.

'Yes, I'll come straight away.' He went and knocked on Anita's bedroom door. 'I've got to go and see my boss right away. Will you be OK on your own?'

'I'll be fine. When will you be back?'

'I'll be back as soon as I can. Lock the door and don't let anyone in for any reason.'

He returned to his car and drove to his headquarters which took him half an hour. He parked in the underground car park and went up to Office 26. Sarah was not at her desk so he knocked on Mrs B.'s door and went in. She was sitting behind her desk as usual.

'Did you have a good trip back?'

'Yes, thank you.'

'What have you done with Delia?'

'How does she know I was with Delia?' he wondered. This woman knows everything. 'I've left her at her flat and told her to lock the door and not let anyone in,' he said.

'Good. I want to speak to you about her later but first tell me what happened.'

Johnson spent the next fifteen minutes telling Mrs B. all that had happened in Northampton. He emphasised that Delia had been petrified at the part she had to play which had caused her to faint and have a miscarriage. Tactfully, he didn't say that he blamed her and Colonel Rutherford. He said that he threw the bomb out of the window because he thought it was the safest thing to do with all the people standing around. He said he decided to stay on in Northampton whilst Delia was in hospital for her safety and because she was a witness and had no-one else to rely on. She did not want to speak to her parents. He added that he had been told by Sergeant Nelson that the murderer had been arrested and hoped this might work in his favour.

'Yes, I am aware that there was an arrest and that you threw the bomb out of the window. I understand that you also shouted to everybody that it was a bomb.'

'No. I shouted at a Muslim woman who was watching me and who had a similar bag that it was a bomb, but she just walked away.'

'What happened to Delia's escort?'

'I don't know. He just walked off and left her.'

'Why did you not follow him? Surely you must have realised that he was the man who controlled her, Suleiman, I think you said he was called. In fact, that is what I told you to do.'

Johnson felt chastened. Of course, he should have left Anita to the people in the hall who were looking after her anyway and gone after someone who was a suspect terrorist. 'I felt concerned for Delia who was obviously in pain,' he said rather lamely.

He could see by her face that Mrs B. was not impressed. She changed the subject. 'You realise that if there is a trial Delia will probably be called as a witness, and possibly even you?'

'I assumed she was a witness. I don't know about myself,' he said.

'Yes, she is definitely a witness and I am concerned about her safety. Do you have any suggestions?'

Johnson paused. He was not quite sure how to say it. Then he said, 'I could look after her myself.'

'Yes. I thought you might say something like that. Does she know?'

'No.'

'Well if she does not want you to protect her let me know immediately and I will arrange for a normal police protection system to be set up. She must not come to any harm.' Johnson nodded.

'We now come to your future,' she said. Here we go, he thought. It was what he was expecting.

'I've spoken with the Director. We are not happy with what happened at Nottingham. You have blown your cover and become emotionally involved with an agent: and worst of all you allowed your suspect to escape.' She looked sternly at Johnson. Johnson just sat there looking back at her, his face expressionless. She went on. 'In view of this I'm afraid we have to terminate your services.'

'I understand,' he replied.

'I'm sorry it has come to this, but you know the rules.'

'Yes,' he replied again. There was nothing else he could say.

'Personnel will sort out your final payments and pension refund.' She paused to let the message sink home. Then she continued; 'I hope it won't be the last we hear of you. I want you to meet someone,' and picked up her phone. 'Come in Number 4.'

The door opened and in walked a Muslim woman wearing a black hijab over her head and with black heavy framed spectacles. Johnson was speechless. He recognised her immediately as the Muslim woman who was watching him attend to Anita on the floor at Nottingham. She removed her hijab and spectacles. It was Sarah, the receptionist.

'I think you know each other,' said Mrs B, smiling. 'Sarah will be taking over from me when I retire at the end of the year.'

Johnson was flabbergasted. He just sat in his chair with his mouth open not knowing what to say. Eventually he said the only thing he could think of, 'I'm sorry.'

Sarah was laughing at his embarrassment. 'I think we have a date,' she said, 'didn't you want to take me out to paint the town red?'

It broke the ice. Johnson laughed in turn. 'I'm sorry. I didn't realise,' he said.

Mrs B. broke in. 'Seriously though, Number 8, whilst you will not be directly working for the firm, you have built up a good network of contacts. We hope you will still keep in touch with them and your ear to the ground and pass on anything you hear to Sarah.'

'Yes of course. I'll do what I can.' He felt vindicated to some extent. At least he was not leaving completely under a dark cloud.

'In that regard, we will leave your direct line for the moment, but we may have to disconnect it on the grounds of expense.' She put her hand into a drawer and pulled out a brown envelope. 'This is the balance owing to Delia. I have added a further five hundred pounds to compensate her. Look after her'.

The meeting ended and Johnson shook hands with both and left. He drove back to Mandela house and up the stairs to Anita's flat. He knocked and she let him in, looking much better.

'You took a long time,' said Anita, 'everything alright?'

'Yes.' He decided not to tell her he had been sacked. She was standing by a table so he handed her the envelope with the money. She put it on the table without checking it.

'We have got to think about your future,' he said, 'what do you intend to do?'

'Well, I can't stay here. I don't want to go on living here.'

'Where do you want to go?'

'I don't know. I suppose I'll have to beg from my parents again.'

Johnson thought. He didn't know how to put it. He didn't want to embarrass her; then making it sound as casual as possible, 'do you want to live with me?'

Anita glanced at him, looking relieved. 'Oh Jimmy,' she said, 'do you really want to put up with me?' He moved closer to her and took her into his arms,

'I can think of nothing else I want to do,' he replied.

32

It was Monday morning. Fitzgerald and his staff were setting up their new incident room at CTC Headquarters. Catchpole reminded him that he still had the weapon in the safe and Tommy's fingerprints.

'Oh yes. You had better get that round to Ballistics as soon as possible. Ask them to pull finger as we have the suspects in detention. Leave the fingerprints here. I will arrange to have them sent to scenes of crime.'

Catchpole collected the weapon still in its exhibit bag and set off for the London Hub of the National Ballistics Intelligence Centre. On arrival, he told the receptionist he wished to speak to the person dealing with the "Baxter" murder case. 'That will be DCI Smith,' she told him and put through a call on the internal line. A few minutes later DCI Smith appeared. Catchpole introduced himself.

'Is that the weapon?' asked Smith.

'Yes. I recovered it on Saturday.'

'Come through.' Smith led the way through a side door to the laboratory and his work bench. 'Put it there,' he said pointing to the bench. Smith went off to a strong room and after a short while returned with some papers and a small plastic container with cotton wool in it. He placed them on the bench. He carefully opened the exhibit bag and pulled out the towel with the weapon wrapped inside and opened the towel.

'Ah. Italian made starter gun; "Precise 880",' he said. 'Looks like it has been converted to fire live ammo.'

'Watch out it's loaded,' Catchpole warned.

Smith opened the cylinder and tipped out seven rounds. 'He said, ·22 short. Must be a tight fit, normally they will only take blanks; and there is usually an obstruction in the barrel to prevent a live round being fired.' He looked at the end of the barrel. 'It's full of shit, I can't see a thing ... Mind you it looks pretty old; it's certainly seen better days,' turning the weapon over showing blemishes to the bodywork. 'Maybe they didn't put the obstruction in when this one was made. Where does it come from?'

'I'm not sure yet but we think Bristol University.'

'And how did your suspect get hold of it?'

'He was a student.'

'That's the problem with these weapons. The regulations that apply to normal firearms don't apply so they don't get the same degree of security.'

'Is it easy to convert them?' Catchpole asked.

'Yes so long as there is no obstruction in the barrel, but it's not recommended. They can be highly dangerous apart from being illegal. Look he's tried to do some modification. See the front of the cylinder has got marks on it, some of the blueing is missing. It looks as if he has poked something down the barrel to ensure the bullet will pass through.'

He then opened the small plastic container. Lying on a wad of cotton wool was a small lead bullet, slightly misshaped. 'Is that it?' Catchpole asked.

'That's it,' Smith replied.

'It looks so small and insignificant. You would hardly think that such a small thing could cause such a catastrophic result.'

'It depends where it went. I'll test fire one of these bullets and then check under the microscope to see if it matches this one,' pointing to the container. 'If it does, then you'll know you've got the right weapon.'

'We've got the suspect in custody. How long will it take to do the test?'

'You'll get your report by the end of the week.'

'Excellent.'

'One thing before you go, is this towel part of the exhibit?'

'Yes. I found the weapon in the glove pocket of a car, wrapped in that towel.'

'Strange, because these weapons normally come in a holster.' Catchpole left and returned to headquarters.

In view of the urgency of the case Smith got on with the testing straight away. He first cleaned the barrel with a cleaning rod and piece of 4 x 2 lint. It was full of fluff and dust and obviously hadn't been cleaned for a long time. He then thoroughly checked the weapon to satisfy himself that it was safe to fire. There were signs that an instrument, probably a drill bit, had been pushed down the barrel which had caused scoring to the inside; but he could see nothing to stop the bullet passing through the barrel. The scoring had obviously caused the marks on the bullet that he could not identify. There was no sign of any obstruction ever having been fitted in the barrel. He was worried about the weapon being robust enough to take the force of firing a live round. He checked the bodywork for any signs of failure but found nothing. Satisfied, he loaded one round into the cylinder and placed the weapon in a clamp with the barrel pointing towards a trap. Wearing protective clothing he remotely fired the weapon. There was a loud crack in the confined area but the weapon fired without mishap. He was satisfied it was safe.

His next task was to recover a sample bullet from the weapon. This would be done in a water trap. The trap was a large water drum with the bottom chamfered to a point where there was a valve and a container. He loaded one round into the cylinder of the weapon and climbed to the top of the drum. He pointed the weapon down into the water and fired. Again, there was another loud crack. He climbed down and shut the valve, unscrewed the container, tipped out the water and recovered the bullet lying in the bottom.

Next, he placed the test fired bullet and the exhibit bullet side by side into a comparison microscope. By twisting the knobs, he could turn each one in either direction. He noticed that the test fired bullet had the same markings as the exhibit bullet. He twisted them around and under the microscope, could place one image directly over the other. The markings matched exactly in shape and size. He attached a camera and took several photographs.

To prepare the evidence for court he mounted the photographs side by side on a card and marked the points of similarity. This card would be prima facie evidence that the weapon recovered from the car was the one which fired the bullet that killed the victim.

He then had to check the accuracy of the weapon. The weapon had no rifling in the barrel so accuracy would be limited. Again, he clamped it and set up a moving target on a scale. He adjusted the weapon so that it pointed exactly to the middle of the target. Starting at one metre he remotely fired the weapon, moving the target half a metre away each time. He found it was accurate up to three metres. After that the bullet started to tumble.

He was intrigued by the towel. It was a medium sized bath towel folded into four. He noticed oil and what appeared to be singeing on one side. He looked long and hard at the singeing, and then had an idea. 'Of course,' he said to himself. 'It has been used for muffling.'

The weapon made a very sharp and distinctive crack when fired, amplified in the confined space of the test area. He loaded the weapon and placed the towel carefully over it in the clamp. When he fired, there was a definite muffled effect. He tried two more shots, firing without the towel and then again with the towel; there was definitely less noise with the towel. This was something he had never seen before so he called a colleague and together they carried out further tests. Both agreed that the towel had a definite muffling effect on the sound of the shots. He then measured the decibel strength of the shots with and without the towel. The towel reduced the reading by about 30m decibels. They both realised something else. If the weapon was fired with the towel over it, it would be hidden from the victim. He was ready to write his report.

The trial of the two Khalids, father and son, was set down for the third week in January at the Central Criminal Court in the Old Bailey. Fitzgerald had two and a half months to assemble all the evidence and prepare the docket of case. He decided to appoint Catchpole and DC Fox to be his main assistants together with two civilian typists.

After Catchpole returned from dropping off the weapon with Ballistics, Fitzgerald called him into his office and they had a brief discussion as to the order in which they should proceed. Fitzgerald decided that the first thing he should do was to have a chat with his boss, Commander Birch, to bring himself up to speed with all that had been going on. He put through a call.

'I'm on my way to a meeting with Colonel Rutherford and MI5,' Birch said. 'Come and see me later and I should be able to put you in the picture completely. I was looking at the news last Saturday night and was horrified to see a report about a bomb at the Nottingham meeting. Did you know anything about a bomb?'

'No sir. Catchpole said nothing about a bomb when he phoned me. Just that he had arrested Lewis.'

'Well when no-one phoned me afterwards I presumed it was false. Anyway, I should know more after my meeting this morning.'

Whilst Birch was at his meeting Fitzgerald decided it would be an appropriate time to have a chat with DC Fox. He called him into his office. Fox was dressed in jeans, polo shirt and jumper.

'Are you going anywhere?' Fitzgerald asked.

'No sir.'

'Then why are you dressed like that?'

'Mr Birch told me I should dress down.'

'Right, understand this. The dress order when you are working in the office is a suit. If you are going out in the field you dress in whatever clothing is appropriate.

'Yes sir'.

'What I want to know is what you have been up to during my absence.'

'I kept a diary, sir, which I sent to Mr Birch every Monday. I have a copy here.' Fox handed over a file with his diary and other papers in the back.

'Sit there whilst I read through it.' Fitzgerald opened the file and started to read, making comments as he read.

'I see you were at the post-mortem. Is that the first one you have attended?'

'No. I attended one at Hendon on a cancer patient. This is the first one involving a criminal case.'

'Not very pleasant, is it?'

'I was in the visitor's galley looking down on it. I found it very interesting. My only problem was the strange smell. I couldn't work out what it was.'

'Yes. I always think it's the smell of death. I am sure it is all the chemicals they have there. Anyway, that'll be the first of many you'll attend during your service.' He carried on reading. After ten minutes he asked, 'did they ever recover the two number plates they found in the boot of that car?'

'No sir. They left them as there was nothing illegal about them.'

'Did you get statements from the two constables who found them?'

'Yes sir. They are at the back.' Fitzgerald looked to the back of the file and pulled out two statements. 'Did you type these?'

'No sir. A civilian did. They had them ready for me when I arrived.' Fitzgerald raised his eyebrows, obviously impressed. He read on whilst Fox sat in his chair watching his expressions.

'When you carried out the search at Barnet, were you there when they found the letters?'

'Yes sir. They're at the back of the file.' Fitzgerald pulled out the letters. 'Were they sealed?'

'One was open, the other two were sealed. I opened them.' Fitzgerald said nothing. Another ten minutes and then ..

'When you went into the shop in Pinner, did you tell the woman who you were?'

'No sir. I just pretended I was a customer. I bought some vegetables.'

'What made you go and look for the allotment?'

'Mr Birch told me to check whether the fertilizer found in the garage was being used to grow vegetables or not. He said we would look very silly if we charged them with using it to make explosives when they could prove they were using it to grow vegetables.'

'And were they using it to grow vegetables?'

'I don't know. The vegetables were very healthy looking. I know because I bought some.'

'What about the old man. Did you ever find out who he was?'

'No sir.' Fitzgerald read on.

'I see you made the arrest of the elder Khalid. Why didn't Sgt Kirkwood?'

'Sgt Kirkwood said I should do it because I was on the case. He was there and put the handcuffs on him.'

'Did you give him the correct warning?'

'Yes sir, though I don't think he was listening because he was shouting that his name was "Patel".'

Fitzgerald finished reading and closed the file. 'Very good. You've done well. How are you enjoying your work in CTC?'

'Very much sir and I'm learning a lot.'

'Carry on like this and you will go far. I'll keep this file. You can start a new diary from here on.' Fox got up and left the office.

33

Johnson and Anita arrived back at his flat mid-afternoon. Anita had packed two suitcases of her clothing which were in the boot of his car. He took them out and led the way to the back of the house where his entrance was. He unlocked the door and stood back for Anita to enter. He followed and placed the suitcases on the floor.

They stood there looking at each other. He had been dying to get Anita back to his flat but now that she was there he suddenly felt awkward, not knowing what to do or say. He realised Anita had never been to his flat before. She seemed a little shy.

'Welcome to my home,' he said. 'It's not much but it's where I live.' She smiled but said nothing.

'Can I make you some coffee?' he asked after what seemed a long embarrassing silence.

'I'd rather have tea,' she replied.

Tea, tea. He never drank tea and did not think he had any. He went to the wall cupboards in the kitchen area and searched through them. All I want is one bag, he said to himself, surely there must be at least one bag here – but there was nothing.

'Sorry I seem to be out of tea,' he said.

'Never mind. Fruit juice will be fine.'

Fruit juice. He never drank that either. 'Sorry I don't have any fruit juice either.' Not a good start. 'Would you like some wine or a beer?' He asked.

'No I won't have wine or beer. Water will be fine.'

'Water; I'll have water as well,' he said. He couldn't remember when he had last drunk a glass of water in his house. He went to the kitchen wall cupboards again to look for a glass. He owned ten tumblers, all different shapes and sizes. He found a glass for Anita and another for himself and filled them from the tap over the sink and handed her a glass.

She just held her glass in front of herself. He felt self-conscious with nothing to say. He knew the embarrassing question had to be asked but did not know how to approach it. Anita was not like any other girlfriend he had brought back to his flat. She had class and he didn't want to blow it by being clumsy.

'Cheers,' he said raising his glass and taking a sip. Anita still stood there and did not respond.

'Where? Um, where do you want to sleep?' he asked making it sound as casual as possible.

'With you I hope,' she replied. She spoke so quietly he thought he hadn't heard what she said. She was still looking at him, straight in the eye. But he had heard.

'Phew'. He heaved a sigh of relief, looked at her face and smiled. She smiled back. 'I can't tell you how relieved I am,' he said, 'I didn't want to embarrass you.' He put down his glass and took her in his arms, giving her a bear hug, squashing her arm holding the glass against her tummy, spilling some water. 'I've been wanting to do his ever since I first met you,' he whispered.

She dropped the glass on the floor and put her arms around his neck. 'I've been wanting to do this ever since you took me to lunch at that pub.' They had a long embrace.

He broke away. 'Let me show you the rest of the flat,' he said and led her to the stairs. Immediately at the top of the stairs was the bathroom; on the left his bedroom. He took her to the bedroom first.

It was furnished with a double bed, a bed-side table and lamp on one side and a chair on the other; another chair against the wall on which he had slung some of his clothes, and a double wardrobe. At least, he noticed, he had pulled up the duvet so the bed looked respectable. 'Not much,' he said, 'my bachelor pad.' It suddenly all looked terribly empty and bleak. Anita said nothing.

He then led her next door to the bathroom. It contained a bath with shower over, a loo and hand basin. He noticed his shaving brush covered in soap suds standing on the basin. He went over and rinsed it under the tap trying to make it look as casual as possible. Then he noticed his toothbrush lying on the floor under the basin so he picked it up quickly hoping she wouldn't think he always kept his toothbrush on the floor under the basin. He suddenly remembered he had run out of toothpaste and forgotten to buy any.

'And this is my spare room,' he said as he led her to the only other room. It contained a single bed with a lot of his clothing scattered over it; a chair and single wardrobe. There were two suitcases on the floor, two cardboard boxes and some weights in the corner. 'Not very tidy, I'm afraid.'

'I think your flat is absolutely lovely,' said Anita, 'it is like a palace compared to what I have been living in. Shall I bring my suitcases up and put them in here?'

'I'll get them,' he said and rushed downstairs immediately, almost embarrassed that Anita should even think of having to carry her own suitcases. He returned with the suitcases. 'We'll have to find some room for you to put your things.'

'There's no rush for that,' she said, 'tomorrow will do fine.'

When they went downstairs he suggested that they go out for a meal.

'I would rather we stayed here and had a romantic dinner on our own. I'll cook it.'

He hadn't thought of that. He was always used to going out whenever there was anything special to celebrate.

'That sounds very nice,' he said. 'What would you like?'

'Whatever you want. What about fish?'

'Excellent. Prawns?'

'I love prawns. How does curried prawns followed by ice cream sound?'

'Can you cook curry?'

'Of course, I can, I'm Pakistani,' she retorted.

'We'll need some supplies. Let's make a list. Do you want to write out a list?

'No, I know what we need.'

'Then let's go. There's a small supermarket at the top of the road. It normally has everything I want.'

They left the flat and went out to his car. The supermarket was on the corner at the end of the road with a small car park behind. He parked and they went in. Anita pulled out a shopping trolley.

'I think you'd better do the shopping,' he said 'because you know what you want. Don't hold back. Don't worry about cost. Get whatever you need. I've got to go somewhere. I'll be back shortly.' She thought he was going to the gents.

He saw her disappear between the shelves and he went back to the entrance where the flowers were on display. He grabbed half a dozen bundles of assorted colours off the stand and then some red roses. At the checkout, he paid for them with his card. It was nearly forty pounds' worth. He didn't know if this was fair value or not, but he took them out to his car and locked them in the boot.

When he returned to the store Anita was standing with her trolley at the end of the shelves, waiting for him. 'Is that all?' he asked. It didn't look very much.

'That's all we need for the moment. We can come back and do a proper shop tomorrow.' Together they passed their purchases through the check out and loaded them into bags and into the trolley. They pushed the trolley to the car where he placed the bags onto the back seat. They then drove back to his flat.

He parked the car and pulled the bags off the back seat and carried them to the door. 'If you put your hand into my right trouser pocket,' he said to Anita who was following him, 'you will find the keys.

Could you get them and unlock the door?' Anita obliged and unlocked the door. They went in and he placed the bags on the kitchen worktop.

'Can I leave you to put things away? Put them wherever you want,' he said. Before she could say anything, he went straight out of the door back to his car. He opened the boot and collected all the flowers. There were so many that when he held them up they completely hid his face. He returned to the flat.

As he entered Anita was bending over putting things into the fridge.

'Welcome to my humble home,' he said to her.

She looked up and stopped. Tears welled up into her eyes and ran down her cheeks.

'What's the matter?' he asked, placing all the flowers onto a chair and walking over to her, taking her into his arms to comfort her.

'No-one has ever given me flowers before,' she sobbed. It sounded so pathetic a surge of love and pity came over him, and even his eyes became moist. They stood like this for at least a minute. He then pushed her gently away and said, 'what are we doing? Here we are, two adults standing together crying over a bunch of flowers. How daft is that?'

She collected herself and laughed through the sobs. He took out his handkerchief and gave it to her. She wiped her eyes and blew her nose. 'Keep it,' he said, when she tried to hand it back to him.

'I've still got your other handkerchief you gave me. Do you remember?' He nodded.

'They are lovely flowers and so many! We had better put them into vases. Do you have any?'

'No.' He thought for a moment and then remembered 'I've got a bucket in the glory hole. I'll get that.'

He went to the glory hole. The plastic bucket was being used as a rubbish bin. He tipped the contents onto the floor and returned to the kitchen. Anita half filled it with water and carefully placed all the flowers into it. There was nowhere to put the bucket but on the floor.

'I'd better get on with the cooking. What about you setting the table?'

Table. Table. The only table he had was a low coffee table or an old card table on which the TV was standing. That will do, he thought, removed the TV and placed it on the floor. Then he placed two chairs at the table.

Next, he looked for a tablecloth. He knew there was one somewhere but couldn't remember where. He searched through the drawers in the kitchen units and found it at the bottom of a drawer. It was covered with crumbs and dust. He took it out and opened it, shaking all the debris onto the floor. It had an embroidered pattern on the surface but when he placed it on the table, the dirt had discoloured one corner. He turned it upside down; it looked much cleaner but crumpled and the embroidery was the wrong side up.

He then went to the cutlery drawer in the kitchen and collected two knives, two forks and two spoons, all different shapes and sizes, and placed them on the table. It still looked a bit bleak. He didn't have any candles but flowers, he remembered. He collected a beer glass, put in some water and stuck the roses in the glass. They just flopped about and were very unstable.

Anita, who had been concentrating on the cooking looked up and saw him struggling with the flowers. She burst out laughing. 'Don't worry,' she said, 'they'll fall over. I'll sort them out later.'

He took the flowers out and replaced them in the bucket. 'What about wine?' he asked, 'are you going to have some wine? I've at least got two wine glasses.'

'Yes please'

'Red or white?'

'White please.' Of course, he should have known. White with fish. He was trying hard to impress her but seemed to be making mistake after mistake. He collected the two wine glasses and the table was laid.

'Dinner will be another thirty minutes. Why don't you help

yourself to a drink and relax?'

'What about you?'

'I'll have some mango juice please.'

He went to the fridge and got himself a can of beer. There was a carton of mango juice there which she must have bought in the supermarket. He opened it and poured the juice into a glass. He had never experienced such domestic activity before and he found he was rather enjoying it, especially with such a pleasant companion as Anita. The smells coming from the kitchen were mouth-watering. He couldn't wait for dinner.

Eventually Anita called that dinner was ready. She brought two plates to the table loaded with curried prawns on a bed of rice with green beans. He collected a bottle of white wine from the fridge and they settled down to this, their first meal together. It was divine, the best curry he had ever tasted.

After the ice cream, he asked her if she would like some coffee.

'Yes please. I know you have been dying to show me your coffee machine so let's have some. I only want a small cup though.'

At last he could show that he was not completely useless but he didn't have any small cups. He only had mugs, but he did have an egg cup.

'I don't have any small cups,' he said, 'will an egg cup do?'

'Not really,' she said laughing, 'just pour a little into the bottom of a mug with a little milk. That will do nicely.'

He made the coffee and poured a full mug for himself and about a quarter of a mug with milk for Anita.

'I must say it is absolutely lovely coffee,' she said, 'I can see why you like it so much.'

They finished their dinner and washed up. Johnson suggested they leave the washing up until tomorrow but Anita insisted they do it then and there. She washed and he dried. He'd never done that before.

'What's the time?' she asked.

He looked at his watch. 'Just gone half past nine,' he said. 'What time do you want to go to bed?'

'When I was in my own flat I would have been in bed by now,' she replied.

'Do you want to go now? You go first and I will come up when you're in bed,' he said.

'No, let's go together,' she said.

They put out all the lights and went up to his bedroom. When they were there Johnson took her by her waist and, looking into her eyes, asked, 'in view of what happened to you are you sure it will be alright?'

'Yes'

'Did you ask a doctor?'

'Yes'

'I'm getting the impression that you planned this whole thing.'

Anita put her arms around his neck. 'Yes,' she said.

Their embrace was long and passionate. They fell onto the bed and made love. It was gentle and natural. Johnson had never felt like this with a woman before. Anita was certainly someone very special.

Afterwards they fell asleep in each other's arms.

Johnson woke up and saw that there was light coming through the curtains. He looked at his watch, it was ten to seven. He hadn't slept like that for years. They had parted in the night. Anita was still asleep and he lay and gazed at her. She was just as beautiful asleep as she was awake, he thought. So innocent. He noticed she was wearing a night dress which she certainly was not wearing when they went to sleep. She must have got up in the night and put it on. He decided he would go downstairs and make some tea for her.

He got out of bed and put on his dressing gown. He thought he had better put on some boxer shorts as well otherwise he was naked.

In the kitchen, he contemplated what to do and then decided that it would be best to make the tea in the bedroom. He collected all the paraphernalia needed and an old tray he had in the glory hole. He loaded the tray and carried it up to the bedroom. There was nowhere to put it but on the floor. The clinking of the mugs woke Anita. She stretched and smiled at him.

'Did you sleep well?' he asked.

'Yes. Beautifully.'

'I'm making some tea.'

'Good. That's a lovely idea.'

He took the kettle to the bathroom to fill it and then plugged it in and switched it on. He then took off his dressing gown and got back into bed, leaning against the headboard waiting for the kettle to boil.

Anita put out her hand and placed it on his arm. 'I'm so happy,' she said, 'thank you.'

He snuggled down into the bed and they made love again. It just seemed so natural.

After a while he got up. The kettle had boiled and switched off. He was about to go to it and then remembered he was naked. He grovelled under the duvet for his boxer shorts.

'Don't worry,' said Anita, 'I like seeing you as you are.' She thought he had a lovely athletic looking body. So completely naked and feeling a little embarrassed he switched on the kettle again. It boiled almost immediately.

'How many bags do you want in your tea, one or two?'

'One please,' she emphasised.

He made her tea with a little milk and a mug of instant coffee for himself. He placed her tea on the chair by her bed and the coffee on his bedside table. With both sitting in bed and leaning against the headboard they drank their tea and coffee.

'Can I ask you a personal question?' he asked. Anita nodded.

'What about your faith. You are a Muslim, widowed and living with an unmarried male who is a Christian. Will that cause you problems?'

'I'm not really a Muslim,' she said. 'I've never been properly converted. My father is a Muslim and my mother a Christian. They are not very religious and so I am really nothing. When I married Raji he was a Muslim and asked me to go to the mosque which I did. The

Imam who preached was very kind to me and after Raji died he was the only person who showed any sympathy, so I continued going. When I became involved with Suleiman, though, things changed and now I know he was going to kill me I am not very keen to get involved with Muslims again.'

'Don't condemn all Muslims,' he replied. 'Most of them are good and sincere; but I fully understand your feelings after what you have been through. Anyway, I am glad you will be OK. I would hate you to have trouble living with me.'

Anita smiled at him.

Johnson shaved and dressed and then went downstairs.

Anita came down later looking ravishing, dressed in jeans and a colourful top. 'Would you like scrambled eggs for breakfast?' she asked.

'I haven't had scrambled eggs for years. Yes, I do like scrambled eggs.'

'Good. Then I will make scrambled eggs on toast; you make the coffee.'

Breakfast was like dinner last night, completely different but delicious.

'What do you want to do to-day?' he asked.

'We need some more supplies and I want to go to a chemist,' she replied. She remembered she did not have any contraception pills and hoped it wasn't too late after last night.

'I think we should bank that money I gave you before it gets lost and I would also like to take you out to the garage to see my Unc, you know, the one you delivered the fruit to. I told him you were my girlfriend to get him to telephone you, and now you are. He was very taken with you so he will be pleased to see you.' Anita smiled. 'And then maybe we should go to your flat to collect the rest of your things. You can also sign off with the landlord.'

'What about my job?' she asked.

'I suggest you put in your notice and if you want another job find one locally.'

They washed up and went out to his car. First stop in the High Street to bank the money and for Anita to go to the chemist and then off to Hackney to the garage. They parked the car and as they were walking to the door Anita slipped her hand into his. Hand in hand they entered the office. JJ was sitting behind his desk as usual.

'Hello Unc, this is Anita who you've met before.'

'To what do I owe this pleasure?' asked JJ, 'of course I remember, the Fruit Lady.' He stood up and came around the desk and shook her hand.

'We're together,' said Johnson with a big grin.

'Good. About time too. When did this happen?'

'Yesterday. And I have also lost my job,' he added.

'What? All this MI5 stuff? Have you been sacked?'

'Yes.'

JJ paused whilst he digested the situation, then, 'What are you going to do?'

'I don't know. I'll find something.'

'Well don't rush into anything. I might have a plan for you. Ring me next week.'

They chatted for a short while and then Johnson said, 'we'd better go. We've got things to do. I just wanted you to be the first to know.'

'Well I am glad you did.' To Anita, 'you'd better tame him, he can be a bit of a wild bugger at times.'

'I'll do my best,' she replied looking lovingly at Johnson. They left the office, still hand in hand.

On the way back to the car Anita said, 'I didn't know you were a spy. You told me you were a policeman.'

'I used to work for MI5,' he said. 'I don't anymore.'

'A spy,' she thought, 'a spy. I'm impressed. I'm very impressed.'

34

At ten forty-five am the telephone rang in Fitzgerald's office. It was Commander Birch. "Can you come and see me now, Arthur, and I think you had better bring Catchpole with you as I have a lot to talk to you about.'

'Right sir, we are on our way.' He shouted through the door, 'Robin – drop everything we've got to go and see the boss'. Catchpole went into his office with a puzzled look on his face. 'He's had a meeting with the spooks and is going to reveal all,' said Fitzgerald. They put on their coats and went off to Birch's office, knocked and entered.

'Take a seat.' They both sat down. 'There *was* a bomb on Saturday night but I will come on to that later,' he said, 'I have had a very interesting meeting with Colonel Rutherford and an elderly lady known as Mrs B. who is MI5. I will go over the facts as I was told by them …

'MI5 are investigating an organisation called "al-Abdullah" which is recruiting converts to Islam and then radicalizing them. An M15 operative, named Jimmy Johnson, recruited a young Pakistani girl, Anita Hussein, to be his agent. She is British born, the daughter of a lawyer here in London. On the day MP Robinson held his meeting in Wolverhampton, she was taken there by a person we now know to be Khalid Senior. After the meeting, he admitted to her that they had "shot a policeman" i.e. Baxter. I think you know about this, don't you?'

'Yes sir. You informed me by telephone at the time.'

'Well, your witness to this is Anita Hussein.'

'Can we use her as a witness in court?' asked Fitzgerald.

'Yes, but I will come to that later. To continue, Anita Hussein heard nothing more for ages until about three weeks ago she was told by Khalid to be ready to go to Nottingham. No reason was given but we now know it was because of another Robinson meeting. In the meantime, MI5 were becoming more and more suspicious because things had gone quiet, so they set up another agent to investigate whether they had turned to bombs or explosives. If you remember we had found some bomb-making equipment in one of his houses which probably prompted them. They tracked Khalid to a stock-room of a corner shop he owned and in there found a bomb made up in a satchel hidden in a sack of toilet rolls. It was a suicide bomb and the obvious intention was to sacrifice Anita and kill the MP at the meeting, so they set a trap. The bomb was defused and replaced. Anita, who was pregnant, was not told about the bomb, fainted when Khalid pushed her towards the MP and then escaped. She was taken to hospital in Nottingham and lost her baby that evening.'

Fitzgerald and Catchpole were fascinated by what they were hearing. It filled in a lot of holes in the evidence they had. Catchpole recalled seeing the shenanigans going on in the front of the hall at Nottingham but had no idea that it was a bombing attempt. Neither did he see Khalid running away, but of course his full attention was on Lewis.

Birch continued, 'No further evidence has come to light about al-Abdullah and it's thought that it consisted only of Khalid and his son. The schoolteacher, who started the organisation, has apparently said he has nothing to do with it anymore. He and Khalid had a row so he pulled out leaving it to the Khalids. The only persons they converted were a young man named David White who is the son of the bursar of Bristol University and was given the nickname "Tommy". You know about Tommy; I gather he has a mental problem' – looking again at Catchpole – 'and before that Anita's husband. They don't know of anybody else – and that's about it.'

'We've had information of an elderly Asian male being seen around but no-one seems to know who he is. Did you get any information on him?' Catchpole asked.

'No. No mention was made of an elderly Asian male. Special Branch in the Midlands are following up on the schoolteacher, by the way, so we can leave that enquiry to them. We must concentrate on getting the Khalids to court.' He paused. 'I think you know the rest.' They nodded. 'MI5, say you can use Anita and Johnson as witnesses but MI5 is not to be mentioned in any way whatsoever. Anita was not aware that she was working for MI5. Johnson, who was her controller, told her that he worked for the Police Crime Prevention Unit so she thought she was working for the Police.'

'Does she know now?' asked Fitzgerald.

'Yes, she does, but you must ensure she never mentions MI5 and she must also be given full witness protection. Speak to the Crown Prosecution Service. Johnson, by the way, has been dismissed by MI5 for blowing his cover when he went to Anita's aid after she fainted. He knows the score. They are now living together at this address,' handing over a piece of paper with the address and telephone number.

'How very romantic,' said Catchpole sarcastically. Birch smiled. He also handed over a photograph of the bomb in the blue satchel and another of the detonator in its wrapping of P4 explosive.

He continued. 'The person who defused the bomb was a member of the SAS. As far as you are concerned, he is Corporal Tom Smith of the army bomb disposal unit, which is not his name, by the way. I think that's all. If you have any other queries, come back to me. It seems as if we have got a pretty good case; keep me informed.' With that the meeting ended.

Fitzgerald and Catchpole went back to their office. 'Well, well. How the other side operate. We had better work out how we are going to handle this. Should we charge them separately or jointly?'

'I think they should be charged jointly,' said Catchpole,

'On what grounds?'

'Plenty. We've got ample evidence against Lewis for the murder of Baxter. He had the motive and the opportunity – his office was next door to the scene of crime separated by a locked door to which he had the key – and the weapon was found in the glove box of his car. At the time, Suleiman was missing but according to Anita, who was sitting in his car, he came back and told her they had shot a policeman. As we now know, he is Lewis's father so he must have been in Lewis's office. In fact, he could even have been with Lewis when Baxter was shot.'

'That's supposition, not admissible in court. What about the Nottingham case?'

'It is the exact opposite. We've got plenty of evidence against Suleiman intending to sacrifice Anita and kill the MP. Lewis, his son had been missing – not returning from leave – and was seen in the crowd. He must have been there to help his father.'

'Again, it isn't evidence. We have to prove they were acting "jointly and severally" and just being present at the scene of crime is not the same.' said Fitzgerald.

'Why don't you put it to the CPS. They can only say "No".

'OK I will.'

'And what about charging Suleiman with the attempted murder of Anita as well?' Catchpole asked. 'He was going to sacrifice her as a bomb carrier which would seem to me to be attempted murder?'

'I don't think we can. We knew about it beforehand and the bomb was defused. We set it up as a trap. I don't think the court would accept it as attempted murder.'

'But his intention was to commit murder. His intention was to kill the MP and Anita at the same time. That is what really matters.'

'Yeah. But I don't think we would get a charge to murder Anita to stick as we knew the bomb was not live,' said Fitzgerald. He continued, 'I think we had better see Anita as soon as possible. Ring her and make an appointment for us to go and see her, maybe tomorrow if that is convenient.'

'You want to see her in her own home, not here?'

'Yes, apart from keeping her identity secret she will be more at ease in her own surroundings. We'll take along a recorder and record her statement on tape.'

Catchpole went to his desk and telephoned the number on the piece of paper. A pleasant sounding female voice answered.

'Hello. My name is Robin Catchpole from the Police. Could I make an appointment to come and see you please?' He tried to make his voice sound as friendly as possible.

There was a pause as she was obviously thinking. 'Can my boyfriend be present as well?'

'Would that be James Johnson?'

'Yes. Jimmy is my boyfriend.'

'Certainly, he can be present. In fact, it would be very convenient because we would like to speak to him as well. He will know what this is about.'

'He's at work. He won't be back until six.'

'That's fine. Can I ring back after six to make a date and time? Tomorrow would suit us fine.'

'Yes. I'll tell him when he returns from work.'

'Thank you very much. I'll ring you after six.'

'OK. Goodbye.' The line went dead. Catchpole poked his head into Fitzgerald's office. 'I'm making an appointment for ten tomorrow morning. I've got to confirm tonight after six.'

'Right. In the meantime, can you get everything ready? She'll have to do a photo identity. You've got Suleiman's photo. We'll need another five middle-aged Asian males. We will also need the blue satchel which I assume is in the exhibit store. Also, I think we should dress a little less formally. Come in trousers and a jumper. Forget about suits.'

'OK Boss.' Catchpole set about collecting things for the meeting the next day.

Fitzgerald caught up with his investigation diary and planned his next move. He decided he would like another meeting with Mrs Khalid. This time it would be "under caution" and she'd have her solicitor present. He was certain she knew more than she was telling them.

He also had a discussion with the Prosecutor who dismissed his doubts and said they should be charged jointly. "These are not suppositions," she said, "they are facts. Let the jury decide."

35

At nine-forty am the following morning Fitzgerald and Catchpole set off by car for Johnson's flat. They arrived just after ten and were met at the door by Johnson who shook their hands and invited them in. Anita was standing just inside.

'Hello. I'm Arthur Fitzgerald', extending his hand, 'and this is Robin Catchpole who you spoke to yesterday. You must be Anita?'

Anita appeared very shy. She extended her hand and shook Fitzgerald's hand. She then shook Catchpole's. 'Do you mind if we call you "Anita"?' He handed her his card.

'No not at all.' She looked very young and attractive, casually dressed in jeans with a coloured top and pumps on her feet.

Johnson directed them to a couple of easy chairs whilst he and Anita sat side by side on the sofa; the coffee table was between them.

Fitzgerald started the proceedings. 'I presume you know why we are here?' They both nodded. 'Robin and I have to prepare the case for court. That means doing all the paperwork. What we would like to do to-day is record a statement from you, Anita, and then maybe another one from you, Jimmy.'

'Will that mean I have got to go to Court?' asked Anita.

'Yes, but don't worry. Your name will never be disclosed and you will not be seen. You will be quite safe.'

Johnson intervened and said quietly to Anita, 'it's OK. I'll tell you all about it later.'

Fitzgerald continued. 'If you don't mind, I would like to record what you say on this tape recorder and then afterwards I will have it typed out. I will then bring it back for you to check and if you are happy, ask you to sign it.'

Johnson intervened again. 'It's Ok. This is normal. Same as what I did with you at the pub. Remember?' Anita nodded.

'The best way is for you to tell your story in your own words from the beginning. If I have any queries, I will check them with you before you go on. Is that OK?'

Anita nodded.

'Right, I will start the tape recorder now and it is over to you.'

Anita looked at Johnson obviously not knowing where to start. 'Start with the LSE and your marriage to Raji,'.

Anita started speaking, very hesitantly and obviously feeling self-conscious. She started with how she met Raji Khan at the LSE and how they got married despite objections from their parents; how his manner changed and he suddenly said he was going to Pakistan even though she was pregnant. She then told how she had been informed of his death in Afghanistan by an old man and how shocked she was.

Fitzgerald interrupted 'Did you know this old man?'

'No. I had never seen him before and I've not seen him since.'

'Do you know how he knew about you?'

'No. He just arrived at my flat and knocked on the door. Without saying who he was he just announced that my husband had been martyred. I did not know what he meant at first but then I realised he had been killed.'

'Sorry. Please go on.'

Anita continued, getting more self-assured as she went. She described meeting Suleiman and the trip to Wolverhampton ...'

'Sorry, who is Suleiman?' Fitzgerald interrupted.

'He's the person who always told me what to do. He told me his name was "Suleiman" but I don't think it was his proper name.'

'Thank you. Please continue.'

Anita continued ... She thought they were going to talk to people who had converted to Islam, but she spent most of the time sitting in his car waiting for him. She had no idea what he was doing because he told her nothing. They spent the last ten minutes or so at the meeting but she did not understand what was being said as she is not interested in politics. She was then told to wait for him in the car. However, when they got back to their room in the Holiday Inn Suleiman suddenly told her that they had shot a policeman. She couldn't believe what she had heard so asked him again and he confirmed they had killed a policeman. She was shocked and frightened as she was sleeping in the same room as him.

Fitzgerald interrupted again. 'Can you tell me what his exact words were?'

'He was looking very pleased with himself and suddenly said, "we have shot a policeman". It was such a shock to me that I queried with him and he repeated, "we have killed a policeman". I am sure those were his words. The way he said it was as if that was quite a normal thing to do.'

'What time did you get back to the hotel?'

'It was late, about eleven o'clock. I had been waiting for him in the car. It was ages before he came and I was freezing cold.'

'Please go on.'

Anita continued, telling how she was ordered to tell no-one of what had happened when they got back to London, but she told Jimmy during lunch at a pub.

Johnson interrupted, 'I'll tell you about that later.'

Anita carried on. She saw nothing more of Suleiman for ages, until one Friday after prayers he suddenly accosted her outside the mosque and told her she was a bad Muslim and must prepare herself to avenge her husband's death. He also went on about the police being *kufars* and then asked her if she had a boyfriend. That really frightened her because she knew Jimmy was a policeman and she thought they might have been seen together.

Fitzgerald asked, 'what did you think he would do?'

'I don't know. He didn't say, but I have read how some Muslims commit murder to take their revenge on people so I thought that was what he had in mind.'

'So, what did you do?'

'I told Jimmy and he said that he would look after me and that Suleiman was bluffing.'

'Carry on.'

She said the next time she saw Suleiman was when he suddenly appeared at her workplace and sold some vegetables to her boss. She was again shocked as she did not think he knew where she worked. When he left, he signalled for her to go outside and he told her to be ready to go to Nottingham. They left early in the morning and did not say a word to each other on the way. They arrived early and he said they should wait in the car until it was time to go into the hall. Then he suddenly got out of his car and told her to get out. He opened the boot of the car and took out a blue bag which he said she must carry. It was a shoulder bag with a strap. She asked what was in it and he said he wanted to record what the MP was saying at the meeting. She did not believe him and tried to open it to look inside but he put his hand on hers and said she must not open it. There were a lot of people around them and she did not want to cause a scene so she carried the bag over her shoulder. It was quite heavy. She was also very pregnant and felt very uncomfortable with the bag over her shoulder. They were shown to seats near the front. She did not listen to what was being said at the meeting because she was worried about the bag and wondering what she should do.

Fitzgerald interrupted again. 'What did you think was in the bag?'

'I was sure it was a bomb.'

'Why did you think that?'

'Because I didn't trust him. He boasted he had killed a policeman so he was obviously a dangerous man.'

'Please continue.'

Anita then moved on to when the meeting ended and everybody

stood up and clapped. Suleiman also stood up and told her to stand up. He said they must move closer to the speaker who was standing in front of the stage with a large crowd of people around him. She argued and said she did not want to go but he put his hand in the small of her back and pushed her. She tried to resist but he was very firm. They were arguing all the time and were by a window near the front when he suddenly walked off and left her on her own.

Fitzgerald interrupted again. 'How close were you to the MP?'

'About four or five feet I think. He was surrounded by a lot of people so I couldn't see him properly.'

'Please carry on.'

Anita continued. She stood there wondering what to do when she felt a pain in her stomach and wanted to vomit. The pain got worse and she could feel herself falling to the floor. After that she had no idea what happened because when she came to she was in an ambulance with Jimmy sitting by her. She remembered they got to the hospital and she was rushed into a theatre where she was given an injection. The next thing she remembered was waking up in a room on her own.

At first, she felt fine but very tired and then after about half an hour the pain started in her stomach again, but this time it was much worse. She called out because there was no-one in the room. Immediately a nurse came in, looked at her and called through the door for help. A doctor and another nurse arrived and ripped the bedclothes off. It was then that she knew she was losing her baby. She saw a small bloody bundle placed in a basin and the doctor looked down at her with a very sad expression, shaking his head. She asked what it was and he said a little girl. She felt very distressed and started to weep because she badly wanted a little girl.

At this stage tears welled up in Anita's eyes and started running down her cheeks. There was a catch in her voice. She was obviously upset whilst recalling the event. Johnson took hold of her hand and she placed her other hand on top of his. He took out a handkerchief and she wiped her eyes and blew her nose.

'Would you like us to stop?' Fitzgerald asked. Anita shook her head.

'Is there more?' Anita shook her head again.

Johnson then took over. 'She was in hospital for four days after which I brought her back here. That's it really. She has been here ever since.'

Fitzgerald switched off the recorder. 'Wow. That's quite a story,' he said. 'That's quite a story. There are just two other things I would ask you to do. Would you look at these photographs and see if you can recognise anyone?' He put his hand out to Catchpole who handed over a folder with six photos in it. 'Have a look at each one first and if you recognise anyone, please indicate to me.' Anita took the folder and opened it on her lap. She looked at all six and then went back to the fourth one which she pulled out. 'That's him. Suleiman. No doubt about it'. Fitzgerald looked at the name on the reverse side – "Usman Khalid".

'Are you absolutely sure?'

'Absolutely. In fact, it makes me sick just looking at him now.'

Fitzgerald showed the photo to Johnson. 'I've never seen him,' he said. 'At Nottingham, I was at the back of the hall and only saw the back of his head.'

'Did you ever know what his proper name is?' Fitzgerald asked Anita.

'No. I only ever knew him as Suleiman.'

'His real name is "Usman Khalid". Does that name ring any bells?'

'No. I've never heard it.'

'Do you know the name of his son?'

'No. I didn't know he had a son. He told me nothing about himself at all.'

'Now the next thing is, will you please look at this bag,' – he put his hand out to Catchpole who handed over a large exhibit bag. He pulled out a blue satchel. 'Is this the one you had?'

Anita caught her breath, looking shocked and surprised. 'Yes.'

Johnson also looked at it and confirmed it was the one he threw out of the window.

So, with the accused positively identified and the exhibit also identified, Fitzgerald felt they had achieved a lot. Anita was the key witness. 'You have been very helpful, Anita, and very brave. This is quite a case. I must warn you the media are very interested and you may get some pesky reporter trying to get a story out of you. Whatever happens say nothing. They don't know of your existence and they are not allowed to question witnesses before a trial so if you get any trouble just ring me, the number is on my card, and I will deal with them. I am sure you are in very safe hands here,' looking with a smile at Johnson.

'Well thank you both again. We'll leave you in peace. I'll contact you when the statement is ready and we can make a date for you to check and sign it.'

Fitzgerald and Catchpole got up, cleared up their things, shook hands all round and left. On the way back in the car Fitzgerald said, 'that is a very brave young lady. To lose her baby in those circumstances is absolutely shocking.'

'Yes, but just imagine how it will go down with a jury.'

36

The following morning Fitzgerald was at his desk. He called Catchpole into his office. 'I have sent the tape of Anita's statement to be typed in draft. When we get it back we'll go through it. I don't think we need it all, especially the beginning bit about her husband.'

'Except that was what started the ball rolling. It was when her husband was killed that she was approached by the old man and told to join his organisation to avenge her husband's death,' Catchpole replied.

'We must remember not to put in anything that would lead to her identity. If we start talking about her husband being killed in Afghanistan, etc. and mention his name, it will be obvious that she is Pakistani. To listen to her talking you would think she is a well brought up middle class English girl.'

'True but we will have to let the CPS know, and of course both the defendants will know.'

'But none of the public will know and that's the main thing. We will make a note on the statement that we have this evidence if it is needed,' Fitzgerald decided. He continued...

'I would like to have another chat with Mrs Khalid, this time under caution. I will write to her and make a date. We can't do this by phone. In the meantime, can you get out all the various documentary exhibits we've got on the case and check them. I've got to work out the order in which they will be presented in court and index them.'

'OK Boss. I've also got the register from the Holiday Inn in Wolverhampton and some statements. I'll assemble the whole lot. Oh, by the way. I've heard back from Bristol University. They did lose a starter gun about two years ago and reported it as lost property. I've sent Fox off to Bristol with the weapon to get a positive identification and statement.'

Fitzgerald wrote a formal letter to Mrs Khalid inviting her to attend the police station on a date and time convenient to her for a "statement under caution" to clear up certain points that had come to light during the investigation of the charges against her husband and son. She was advised to bring a legal representative with her.

Two days later he received an urgent telephone call from Mrs Khalid. 'What is this all about?' she asked. 'Am I going to be arrested? Do I have to attend?' Fitzgerald told her he could not discuss the matter over the telephone but if she was worried, she should ask her legal representative to telephone him and he would explain. An hour later she telephoned again and said she would attend at two pm the next day.

The following afternoon Mrs Khalid arrived promptly at the agreed time, accompanied by a young lady who introduced herself as Emily Watson of the legal firm Jones, Rogers and Jones, who had been representing the Patel family as their lawyers for years.

'I take it you are familiar with the "statement under caution" procedure?' Fitzgerald asked her.

'Yes, and I have explained it to Mrs Khalid.'

Fitzgerald led them to the interview room. They sat together on one side of the table and he and Catchpole on the other. Fitzgerald produced two new tapes in their packets, undid the packaging and placed them in the tape machine. He then made the normal introductory statement for the tape and they were ready.

'I must first caution you. You are not obliged to answer any questions that may incriminate you but if you fail to say something that you later rely on in court it may affect your defence. Do you understand the caution?'

'Yes.'

'You may consult with your legal adviser at any time.'

'Yes.'

'The other day we had a meeting and you made a statement which was recorded. Here is a typed copy for your information.' He handed her a typed statement with a copy for the lawyer. 'If you wish to make any changes to that statement then you may do so without penalty.' Mrs Khalid nodded.

Fitzgerald continued. He first asked her about the number plates found in the boot of her car. She admitted they were from an old van they used to own and her husband kept them in case he was caught in a speed trap. She admitted he used to put them on their car whenever he went on a long journey to avoid being caught by the police. He then asked her why they had moved from Barnet to the flat in Pinner, much smaller accommodation. She insisted it was her husband's idea to be nearer the business and for no other reason. He asked when they moved but she could not remember.

He went on and asked if there was anyone else living with them. She replied that it was only her and her husband; their son moved out three years ago when he went to university. He asked about the presence of an old man reported being seen in the vicinity. She said her husband was friendly with members of the Pakistani Community who did not speak English, because he could speak Urdu. He sometimes gave them little jobs. One job was working on their allotment. She did not know any names or meet them because she did not speak Urdu.

Fitzgerald showed her the correspondence concerning the purchase of the satchels. She said it was her husband's idea because he suggested they could sell them in the shop. She had refused as it was not the sort of thing they usually sold and she had nowhere to display them. They had had a row about the satchels and she had refused to pay for them. Catchpole produced the blue bag and she agreed it was one of the satchels that had been purchased. She did not know what it had been used for. She assumed they were kept in the stockroom, but she seldom went there. Her husband did all the ordering of stock.

She knew her husband had gone to Nottingham on Saturday but did not know why or who he was meeting or who went with him. He often went off on his own and did not tell her what he was doing. He got back at about one in the morning. She denied that she was delaying opening the front door when the Police arrived. She was surprised to see them and had left her husband sleeping in bed when she went downstairs. She did not see him come down and go to the back door.

She had never heard of al-Abdullah and did not know what it was. She admitted her husband and son were devout Muslims and did try to persuade others to adopt Islam but they never forced anyone. She did not know if they were ever successful. She was also a Muslim but not as devout as them. They used to go to the Mosque quite often but she did not go with them, but she always went to Friday prayers. Men and women were always segregated and she normally came home on her own, leaving her husband and son at the mosque. She arrived in England with her parents from Pakistan as a very young child and was educated and brought up in England. Her husband arrived when he was eighteen and they were married a year later.

Fitzgerald terminated the meeting and gave one copy of the tape to the lawyer. The other he removed, packed and sealed in front of them. They were free to leave.

'What do you think?' he asked Catchpole when they were alone.

'I think she anticipated the questions we were going to ask her and has rehearsed the answers. She was far too pat for my liking. Too glib. That bloody woman knows more than she's let on, but we'll never be able to prosecute her unless we find out what she's hiding from us.'

37

The trial of the two Khalids was held in the Crown Court at the Old Bailey starting on the third Monday in January before Mr Justice Davies and a jury of eight males, three of whom were Asians, and four women, one of whom was Asian.

Leading for the Crown was Mr Robert Pascoe QC. His junior was Miss Janette Arbuthnot. D/C/Superintendent Fitzgerald was asked to sit in the body of the court behind the prosecutor to be available to answer queries. The defence was led by Sir David Ramsbottom QC instructed by solicitors Jones, Rogers and Jones, speaking for both defendants, who were represented in court by Miss Emily Watson.

The case had created much media interest and the press gallery was packed. The visitors' gallery was also packed and seated by himself was an elderly Asian male with unshaven appearance and wearing traditional clothing. No-one spoke to him and he spoke to no-one. Johnson also took a seat in the visitors' gallery.

It had been decided that the defendants should be jointly charged firstly with the Murder of PC Baxter and secondly with the Attempted Murder of David Robinson MP. The indictment read – "that the defendants Usman Khalid and Rhana Khalid did both and each or one or other wrongfully and unlawfully, jointly or severally and with malice aforethought Firstly on the 17th August 2012 kill and murder Edward Arthur Baxter, a police constable with the Metropolitan Police, contrary to the common law; and Secondly on the 25th September 2012 Attempt to Kill and Murder David Robinson a

Member of Parliament, contrary to the common law". The charges were read out by the Clerk of Court and both defendants pleaded "Not Guilty".

It had been agreed by the judge, after an application made by Fitzgerald, that the witness Anita Hussein deserved being granted Special Measure consideration, would be given a code identity "Miss X" and give her evidence from behind a screen. It had also been agreed, after discussion with the Crown Prosecution Services and the defence, that no mention would be made of Anita working for the intelligence service and unless there was a dramatic change of circumstances, Johnson would not be required as a witness.

The jury was sworn in and the trial started. Both Counsels made opening statements outlining their cases. The prosecution went first which took up the rest of the morning and the defence in the afternoon. Various procedural matters were then dealt with and at three-thirty the judge adjourned the trial until ten am the following morning when the first witness would be called.

The first witness was D/Inspector Catchpole. He outlined the investigation of the case and how he arrested defendant Rhana Khalid, whom he knew as Lewis, trying to escape in his car; and finding the weapon wrapped in a towel in the glove box. The weapon and towel were produced as an exhibit. Then came Detective Constable Burns who described finding the body of PC Baxter slumped over a table in the pantry. He was followed by Detective Constable Fox who described how he had arrested defendant Usman Khalid whilst trying to get into his car. Next witness was Professor Fraser, the pathologist, who described and produced as Exhibits the post-mortem report with photographs and forensic reports on the samples taken. He also stated how he found a bullet in the brain which was produced in a small plastic container.

Then D/C/Insp. Smith of Ballistics. He first explained how the weapon, a starter gun, had been modified to fire live ammunition, and explained how he tested the weapon and compared the test fired bullet on his comparison microscope, with the one recovered by Professor

Fraser, and found the markings to be identical. He produced photographs to prove the point. He also explained how he carried out accuracy tests and showed the results with photographs. Finally, he explained how he tested sound muffling with the towel ...

'Objection My Lord,' Sir David for the defence interrupted. 'This is an opinion, not evidence.'

'I don't agree,' the Judge replied. 'The witness is an expert in ballistics and can give his opinion on tests he carried out. It is up to the jury to decide whether they accept his evidence.'

D/C/Insp Smith continued; he had made a note of the decibel readings. The pistol on its own was 160 decibels and with the towel, 130 decibels. 'However,' he continued, 'the tests were carried out under controlled conditions in an empty laboratory, whereas the shot was fired in a hotel with carpeting and furniture and probably with the door shut. This would have increased the muffling effect.'

'There's your answer,' The judge said to Sir David.

The judge nodded at Mr Pascoe, the prosecutor, to continue with his examination of D/C/I Smith. 'I have no further questions,' he said.

The next witness was Detective Sergeant Davies, an expert in forensics who carried out the search at 44 Grenada Avenue in Barnet. He explained what he had done and produced the samples of fertilizer, the long slim plastic bags and the electronic detonator found in the garage. He also produced the letters addressed to "Patel Provisions" found in the house.

Then came Corporal Tom Smith who stated he was in the army bomb disposal unit. He explained how he was directed to a garage being used as a stock-room and in a large bag of toilet rolls found a blue satchel in which there were explosives made from ammonium nitrate and diesel in long slim plastic bags This had been made up into a bomb which could be electronically detonated by a mobile phone. He produced photographs showing what he had found. He had defused the bomb, replaced the explosives with bags of sand and fitted a dummy detonator. He then put the satchel back into the sack of rolls. He produced the blue satchel, empty, as an Exhibit. It was put to him by the defence that the bomb was in fact crude and would not work.

'I have defused many explosive devices and this one was as sophisticated as any and if it had detonated in a confined space would have caused considerable damage and many casualties.'

'So why did you put the bomb back into the sack of toilet rolls?'

'Because the police instructed me to do so.'

All the exhibits were now on record, had been numbered and placed on a table in front of the clerk's desk for easy access if needed during the trial. It was twelve-thirty, so the judge adjourned the court until two-thirty. The next witness would be Anita.

Johnson and Anita had arrived in good time for the usual ten am start of proceedings. Anita was immediately directed to a side office and told she must wait there until called. Johnson had to leave her there. On entering the office, Anita was met by a kindly looking middle-aged lady.

'Hello. I'm Brenda,' said the lady coming forward and shaking Anita's hand. 'You must be Anita?' Anita nodded. She wasn't expecting this. 'I'm here to look after you until you are called. Unfortunately, you must stay with me, it's for your safety. I believe you have been told about this?'

Anita nodded again. She had been told that special measures were being taken to protect her, but she did not expect she would be isolated.

'Give me your anorak, luv, and I'll hang it up. Is this your first time in court?' she asked as she was hanging the anorak.

'Yes.' Anita replied. 'My boy-friend told me what to expect but I have never been inside.'

'Well it can be awe-inspiring the first time. All the panelling, the benches upholstered in red, the officials in wigs and gowns. Don't let that put you off. It is all for show. You have probably seen TV plays of court proceedings, have you?'

'Yes, but they are not the sort of programmes I normally watch so I have not taken much notice.'

'Never mind. The court will look the same. Don't be put off by stories of barristers asking you trick questions. Just remember you are a witness in this case and the court just wants you to tell them what happened as you saw it. You're here to help them and so long as you stick to that and don't try and invent anything, you will have no trouble.'

'Oh. I hadn't thought of that. I was afraid I would be asked something I cannot answer, and ... '

Brenda interrupted her. 'No. Not at all. In fact, they try to help you, not trick you. Also remember if you can't remember something, say so. A lot of the events took place months ago so you could well have forgotten some small detail.'

'I read my police statement last night,' said Anita. 'Is that all right?'

'I was going to ask you if you had done that, yes, absolutely fine.'

Anita was feeling a little less apprehensive after this talk with Brenda. Suddenly the phone rang. Brenda answered. 'Yes she's ready .... OK.' To Anita. 'They are nearly ready for you, just putting up the screen. You know you will be hidden from the defendants. The only people who will see you are the judge, counsels and jury.'

'Yes, I had been told that; also, I'm to be called "Miss X".'

'Well let's go then. Best of luck.' Brenda opened the side door directly into the court and went ahead. Anita immediately saw the judge in red robes and a wig, various court officials in black robes and wigs and on the far side a group of civilians sitting in two rows behind a barrier. Brenda indicated the witness stand, Anita entered and faced the court. The grandeur took her breath away.

A robed clerk approached her with some cards in his hand. 'Oath or affirmation?' he barked. Anita hadn't the faintest idea what he was talking about and just looked at him. Brenda quickly realised the problem. 'What religion are you?' she asked.

Anita was surprised to be asked such a question. 'Christian.'

'Read from this card please,' said the clerk, and handed her a card.

Anita looked at it and read the short statement, "I hereby swear that I will tell the truth, the whole truth and nothing but the truth; so help me God." The clerk signalled for her to hand the card back to him and then resumed his seat.

The judge and both counsels had been told in advance of her situation and that the start of her evidence would be confined to her "husband dying in an accident".

Mr Robert Pascoe, the prosecutor, saw she was apprehensive and did his best to put her at her ease. He thanked her for coming and asked if she would like a chair as she had a long story to tell. Anita said she was fine standing. He continued ...

'After the unfortunate death of your husband, could you tell the court in your own words what happened?'

Anita started off, hesitantly, but as she continued became more confident. She spoke in a clear voice without emphasis or dramatizing any point, relating almost word for word what she had said in her original statement, just telling her story as it happened. She said she knew the first defendant as Suleiman. She did not know his proper name and she did not know the second defendant because she did not know Suleiman had a son. When she came to the bit about Suleiman saying she was a bad Muslim and warning her about the police, Robert Pascoe interrupted her and asked if she could expand on that bit.

'He said I was a bad Muslim because I had not avenged my husband's death.' She continued, '... and then he asked if I had a boyfriend which alarmed me because I did have a boyfriend who was a policeman. I later told my boyfriend and he said I was not to worry as Suleiman was probably bluffing and that he would look after me'.

'Thank you. Please continue,' said Pascoe.

Anita carried on speaking, sounding much more confident and told what happened at the meeting in Nottingham. When she came to the blue bag Pascoe interrupted again. He pointed to the bag which was lying on a table in front of the clerk's desk.

'Is that the bag?'

'Yes'

'What did you think was in it?'

'I thought it was a bomb,' she said.

'Why did you think that?'

'Because I didn't trust him.'

'What made you not trust him?'

'When he told me they had killed a policeman I knew he was a dangerous person.'

'Thank you. Carry on.'

She continued and told how Suleiman pushed her forward after the meeting. They were arguing because she didn't want to go and then he suddenly left her standing on her own. She felt pains in her stomach and wanted to be sick but fainted and fell to the floor. She remembered waking up in the ambulance and seeing her boyfriend sitting next to her. She knew she arrived at a hospital but the first time she really knew what was happening was when she woke up at night in a room by herself. Then the pain started in her stomach and she called out to a nurse and she knew she was having a miscarriage. She hesitated here and there was a catch in her voice. Then, sounding tearful she said, 'it was a little girl.' She went silent.

Fitzgerald looked at the jury and saw two of the women jurors were also emotional and wiping their eyes with tissues. The judge realised the situation and said, 'this will be a convenient time to adjourn.' The court rose and Brenda indicated Anita should follow her back to her office.

'You are doing very well,' said Brenda. 'Very well. Would you like a glass of water, I don't think there will be time for tea?'

'Thanks. Yes. My mouth is very dry.'

'Probably nerves. You should be alright now,' and handed her a glass of water. Anita drank it and felt much better. The court reconvened and Anita was ushered back into the witness box. Pascoe asked her if she would like to continue. She added that she was in hospital for four days and then her boyfriend brought her back to London. Pascoe sat down. Her evidence-in-chief was over.

Defence Counsel, Sir David Ramsbottom, stood up and trying to sound as gentle as possible said he just had a few questions he would like to clear up with her. He took her back to her night at the Holiday Inn.

'You said the defendant, Suleiman, told you that he had "shot" a policeman. Are you sure he said "shot" and not "got"?'

'No, I'm sure he said "shot" because later he said they had killed a policeman.'

Sir David went on 'I suggest to you Suleiman did not say he killed a policeman, you imagined he did because you were frightened of him.'

'I was frightened of him, but I am sure that's what he said.'

Sir David continued, 'it is very important that we get this right. In the confines of your bedroom and you being afraid of him, are you sure you are not imagining what he said, in other words this is what you expected him to say?'

'No. I'm quite sure that is what he said. But a policeman was shot, wasn't he?'

Sir David moved on. He took her to the blue satchel.

'You said this was the satchel you had over your shoulder. You didn't really think it was a bomb, did you?'

'Yes, I did,' said Anita.

'Didn't you know it had been defused?'

'What does defuse mean?'

'There were no explosives inside, only sand.'

'Oh,' said Anita in all innocence. 'That must be why it was so heavy.'

Sir David sat down. He was obviously only going to make things worse by questioning her. There was no re-examination. The judge turned to Anita and thanked her for her evidence and the time she had spent in court. He commended her for her bravery. He said she was now dismissed and could go home. Anita said nothing. Brenda signalled for her to step down and together they went back to the office.

'You did very well,' she said. 'The judge was obviously impressed as he commended you. They don't do that often, and I would think the jury were as well.'

'I'm just glad it's over,' Anita replied.

Meanwhile Johnson, who was sitting in the visitors' gallery went straight to the office where Anita was. He knocked and entered. Anita was still talking to Brenda and smiled broadly when at last she saw someone she knew. Johnson smiled at Brenda and said to Anita, 'come on. Get your coat and let's go.' Anita put on her anorak and taking Johnson's hand, said goodbye to Brenda and left. It was only when she got into his car that she finally relaxed.

'Phew. I'm glad that's over.'

'I'm not surprised. You did very well.' They couldn't talk because it was the start of the evening rush hour and he was concentrating on negotiating his way through the traffic. Finally, they reached home and took off their coats. It was only then that Anita felt that her ordeal was over. Johnson went up to her and put his arms around her waist, pulling her towards him. 'You were absolutely marvellous,' he said. 'I am very, very proud of you. Even the judge was impressed.' Anita put her arms around his neck and they embraced. Suddenly she pulled away. 'Marry me,' she said.

Johnson was taken aback by her sudden outburst. 'What?'

'Marry me. Let's get married.'

'Whoa. That's a tall order. I'll have to check that I have the means to keep you in the manner to which you are accustomed,' he said with a smile.

'I don't care if we live in sackcloth and ashes so long as we are together. Forever.'

He was still holding her by her waist. 'We'll have to talk about this later. Tonight, in bed.'

'What about now?' she replied. She had the trace of a smile on her face.

He looked into her eyes slowly shaking his head in wonderment at this lovely woman. 'What about now indeed.' He took her hand

and led her towards the stairs.

In their bedroom, Anita put her arms around his neck and they embraced again. They started to undress each other until finally falling onto their bed they made love. Anita became more and more passionate as they progressed. Over the past months in her dealings with Suleiman she had been through periods of trauma, stress, anguish, and at times outright fear culminating in the loss of her baby; and finally, she found today giving evidence in the high court with all its grandeur, procedures, wigs and gowns very intimidating. All these tensions had now come to a head and were exploding to escape her body in her lovemaking with a man she adored and trusted.

Johnson read the situation. He had had many girlfriends, but none had been as passionate as Anita was now and for no-one did he have such strong feelings. Subconsciously he felt guilty that he had been the cause of so much trauma by making her his agent.

Finally, exhausted they flopped down and pulled up the duvet to keep out the cold. Anita turned her back and snuggled up against his body; he put his arm around her and they fell into a deep sleep.

Johnson was the first to wake. It was pitch dark. He switched on the bedside lamp and looked at his watch. It was just after six-thirty pm. 'Crikey,' he thought, 'it was only two hours ago we were leaving the high court.' He looked at Anita still fast asleep. She looked so innocent. He felt a surge of warmth in his heart. Of course, they would get married. He could not imagine life without her. He gently pulled back a frond of hair covering her face, bent down and kissed the side of her forehead.

Anita woke with a start, swivelled around and looked at him with a strange expression on her face. She grabbed him and held onto him as if her life depended on it, burying her face in his chest.

Johnson was alarmed at this sudden change. 'What's the matter?' he asked very concerned. There was no answer.

'Anita darling, what's the trouble,' he asked again. He could feel her sobbing quietly against his chest.

Finally, she answered. 'I had a nightmare about Suleiman,' she said between sobs. 'I was carrying his bomb in that bag and he was pushing me from the back saying. "Go closer. Go closer". I was looking desperately around the crowd for you, but I couldn't see you. I knew that if you didn't save me, I was going to be killed.'

Johnson hugged her closer resting his chin on the top of her head. 'Anita, Anita,' he whispered, 'please try and forget about Suleiman. He's gone. Finished. He will get a long prison sentence from this trial and be out of our lives forever. Remember I will always be around to protect you. Forever. For the rest of our lives.' They remained like this for a while until Anita stopped crying. She turned her face up to look at him. There were still tears in her eyes. Johnson bent down and kissed her gently and then kissed her eyes to wipe away the tears. She smiled at him.

'That's better. That's more like the Anita I know and love.' They looked at each other for a few moments more. Then he asked, 'what about dinner?'

'I haven't prepared anything.' She was more composed now.

'Shall we go to the George?' He was referring to the small family-owned pub they had found recently, just off the High Street where they had become friendly with the proprietor and his wife.

'Fine but I need a bath,' she replied.

'OK you have a bath and I'll wash in the basin.' He looked at his watch. It was ten to seven. 'We had better get a move on or the kitchens will be closed.' He threw back the duvet. The central heating had come on and taken the chill out of the air and so both, completely naked, got off the bed and went to the bathroom. Anita ran the bath and lay back in the warm water. Johnson stood on a towel and washed himself at the basin with a flannel. Anita loved looking at his body. It was so athletic. Like a god. Johnson finished before Anita had even started to soap herself. He dried himself and wrapped the towel around his waist. He looked at Anita lying in the bath. She looked like a beautiful nymph.'

38

The trial resumed the following morning at ten am. The screens had been removed and the court was back to normal. The first witness to be called was Mr Japour, manager of the Old Plaza Hotel. He produced a floor plan of the hotel showing Lewis's office, the pantry where the shooting had happened and the suite occupied by the MP and his Police guards. He gave an account of Lewis's duties and stated Lewis had organised the suite for the MP, chosen by the Police. He added, 'you did not have to be a brain surgeon to know that the waiter provided to serve him was a policeman.' He was told to moderate his language by the judge.

Next was the receptionist who saw Suleiman collect the cash tin from the table by the door and who thanked him. He was unable to identify him in court saying he only saw him very briefly as it was dark. After the receptionist was Ahmed Mustafa, the barman and Lewis's flatmate. He identified Lewis and was outspoken about how he disliked him, because of his extreme views. He stated the hotel staff were afraid of him because he was a senior manager and they thought he was a Jihadist. He said Lewis had complained to him how he hated having to assist the police after the shooting but had to pretend to be helpful.

'I put it to you that you are exaggerating to try and influence your employer and hope to get promotion to Lewis's job,' Sir David asked him.

'No. I am not exaggerating. He was also always talking about reports of bombings from Iraq and Afghanistan being committed by martyrs and how he would like to be a martyr.'

He went on and admitted he had never seen him with a weapon and had never heard him make any mention of shooting the policeman. He was given a grilling by the defence but stuck to his story.

The final two witnesses for the Crown were from Bristol. They were summonsed to be at the court the next day, but to the annoyance of the judge, were delayed by the train running late. The trial eventually got under way at eleven-thirty am. First was Mr Roland Ashworth, assistant bursar at the university. He confirmed that the weapon was the missing starter's gun from the university. It had been noticed missing over a year ago and had been reported to the police, but it could have gone missing at any time, because it was seldom used. Rhana Khalid was a student at the time.. 'We thought it had just been lost,' he said, 'but now we know differently.' He was rebuked by the defence for making assumptions without proof.

The final witness for the Crown was Mrs Judith Morris, secretary of the Bristol Gun Club. She confirmed that Rhana Khalid had been a member of the club and had been taught how to shoot by a club tutor. He had been very good and won a certificate for small arms shooting. She also described how the ammunition used to be issued on trust but emphasised that much tighter controls were now in place.

Pascoe decided that there was no need for any further witnesses to prove his case. He therefore closed the Crown case.

'The case for the Crown, My Lord,' he said and sat down. The judge turned to the defence.

'Do you have any witnesses, Sir David?'

'No, My Lord.' That surprised Fitzgerald who thought that the defence would at least call Suleiman's wife.

'Are you calling your clients?' asked the judge.

'No, My Lord.'

Again, Fitzgerald was surprised but could not say anything. He thought Lewis would want to give evidence but assumed he had been discouraged by his lawyer in case he turned the occasion into a publicity stunt.

'Well if you have got nothing more to add we will go for closing addresses. Mr Pascoe please,' said the judge. There followed closing speeches by each counsel. First the prosecutor who went through all the witnesses, highlighting the bits that proved the charges against the defendants. He had a compelling case, Fitzgerald thought. His address lasted over an hour. Then it was the turn of the defence. His address was about half an hour because he had no witnesses of his own. He went through some of the prosecution witnesses and picked out bits that he suggested were exaggerated or biased and therefore could not be counted against the defendants. He pointed out that his clients were both upstanding and respected citizens who were making a positive contribution to society and this sort of behaviour was completely out of character. 'Clutching at straws.' Fitzgerald thought.

Eventually the speeches ended. The judge addressed the jury saying they must make their decision only on the evidence they had heard in court and dismiss anything they might have read or heard from the media. He instructed them to retire and consider their verdict. The Clerk of the Court called 'All Rise.' Everybody stood and the judge left the court. The long wait started.

Fitzgerald left the court and went to the small Police office where police personnel gathered. He was relieved to see that there was a kettle to make a much-needed cup of tea. He met Catchpole there.

'Seemed to go alright Boss,' he said.

'I am surprised at the defence,' Fitzgerald replied. 'It just seemed to collapse. They had nothing to say.'

'Anita,' said Catchpole. 'She was perfect.'

'I agree. It was her manner and demeanour. She was so quietly matter-of-fact, and had an air of complete innocence, no emotions or exaggerations. You just could not imagine she was telling anything but the truth.'

'I couldn't see her,' said Catchpole, 'but l was looking at the jury and they seemed to be transfixed by her. Some of the women members were weeping when she spoke about her miscarriage.'

'Well, we must wait and see. I am quietly confident. I doubt we will get a verdict tonight. It is too late, but I think tomorrow.' It was now four pm.

The next day Fitzgerald and Catchpole were both at court. They had to be there in case there were any queries. Fitzgerald brought a newspaper with him and sat in his place in the well of the court as it was the only place where he could find peace and quiet. At twelve-thirty the Clerk of Court appeared and said the jury had reached a verdict. It took twenty minutes for the court to re-assemble. The Clerk of Court stood up and asked, 'would the foreman of the jury please stand.' One of the Asian males stood up. Fitzgerald recognised him as a prominent businessman in the city.

'Have you reached a verdict on which you are all agreed?' asked the Clerk.

'We have.'

'In respect of defendant Usman Khalid, count one, do you find him guilty or not guilty of the murder of PC Baxter?'

'Not Guilty.'

'In respect of defendant Usman Khalid, count two, do you find him guilty or not guilty of the Attempted Murder of David Robinson MP?'

'Guilty.'

'In respect of defendant Rhana Khalid, count one. Do you find him guilty or not guilty of the murder of PC Baxter?'

'Guilty.'

'In respect of defendant Rhana Khalid, count two. Do you find him guilty or not guilty of the attempted murder of David Robinson MP?'

'Not Guilty.'

The clerk sat down. The judge addressed the jury thanking them for their deliberations and said they were now dismissed. The jury rose and left. He then addressed counsel, asking for anything in mitigation. The prosecutor rose and said neither defendant had any record, and sat down. Defence counsel rose and gave a long speech saying the defendants were both hardworking members of society. Usman Khalid had arrived in this country from Pakistan as a penniless refugee and by his own endeavours was now running a successful business with his wife. Rhana was his only child who was now a hotel manager. Both were devout Muslims and were offended by the anti-Islamic rhetoric that filled the media after nine eleven. These were their first offences and pleaded for leniency.

All this was, apparently, completely ignored by the judge who said the defendants had been convicted of very serious offences and must expect long custodial sentences. In the meantime, they would be remanded in custody for thirty days. The judge stood up. The Clerk of Court called, 'All Rise'. Everybody stood up. Counsels bowed to the judge who left the chamber. That signified the end of the trial.

Counsels removed their wigs and there was a murmur of voices as people started talking. A huge sense of anti-climax descended on the court. Fitzgerald left the chamber and met Catchpole in the foyer. 'Congratulations Boss. Another one you can notch onto your bedpost, or wherever you notch them. Are we going to go and celebrate?'

Fitzgerald, the family man, just wanted to get home. 'I'm feeling pretty wacked. I tell you what, instead of celebrating now why don't we arrange a night out with our wives to thank them for all the time we were away in Wolverhampton?'

'Excellent idea. I know just the place.'

'Good. You do the booking. I'll do the paying.'

'Even better.'

39

It was Friday morning exactly six weeks after the end of the trial. The two Khalid's had been sentenced. Suleiman was given 12 years for attempted murder. The judge noted that he was prepared to sacrifice another life to achieve his aims which made his crime more serious. Lewis was given life with a minimum tariff of 15 years.

Johnson had gone off to work. He was working for his uncle JJ, learning the business before taking over when JJ retired at the end of the year. Anita was alone in the flat cleaning the kitchen cupboards. Johnson had given her carte blanche to turn his bachelor pad into a home. He trusted her implicitly to do the right thing. Anyway, he thought, what do I know about it.

Anita was in her element. She had brought over her things and added them in with his, diplomatically suggesting they throw out all the broken and cracked pieces that Johnson had. They now had a full set of glasses, clean tablecloths, napkins, vases in which she had arranged flowers, a proper set of cutlery and the flat was looking much tidier than before. She was living with a man she loved and he clearly loved her and they were engaged to be married. He had given her a beautiful diamond and emerald engagement ring and for the first time in ages she felt safe. She could not be happier.

At about eleven o'clock the front doorbell rang followed by knocking. Who could that be? She wondered as she opened the door.

Standing on the doorstep was an Asian man dressed in a long sleeved *bisht* and wearing a *taqiyah* on his head. He was holding a parcel in his hand. He looked old and had an unshaven appearance. His face was completely expressionless, but he looked vaguely familiar.

'For you,' he said holding out the parcel to her, then turned and limped away without saying another word.

She went back inside, shutting the door behind her and placed the parcel on the kitchen worktop. She was sure it was a present from Jimmy.

Excitedly she cut the string and unwrapped the brown paper covering exposing a shoe box. She lifted the lid and ...

There was a monumental explosion. All the windows were blown out, the ceiling collapsed and a huge cloud of dust billowed into the air.

Meanwhile a hundred yards away walking down the treed avenue was an elderly Asian man with a limp. He heard the explosion, but his expression did not change one iota. '*Insha'Allah*' (The Will of God) was all he said.

***

About the Author

This book is dedicated to my dear wife Moira who gave me many ideas and suggestions which I incorporated into the story, and to my daughter Susan Hubert whose help was invaluable. The story is complete fiction.

I started my working life in Southern Rhodesia (now called Zimbabwe.) In 1954 I attested into the British South Africa Police, Rhodesia's much admired police force and served for twenty-two and a half years during which I was involved in the bush war. There I experienced many incidents on which I based the incidents in this story. In 1977 I retired and was appointed as a personnel manager to a large factory in Bulawayo. In 1985 we emigrated from Zimbabwe, as the country had become, to the UK and stared up a small engineering business. We sold the business in 2012 and retired. I took up writing as a hobby and joined a writing group in Sherborne, Dorset. I have written four books.

Moira and I have been married for sixty-two years and have three children, all married and have given us six grandchildren.

***

If you enjoyed this book and found some benefit or pleasure in reading it, I would like to hear from you and hope you could take some time to post your review or rate it on Amazon. Your feedback and support will help me greatly to improve my writing skills for future books as well as help on this book. Your review is important, so, if you are able to write one, thank you very much for doing it.

For Better, For Worse
(Book 2) of The Pursuit of Evil Series

1

The LED light started flashing indicating an in-coming call. Tracy White put on her head set, 'Police Control Room.'

' Ello . . . Ello. . . I'ya . . I'ya. . .'

'This is the Police . . . Can I help you? . . . Have you got a problem?' Tracy White was one of several telephonists in the control room managing the Terrorist Hot Line. She realised she had a foreigner on the other end who had difficulty speaking English. She covered her speaker with her hand. 'Jean,' she said to her neighbouring telephonist, signalling for her to listen and turned on the speaker phone; two sets of ears are better than one.

'I'ya . . . I'ya. . wana help. . .'

'Alright luv, just speak slowly. What - is - the - problem?' she said speaking very slowly and clearly.

'Big Bang. Very Big Bang. Big Smoke. . . too much smoke.'

Inspector Thomas, who oversaw the control room, went and stood behind Tracy's chair to listen as soon as he heard the speaker phone. 'Ask where he is,' he said.

'Where - are - you - luv?'

'I donna know. I no live . . .'

'Ask him if he knows the street,' Thomas instructed.

'D'ya - know - the - name - of - the - street?'

'I see name . . . De wil. . . De wil. . .'

'Can - you - spell - it?' asked Tracy.

'Control. This is Delta 4.'

'Go ahead.' Monica Williams was one of the radio operators at the other end of the control room. Delta 4 was a police patrol car.

'Control - Delta 4. We've just heard a massive explosion nearby. Have you had any reports?'

'Stand by.' She turned in her chair to look for Thomas.' SIR,' she shouted as she saw him at the far end of the room; 'DELTA FOUR REPORT HEARING AN EXPLOSION.'

Thomas heaved a sigh of relief. 'Tell him to hold on. I'm coming.' To Tracy, 'get Fatima to speak to him. We want his name, address and place of work. Someone will go and see him later.' Fatima was Pakistani, spoke several Middle Eastern dialects and was invaluable in situations like this. Thomas moved quickly to the radio.

'Delta 4 – Control. What's your position?'

'We're opposite the Leisure Centre in Camberwell. We heard what sounded like a very loud explosion nearby but can't place it.'

'We have a report coming in right now from a foreigner who speaks bad English. The nearest we can get to a location is a road that sounds like "De-wil". Does that mean anything to you?'

'Hold on, I'll ask my colleague. She lives here. . .' After a pause, 'Control – Delta 4. The nearest we can get is "The Willows" which is an avenue not far from here. We'll investigate. I'll take about five minutes.'

'Roger. Get back asap.' Thomas handed the microphone back to Monica and called his deputy, 'John, bring the file. Looks like we've got a major.'

Sergeant John Wilkins grabbed the file and sat down with Thomas at his desk. The file had a checklist of actions to be taken whenever a major incident was reported. Thomas opened it and went through the list of people to be informed.

'I'll contact Commander Birch, CTC, and I'll get the Charge Office to send more vehicles for crowd control and erect a cordon. You do Scenes of Crime; Bomb Squad; Ambulance and Fire Brigade. Also get someone to put hospitals on alert.'

'Right sir.' Wilkins got up to go to his desk.

Four minutes later, 'SIR,' Monica called again. 'Delta 4 is on the air.'

Thomas hurried to the radio. 'Tell him to go ahead.'

'Delta 4. Go ahead. Boss is listening.'

'Sir. I'm on the ground at No 22, The Willows. It's a house converted into flats. The flat at the rear has been completely destroyed. Looks like the upper floor has collapsed onto the ground floor. There's dust everywhere.'

'Any smell of gas?' Thomas asked.

'Negative.'

'Fire?'

'Negative.'

'What about casualties?'

'It looks as if there is one female casualty under a pile of rubble. There is no sign of life.'

'Are you sure?'

'Absolutely. She's got no face and one arm is missing. There is blood everywhere. Also, she's pinned down with a heavy beam across her body.'

'Roger. Keep away from the building, it is probably unsafe. Keep a guard on the place. Help is on its way.' 'JOHN,' he shouted to his deputy, 'add the undertakers to your list.'

Commander Birch was in his office when the internal phone rang. He lifted the receiver, 'Birch!'

'Inspector Thomas from the Control Room, sir. There has been a report of a major incident, an explosion in a house in Camberwell. One female casualty – deceased. The address is 22 The Willows, Camberwell. We have notified all persons on the list who on are on their way.'

'Who are the occupants?'

'We don't know sir. The report has just come in.'

'OK. Thank you,' Birch replaced the phone. He sat and thought for a while. Adrenalin surged through his body. It had been nearly two months since a serious incident had occurred, so he knew something was bound to happen soon. He called up his chief investigator, Chief Superintendent Arthur Fitzgerald, on his mobile. 'Arthur. Drop what you're doing and report to me as quickly as you can.'

'Yes sir. On my way.'

Whilst waiting for Fitzgerald to arrive he mused on a subject that had always amused him. Police work is highly ironic. If the police apparently have very little to do it can be assumed they are doing their primary task, prevention of crime. Governments see this as an opportunity to cut funding. If, on the other hand, the phone never stops ringing and new cases are coming in all the time, then the police have failed in their primary task and fall back on the secondary task, detection of crime. Governments never refund the cuts.

There was a knock on the door and Fitzgerald poked his head in. 'Come in Arthur and take a seat. Looks as if we may have a major incident. There has been an explosion at a house in Camberwell. One female deceased.'

'Do we know who it is?'

'No. It's been quiet for nearly two months, so I suppose something major was bound to happen sooner or later. What are you doing now?'

'Two male prostitutes blackmailing an MP. I think it's a lot of baloney, a civil dispute, not a crime, but the MP insists we charge them.'

'Why are we wasting time on that. It's not our type of crime. It's not even a security matter?'

'Prime Minister. The MP is a personal friend.'

'Well leave it. Pass it on to someone else. I want you to concentrate on this matter.'

'Thank you.'

'I think you and I should visit the scene now.'

'Have you got the address?'

'Yes.' Birch sorted out his notes. '22 The Willows, Camberwell.'

Fitzgerald's blood froze. Birch looked at him.

'What's the matter?'

'I know that address . . .That's the home address of James Johnson, the ex-MI5 Officer and his girlfriend, Anita Hussein, who was our main witness at the trial of the Khalids.' . . . . . .

Printed in Great Britain
by Amazon

84743902R00162